W9-BED-234

EAT MY HEART OUT

EAT MY HEART OUT

a novel by
ZOE PILGER

THE FEMINIST PRESS
AT THE CITY UNIVERSITY OF NEW YORK
NEW YORK CITY

Published in 2015 by the Feminist Press
at the City University of New York
The Graduate Center
365 Fifth Avenue, Suite 5406
New York, NY 10016
feministpress.org

First Feminist Press edition 2015

First printing May 2015

Cover and text design by Suki Boynton

Library of Congress Cataloging-in-Publication Data Available

For Joe Silk

1977–2003

Too bad I'm not stronger. I'd be worse.

ARIANA REINES, *Cœur de Lion*

ONE

THE SKY WAS still black when the butchers began unloading the pigs from their vans at Smithfield Market. It was five in the morning. I had been to a party nearby. There he was, loitering across the road. He was watching the meat with terror and awe.

His black hair was lank, and, as I approached, I could see that a military medal of some kind was pinned to his beige crochet sweater. He was freakishly tall, about six foot seven. He wore a red hat and he was shaking with cold.

"Hi," I said. "I'm Ann-Marie. I'm twenty-three. How old are you?"

He seemed shocked that I was talking to him. "Thirty-six."

"That's a good age." I shoved my hands deeper into my vintage structured tweed and asked him if he wanted to go for a coffee. "Maybe we've got something in common," I suggested.

"I doubt it."

"I adopt loads of pussies from a refuge," I said. "Yeah, and I love to feed the pussies condensed milk in tiny china dishes. I lounge around on my chaise longue in my red silk kimono and I watch their pink tongues lap it up." I paused for effect. "They *love* to lap it up."

Vic gave me his email address.

That was yesterday.

Dear Vic,

It was lovely to meet you! What are you up to later? I'll come to where you are.

Ann-Marie X

Today I was waiting at the window on the first floor of a waxing salon across the road from Chalk Farm station, where Vic had chosen to meet. The manager had told me that they were nearly closing, but I'd made my eyes look beseeching like a spaniel and the drowned aesthetic must have helped because she let me in. I could hear a panpipe rendition of "These Boots Are Made for Walkin'" emitting from a closed door; I couldn't smell the floral notes of wax. I waited.

And waited.

To wait is a woman's prerogative, according to Stephanie Haight, whose book *Falling Out of Fate* had recently been short-listed for the Samuel Johnson Prize for Non-Fiction. To wait is a woman's raison d'être. To wait and see what a man will do for you. Do *to* you. I hadn't bought the book yet because I had no money, but I'd heard her speak on *Start the Week*. Her accent had a twang;

I couldn't tell if she was American or English. "Waiting for the call," she'd said. "Waiting for that fateful ring of the telephone situates woman in a passive position. It is akin to waiting for the Call from God."

November commuters were rushing away from the station in the street below. The rain was torrential; it obscured the stars. There was no one I recognized.

The waxing woman was trudging up the stairs behind me when at last I glimpsed that red, woolly hat. "Have you seen enough?" she was saying.

I watched Vic cross the road.

Now the woman had a hand on my shoulder. She turned me around.

"Do you mind if I wait here for just a few moments longer?" I said.

She returned downstairs so that I was alone again with that music, which had changed to "My Heart Will Go On." Vic was wearing a red anorak. He didn't smoke a cigarette; he didn't look at his watch. He reminded me of a Giacometti: emaciated by the act of living.

I rooted around in my handbag for *Heidegger: An Intro* and read: "Concept of Thrown-ness: One is thrown into the world and one must deal with it." I closed the book. Since I went crazy during my university finals a few months ago, I could only read these terrible comic-style philosophy manuals, and only one or two sentences at a time.

Now Vic was circling a lamppost.

A door to the right of the entranceway opened and a woman appeared with the blank face of one who has just been tortured. Another woman in a white apron followed her. There was an intense smell of sugar—no, cocoa butter. The blank woman was about forty-five, but she was saying in a little girl voice: "Thank you ever so much. I do feel so much better now. It's my anniversary." They disappeared without looking at me.

Now Vic was holding on to the lamppost and looking up into its light, letting the rain fall on his face.

Ten minutes had passed.

Soon he would go.

Would he go?

I watched him reach upward to the void of sky; he seemed to plead with it. And then he *was* going, taking long strides with his gloopy, elastic legs, splashing through puddles that reflected cars and red light. He was leaving, he was leaving.

The music had stopped.

I ran down the stairs and across the street. I had lost sight of him; *Him*. I wanted Him more now, much more, since He was already leaving me.

I found the red hat striding over the bridge toward Primrose Hill. I got close enough to watch the rivulets of water running down Vic's plastic-covered back. I fell into step behind him. The black heavens never answered my questions. Why not?

I pounced.

I got my arms and legs around him, piggy-back style. He grunted, a stuck pig. He tried to push me off, but I clung and clung and clung. Stephanie Haight had said that that is what women are wont to do.

We fell, together.

I whispered into his ear: "Hello Vic, it's very nice to see you again. Sorry I'm late." I paused. "This seems like a good moment to lay my cards on the table. You're my first date since I got out of a really long-term relationship."

We were sprawled on the pavement. People were walking around us, but no one stopped to help. Vic sat up and touched his forehead. He was bleeding.

I went on: "My ex-boyfriend Sebastian was fucking this girl from the Home Counties called Allegra behind my back. I didn't think I'd ever get over it, but now— since I've seen your face, I think I might get over it."

The lights of the fruit machine whirred in the corner, spinning their pictures of apples and bananas as I sipped my large glass of house white wine and tried to seem engrossed in Vic's pronouncements on operation management.

"So you manage the operators?" I said.

"Not exactly. I operate and I manage. I live with other operators who are lower down the pecking order than me, but I don't let that affect things like who can use how much space in the fridge." He shrugged.

A large bullfighting poster was framed on the wall to his left. It showed a blindfolded horse being gored by a bull. A matador stood poised to stab the bull with the final sword. We were squeezed onto the end of a table of graphic designers who had offered to drive Vic to the hospital for stitches because the gash on his forehead continued to bleed.

"At least you didn't break your nose," I said. "My friend Freddie who I live with has got a broken nose. And he's got these eyes like a fawn about to be shot. The juxtaposition is quite poetic."

"Do you always use long words?" said Vic.

"I'm not an elitist."

"I'm an elite," he said. "I'm a one-man elite. That's the way it is in the services." There was no sign of the medal that he had worn yesterday.

"So you were in the army?" I said. "That must have been what drew me to you. Did you, like, get discharged for gross misconduct or something?"

His face looked pained for a moment and then it hardened. "No." He leaned forward. "You know, you're lucky that I'm here with you, that I'm willing to fuck you still, since you gave me a concussion." He touched his wound.

I pulled his hand down. "Don't, Vic. It might get infected."

"I would like to infect you," he said, heartily. "Posh girls like you want to get infected by a real man like me."

I sighed. "Real men are hard to find."

"That's because all you castrating bitches don't know your place anymore."

There was a long silence.

"I went to Cambridge," I said. "Yes, that's right. The real Cambridge. Not the ex-polytechnic. So it's a curse and a blessing in a way because when one elevates oneself above the quotidian, one starts feeling terribly lonesome, as though one will never find a soul mate again." I paused. "I guess Freddie is my soul mate now."

"Do you like the way he fucks you?"

"He's gay."

I felt Vic's hand grope my thigh under the table. We were sitting quite far apart; his arms were as long as an ape's. I moved my thigh away and his hand thudded to the ground.

"Fine," he said.

I downed my drink. "Shall we get another?"

"Great." He leaned back. "Thanks."

The song changed to Curtis Mayfield's "Move On Up." The graphic designers started dancing in their chairs.

"But I got the last one, Vic." I wanted to cry—maybe he didn't love me?

"Only joking, only joking." He laughed. "Shall I get a bottle?"

The next thing I knew I was riding Vic hard in the back of a taxi, muttering into his mouth: "Fuck me right here, right now. Tell me what you want."

"I want you to get off," he was saying. "Get off."

"No, no, no." I slapped his face. "Isn't that the word you like to hear from women?"

"No," said Vic.

I got off and slid as far away from him as possible.

The taxi slowed with the traffic on Chalk Farm Road. A woman wearing a white wifebeater and a pair of acid-washed jeans despite the harrowing cold was crawling on all fours outside the kebab shop, picking up the remains of her fries and cheese and cramming them into her mouth. We drove on, slowly. A gang of girls were swaying together in a long, linked-arm line over the lock, singing some mournful song: "The First Time Ever I Saw Your Face."

I wound down the window and leaned my head out. "That was my parents' song!" I shouted. I turned to Vic: "That can't be a coincidence?!"

One of the girls broke away from the chain and sprinted in six-inch, neon-green heels toward the dark window of a leather shop. She lowered her head like a bull, laughing all the way. Her friends grabbed her arms just before her head smashed into the glass. She fell back into them, laughing harder.

"Close the window!" shouted the driver.

I did.

London is a depressing place to look for things.

The doors on the first floor of Vic's house were all white and all shut. I'd stripped off my clothes downstairs and now I was throwing my naked body against each door in turn. They stayed shut—locked? Vic was mumbling about not waking the operators. He was picking up my clothes.

"Fuck me," I was saying. "Fuck me, fuck me, fuck me."

Finally he produced a key from his pocket and opened a door on the left. "We like our privacy," he explained. "Security is always an issue. Even among friends."

He followed me into the dark room. I hit my shin on

the bed. Vic turned on the light. It was a futon. A NATO aerial-bombardment map was pinned above the mirror. There was a poster of the film *Taxi Driver*. The room was monkish, the perfect place to ask for forgiveness.

Vic was surprised when I rolled away from his hairy body and produced a packet of Performa condoms from my handbag. I snapped one on his penis efficiently.

It immediately began to die.

"Would you rather we didn't use them?" I said.

"Yeah. Thanks. It's just that I don't like the sensation of condoms."

"Well, I don't really like the sensation of abortions." I sat up. "I don't really feel like having a fetus ripped out of my womb, thank you very much."

There was silence.

I felt for it, but now it was dead.

He got out of bed and stood over me. "Why do you humiliate me?"

I waited.

"Hit me, then," I said.

He exhaled, agonized. He lay down again.

Soon he was snoring.

I moved into the crook of his arm. I felt so happy then.

The dawn entered the room. I rolled over and lit a cigarette. I tried to hold on to Vic, but he was pushing me off in his sleep. His head injury had scabbed. Experimentally, I ground the cigarette into his chest.

He woke up, screaming. "What the fuck are you doing?"

I rubbed the cigarette out between my fingers.

Now the room was ablaze with morning.

"Do you love me?" I said. "Now that we've had sex?"

He pretended to sleep again.

Finally he mumbled: "We didn't have sex."

"But do you love me anyway though? Because we might have sex in the future?"

He sat up. "What about the pussies from the refuge?" His face looked dire in the light. "What about the red silk kimono? Who are you?"

"Yeah, I'm not in the habit of going out in nightwear. I do own one though. Freddie's always trying to borrow it."

"You know it's really off-putting for a girl to keep on going on about her ex-boyfriend on a first date."

"Freddie's not my ex-boyfriend, I told you. And this isn't our first date, Vic. We met in a past life. I was your faithful concubine. But now I'm an empowered woman." I corrected myself: "I'm a woman in the process of becoming empowered." I laughed. "If you'll only let me."

Vic lay down again.

I rolled another cigarette.

"No," he said, and tossed it somewhere. "You're desperate."

I laughed. "No, Vic. That's the trouble. I think I'm desperate, I even want to be desperate, but I'm not. The sad truth is that I'm not. Maybe if I was, then you'd love me." I stood up, exhilarated. "But I'm not."

I got dressed quickly.

"You're all the same," he mumbled, face down in the pillow.

The front hall was adorned with black-and-white photographs of Big Ben, captured from a range of surreal angles. This was a terraced house. I could hear operators talking in the kitchen. I went in.

There was a breakfast bar. Operators—two men and a woman—were sitting around it on matching stools. There was a laptop. On the screen, there was a picture of marmalade on toast. A real piece of half-eaten toast was spotlighted on the counter.

"Yeah," the woman was saying. She had brown hair and no distinguishing features whatsoever. "And put the date and time. And say what it is."

"What is it?" said the man, fingers poised over the keyboard.

"Toast," said the woman.

"Hi!" I said. "I'm Ann-Marie! Vic's new friend."

They stared at me.

There was an empty stool—Vic's? I perched on it, taking a bite out of the toast, nodding with approval. I could see that the marmalade on the screen was a more brilliant shade of amber. It had been photoshopped.

"I'll probably be hanging round here a whole lot more from now on," I said.

They continued to stare.

The woman plunged a French press. They didn't offer me any coffee.

"Vic told me what happened in the army," I lied. "It's terrible. I'm really hungover. We got totally trashed. I don't usually get this trashed anymore, not since I went on this mad detox diet for the six months leading up to my finals." I nodded. "I just graduated. I got double-starred first actually, from Cambridge."

They didn't look impressed.

"My director of studies, Dr. Kyle, said that I could easily win a scholarship to Harvard or some other Ivy League place," I said. "Maybe a more progressive one, but I said I just want to be free, you know? Like now." I finished off the toast. My voice sounded dead: "I'm free." I got off the stool. "Well, um. I better . . . go to work."

"Vic never talks about what happened," said the woman. "It's dangerous for him to talk about it. It triggers things." She looked at one of the men. "I told him he shouldn't hang around that meat market. Why seek out what you're most afraid of?" She held the fridge door open. "Vic is terrified of meat."

"Oh?"

"Yeah," said one of the men. "Ever since the accident in the woods when he was in the army, he can't go near it. The doctor told him not to go near it."

"I can empathize with that though," I said. "I only ever want what I hate."

"Well, you're special." She pulled out some raspberries and closed the fridge.

I was about to leave and never come back, but then I changed my mind and ran upstairs. I tried every door before I got the right one. There he was, a corpse. I got out my notebook. I thought about writing him a love poem.

"Vic?" I knelt beside him. "What did you do? What happened in the woods?"

Nothing.

"Did you kill someone?"

Still nothing.

I wrote down my number and left it on the bookshelf, which wasn't well stocked at all. There was a military memoir and *Fifty Shades of Grey* and—oddly—something by Fay Weldon. For all his positive attributes, Vic was not an educated man.

TWO

I NEVER SAID that Allegra could come into my room, but she came in anyway.

Her gift to me was a box of postfeminist cupcakes decorated with tiny gold balls. I had been listening to an Amy Winehouse lament, writing an essay on Montesquieu's *The Spirit of the Laws*. The sweetness of those cupcakes was harrowing. The sponge collapsed in my mouth like a cloud. And she would claim later that I was the witch.

That was three years ago, during freshman orientation, before I got thrown out for calling one of the guards a cunt. The college was supposed to be proud of its all-girls tradition, owner of the second-largest feminist art collection in the world. We ate dinner under a portrait of an Iranian woman wearing a hijab, aiming a Kalashnikov.

"Oh, I can't tell you," Allegra had babbled. "I can't tell you what a relief it is to have found someone who I can really relate to. Someone who makes me feel *real*."

She produced a bottle of cheap red wine, rinsed out two cups, and toasted to our newfound sistahood.

One wall of my dorm room was taken up by a huge window that let in a lot of light. It looked out on to the college lawn, the sign saying "Keep off the lawn," and the red star of the Texaco gas station across the road. I was living for Sebastian's weekend visits, when we would lie together all day and night in my single bed. But he wasn't there that day. It was a Tuesday.

Allegra told me that she was studying law under the duress of her family, that she wanted to be a performance artist, that she was heavily influenced by the Theater of Cruelty, that she felt she couldn't create anything unless she, you know, really forcibly broke some eggs. She feared that the eggs that she would have to break were her family.

I stared at her liquid-black hair, her chalk-white skin.

"Except my brother Samuel," she went on. "He's a chess champion at Eton and simply *too* good-natured." She said that she had waited all her life to meet a great man who would really wreck her youth and break her heart and make her feel *something.* "Anything would do." She looked at me with her gray eyes.

And then she went completely mad.

She grabbed the saltshaker and the packet of coffee and the sugar and started chucking them around the room. Then she grabbed the remaining cupcakes and smeared them over the exposed brick walls, along the ridges of the radiator, over the lightbulb. She seemed to like the sensation of burning her fingers. She mashed the coffee into the sponge on the wall, forming a brown paste. She made abstract expressionist gestures.

I sat on the bed, impassive. I watched her fuck the place up.

Soon she sank, exhausted, beside me. She smiled.

Then she passed out.

I was thinking about Allegra as I journeyed back to Clapham after my night with Vic the war criminal. I was never more than five minutes away from thinking about her; my thoughts looped and returned always to the same point: she had ruined my life.

On Clapham High Street, I stared at the glistening kidneys in the window of the organic butcher for a while, the strung-up pheasants, the stags. Stephanie Haight's face was enlarged on a poster in the window of the bookstore. She had drooping eyes and scraggly blonde hair. Her lips were petulant. She must have been about sixty but the years had been injected out of her face. She wore jeans and a tartan shirt that recalled Generation X, to which she was too old to belong.

I went into the shop.

The bell rang and the man with the ponytail behind the counter looked up and smiled. "Hello there!" he said. "And how is your young man?"

"He's fine, thanks. Don't know where he is actually."

"He came in here just last week and was telling me all about how you two are thinking about getting engaged."

"Did he?"

"He wanted to order a special edition of Vasari's *Lives of the Artists*. For his uncle."

"Oh, you mean Freddie. Freddie's fucking nuts."

I stared intently at the Mind, Body, and Spirit section, hoping that the man would stop talking to me. There was one other customer in the shop. A tiny dog was poking out of her handbag. I moved over to Gender Studies. The man's questions were incessant. Yes, I was glad that that awful psychotic phase had ended. Yes, the standardization of education was to blame for the fact that I'd totally lost my fucking marbles.

"The only thing to do is claw them back," he said.

I found Stephanie's book. *Falling Out of Fate* was printed in pale blue letters above an image of a woman falling out of a cage made of hearts. She was plummeting through an empty blue sky to her death.

"Going like hotcakes," he said.

I flipped to "About the Author:"

Stephanie Haight was born in Bermondsey and educated at her local secondary modern before winning a scholarship to St Anne's College, Oxford. She completed her PhD on romantic masochism in the work of Simone de Beauvoir at Harvard University in 1980. She has written widely for titles including the *New York Review of Books* and the *London Review of Books*. Her books include *Master or Slave? How Submission is Reversed and Other Tales from the Women's Movement*, and a novel, *Abreaction*. After many years of living in New York, she has recently returned to London.

The man was talking to the dog woman.

I put the book down the front of my tights and exited the shop.

I got halfway across the road before I felt a hand on my arm. The light was about to turn green.

"I saw you," snarled the dog woman. Her face was expensive. Her coat was vintage tweed, like mine. I wanted to ask her if she got it from Beyond Retro.

"I'm not a corporation." The ponytail man was shaking his head. His lone dangly earring swung from side to side. It was a Native American dream catcher.

"Have you spent a lot of time in the States?" I asked him.

Dog Woman had perched on the edge of the desk. "Will you take this seriously?" she barked. "It's a serious offense. We could call the police."

"Please do," I said. "Be my guest. I've got nothing to live for anyway. The man I love doesn't love me. I thought it was Sebastian who was the love of my life but now it transpires it's Vic."

"What about Freddie?" said the man.

"Actually my great-great-great-grandmother was a thief too," I told him. "She was a prostitute in Whitechapel. And she got deported for beating the shit out of this gentleman. My mother's got the prison records on the wall."

His face reddened; he flapped his arms.

"What have you got to say for yourself that's serious?" said the woman.

"I don't want to be free," I said, with passion. "Sometimes I feel free but most of the time I feel trapped anyway, in all this freedom." I gestured to Stephanie's book on the desk. "That's why I'm interested in her. She seems to know what she's talking about."

"That's not the point," said the man.

"Call the police," said Dog Woman. "She's not even sorry."

"I thought you were against the system?" I said to the man.

"Not when I am the system," he said. "It's my shop." He trod around the office.

Piles of unsellable books were stacked everywhere.

"I don't have any money," I said. "It's Freddie with all the money. We live in his uncle's apartment, rent-free. That's the only way we can afford to live in such a yuppie area." I looked at Dog Woman.

She bared her teeth; they were perfect.

"We don't belong here," I said. "I don't belong anywhere near here."

The man didn't look convinced.

"I'm crazy, remember?" I said. "Cambridge made me crazy."

I could see him begin to waiver, but then Dog Woman shouted at him: "Can I talk to you in the shop?"

Alone, I turned to the first chapter of Stephanie's book. It was called "Falling."

To fall is a woman's destiny; it is the culmination of her destiny.

Eve fell because she ate the apple from the Tree of Knowledge. Since that first biblical Fall, any woman with a sexual appetite, any woman who fucks outside of marriage, has been deemed "fallen." The woman who fucked for love, lust, or money "fell" pregnant and was shamed by the community.

Bridget Jones—that blueprint for a free generation—fell all over the place. Her slapstick naïveté meant that she could rarely stand up without falling flat on her face and demonstrating her incompetence and the incompetence of women in general for the sake of a few laughs.

While the fallen woman was once a figure of damnation and moral outrage, now we are all fallen. We are encouraged to fall. Because falling endears us. It ameliorates our strength.

We fall in love.

Following the sexual revolution and the second wave women's movement of the 1960s and 70s, in which I played a key role, the values that kept women in her place—albeit in a second, inferior place—seem to have dissolved. In fact, they have merely changed form.

Power metamorphoses.

Culture is an atmosphere.

It is not simply men who do not want to give up their position of dominance over women. The whole cultural atmosphere is tuned to keep women falling.

This atmosphere is what French psychoanalyst Jacques Lacan called the Symbolic.

The Symbolic is everywhere, it is everything.

The Symbolic is what the authorities tell you to do, but, more generally, it is what the world tells you to do. And here's the twist: the world doesn't have to tell you to do it.

Women obey without knowing they are obeying. The choice is always already made.

"We're going to let you go," said the man. He looked devastated. "Because I was young once."

"I was young once too," I said. "I can't quite remember. I think I was happy."

THREE

Dear Vic,

Last night was truly extraordinary. Thank you.

Plato said that we were all born with two heads and four arms and four legs. I didn't have a Hellenistic education because I went to a comprehensive school. I'm the only one of all my friends who went to a comprehensive school— apart from Sebastian, who isn't my friend or my boyfriend anymore. He comes from a decadent, progressive family in Islington. He is one of six siblings who all look intersex, but they are all excellent at a musical instrument. I never did that either. Nietzsche would say I suffer from ressentiment.

Sebastian looks a bit like a Nietzschean blond beast. He started off at an exclusive left-wing boarding school, but then he got expelled at the age of twelve for fighting. He had to fight at my school too. The rude boys hated him because he was upper-middle class. I remember this one time when we were thirteen. We were in the hall between lessons. It was packed with people screaming and fighting and the teachers couldn't control it. Sebastian pretended that he was pushed too close to me and held my hand by accident but I knew he did it on purpose. So I bent his hand backward. He was in a lot of pain but he wouldn't scream for mercy. Instead he grabbed my hair and got me in a headlock. I bit his stomach. He wouldn't let go and I wouldn't let go. Neither one of us would ever let go.

We walked to the next lesson like that—a two-headed monster. It took the teacher at least half an hour to separate us. There was a circle of red marks on his white shirt—it was his blood, but it was my teeth.

Soon after that we fell in love.

Plato said that Zeus got angry and ripped all the hermaphrodites in half and made them into normal humans with only one head, two arms, and two legs. But they were doomed by an overwhelming sense of what they had lost. They were doomed to spend the rest of their lives searching for the half that they lost.

That's how I've felt since I left your terraced house this morning. I spoke to the operators in the kitchen. They seemed really nice. What's the name of their blog again?

With love,
Ann-Marie X

Back at the apartment, I lay on my bed for about three hours, watching Beyoncé's "Deja Vu" video again and again and again. I watched her shimmy across the screen in a colonial-style grass skirt against a fake backdrop of dry earth and deep sky. She waved her beautiful arms around dementedly and kicked up the dust and then collapsed on the floor at the song's crescendo, screaming about seeing her lover everywhere she went.

I pulled on my red silk kimono. The bathroom door was closed. I could hear Freddie running a bath and the squeal of an American cartoon.

"I'm coming to jump in there with you in just about ten minutes!" I shouted.

I had a look in the living room; it was fucked. Freddie's portrait of me had been taken down from the wall and lay on the coffee table, covered in white dust and a rolled note. He painted it last summer on the roof at Hammerton Hall, the stately home where his father keeps all his art but never visits. Maxine, the housekeeper, had decked the roof out in fairy lights and candles because I think she wanted to turn Freddie straight. I had lain on blue velvet with my clothes off while he pretended to be seized by inspiration: a cigarette clenched between his teeth, splattered with paint the approximate shade of my skin. He had insisted that I wear a sapphire necklace that belonged to his mother. The result was a hybrid of Francis Bacon and soft-focus 70s porn. My mouth was a yawning black chasm and there were boxing gloves on my feet, but my lips and nipples were painted a tender pink. Maxine said that the portrait made me look about ten times more beautiful than I am in real life. Freddie loathed it; he couldn't even accept it as self-consciously derivative. He said that it revealed him in a light that he didn't want to be revealed in. I said that I thought the portrait was supposed to be of me? He said no—he had exposed *himself* as sentimental, as sentimental as a dirty old flasher in the park. I asked him: "How is a flasher sentimental?" And he said: "A flasher is just a romantic at heart. He just wants to be naked under the trees." Freddie decided to give up painting altogether and invest his creative potency in video art. Now he only works in 8 mm.

Next to the chaise longue, there was a bust of Freddie's uncle, Professor Timothy Frank, an esteemed anthropologist. The bust was commissioned by Freddie's father who hated Freddie's uncle. It looked like a remnant of an exploded car factory. The face was more or less a steering wheel embedded in a tire.

There was a lot of tribal hunting equipment too: scythes and axes, charged with a preternatural energy. They were full of wrath. They didn't want to be estranged from their country of origin. There was a taxidermied peacock with fanned feathers.

In the kitchen, I ate some chicken livers and stale bread, checking my phone constantly. Vic hadn't called or texted.

I went back upstairs.

Now the bathroom door was ajar. Disney's *The Little Mermaid* was playing on our old mini TV, which stood on a marble plinth at the end of the bath. I watched the screen as I got my tights off in the hall.

"Keep singing!" barked Ursula the sea witch, reaching her phantom fingers down Ariel's throat and usurping her voice.

Ariel spasmed; her tail turned into legs.

"This bit is, like, so romantic," came a voice. It wasn't Freddie's voice.

I pushed the door open.

There was a boy in the bath. He wasn't Freddie.

"Who the fuck are you?" I said.

The boy turned his freckled, crying face toward me.

I knew who he was; he was Samuel, Allegra's younger brother. I hadn't seen him since the day after the night of the crème de menthe—that was nearly two years ago. He used to be a preppy little bastard, but now he had transformed into a hipster of some description.

"Get out," I said.

His hair was ginger, not black like hers. His body was thin and white, but not exactly alabaster like hers. His eyes were not gray like hers, but hazel. He had the same high domed forehead as her and I hated him violently.

I attempted to haul the TV into the bathwater.

He leaped out.

The cord strained. The TV rocked on the edge.

It didn't go in.

Now Ariel was scrabbling on the shore, trying to figure out how to walk.

Samuel clung to me, wet and ludicrous. I pushed him off. He was almost as tall as Vic. With shaking hands, he returned the TV to its plinth. He got back in the water.

A moronic smile appeared on his face. "Look." He pointed to the screen.

Eric the prince was trying to interpret Ariel's damp-eyed sign language. They were standing by a rock on the beach.

Samuel put on my exfoliating mitts and lathered himself up. "Freddie is so analog," he said. "That's why I love him."

I tried to drag Samuel out of the bath by the arm, but he shook me off with ease. He said, sadly: "Yeah, Freddie told me you had a lot of anger management issues after you totally caught the G. She gave you the G. Because even though people are from the same blood buffet, it doesn't mean they're the same type of sick gangster. What she did was Frigidaire."

"What the fuck are you talking about?" I said. "Where's Freddie?"

He guffawed. "Sleeping it off. Last night we got more than shellacked and Freddie boggled and, like, got hit on by a flavorless but then he hit on me and I was like, you can totally tap this. You're a juicer and a hypo but I love you."

"What?"

"Oh, yeah, right." He blushed. "That's how they speak in Brooklyn. In Williamsburg. I'm reading this." A wet copy of *Shoplifting from American Apparel* by Tao Lin lay on the bath mat. "Have you read it? Freddie told me to read it. He's going to improve me."

"That's mine," I said. "I haven't read it."

He laughed. "Where are my manners, babes?" He held out his hand. "I'm Samuel."

"I remember." I didn't take his hand.

"Freddie told me that you two are, like, majorly liquid even though he's not a CK1."

"A what?"

"That you're on a spectrum."

"We're not on a spectrum."

"He said it was like *The Cement Garden* and incestuous and shit all up in this place but that I shouldn't be perturbed if you got jealous because one thing he likes and can't stand about you is your temper." Samuel turned back to the TV.

Now the crazy French chef was trying to murder the blatantly racist rendition of a crab with a cleaver.

Samuel laughed until tears welled up in his eyes again. He addressed me with sincerity: "You're the coolest bitch I've ever seen."

Freddie was concealed inside the silk drapes of his four-poster. The room was fetid and smelled of yeast. Sex. The curtains were closed, but I could see the full blue condom that had belly flopped into a brogue.

I crawled into the bed. "Freddie."

He was asleep.

"Freddie, why did you let Allegra's brother in here?" I pried his eyelids open. His eyeballs were a brilliant red. "Get him out."

Freddie smiled and pulled me down against him so that my face was pressed against his naked chest. "This is nice," he said. "I love you." He kissed me on the forehead.

I lay down next to him and smoked a cigarette. Then I got up and attempted to lock the door, but the lock was broken.

Samuel appeared wrapped in my towel and sang in a falsetto: "Say My Name." He got into bed too.

I was stuck between them.

The gloom was unbearable; I got up and opened the curtains.

"Freddie says you love Beyoncé because you went to a black school and that is sick," said Samuel.

The morning light seemed to wash the room. I saw the full horror: more full condoms; three more. More white dust.

Now Freddie and Samuel were kissing, graphically.

I shook Freddie until he turned away from Samuel and turned toward me. "It's finally happened!" I said. "I felt it—the coup de foudre! Vic and I had sex so hard last night that now I can't even walk properly!"

"Deck," said Samuel.

I spat in his face.

He looked like he would cry again.

"That's not very nice, is it?" said Freddie. "You got on very well with Samuel when we all spent that lovely weekend together in Buckinghamshire." He turned to Samuel: "When your parents were in the Maldives."

"Yeah, it was awful."

I addressed Samuel: "You've changed. You used to be a chess champion."

"Yeah, but now I'm a hipster." Samuel nodded earnestly. Then he shook his head. "No. I forgot. I'm not meant to say that I'm a hipster. But I am one." He bared his private-school teeth: they were straight and white like hers. "I got the braces taken off and everything! I was just waiting to get them taken off before I made my last exit to Hackney."

Dear Vic,

A man with arrested development has invaded the house. If you don't write back to me soon I'm going to kill myself. That is not an empty threat. I never did see the point in living unless some form of meaning was erected out of the raw, overwhelming nothingness. I guess that's the point of being an artist. Are you an artist, Vic? Could you ever be one? I doubt it.

I'm glad. Artists are like megalomaniac aging despots who build halls of mirrors around themselves in order to block out the world that dares to be itself, e.g. autonomous. They veer between arrogance and insecurity.

I think I'm falling more and more in love with you.

Ann-Marie X

I sat in the basement on an upturned plastic bucket and switched on the projector. I had to cover my nose and mouth; the smell of sewage was unbearable. It was dark and I was alone except for the mice. We turned this space into a screening room a few months ago.

Our Super 8 installations flickered like sun on water. There I was dressed up in a mohair sweater and white shirt, my hair coiffed, my ankle socks pristine, preparing milk and cookies in a Formica kitchen, kissing two child actors whom Freddie had hired for the day, laying them down for a nap, duct-taping the bedroom door shut and sticking my head in the oven. There I was dressed up in an Edwardian hat, traipsing into the River Cam in the middle of the night, piling rocks into my pockets, looking depressed though ready. Drowning. There I was gassing myself in a parked car in a garage—that was Anne Sexton. She was less well known, but Freddie had wanted a trilogy. His lucky number was three, but only if pressed—really, he wasn't superstitious at all. He'd won a young filmmakers' scholarship from Sundance.

Dear Vic,

Do you want to Skype? My username is purposedestiny7.

Ann-Marie X

Samuel decided to make a cocktail called Aqua Fortis because a friend of a friend who'd been to Williamsburg had said it was deck, so off he went to Gerry's specialist off-license in Soho to buy marjoram-infused Lillet Blanc, El Jimador Reposado, and Meletti Amaro. He returned hours later, empty-handed.

Samuel couldn't get served. He couldn't get served because he was only seventeen.

"Aren't you supposed to be at school?" I demanded.

"I gave all that up." He was standing against the wall in the kitchen, his hands behind his back.

Freddie sat at the table, morose and smoking.

"Samuel." I spoke very slowly. "Do your parents know where you are?"

Samuel started to nod, but then he shook his head. I saw the tears. "They think I'm at the Custard—" Now the tears flowed.

"Is that your candy store?" I said.

"No. The Custard Collective is my squat. East. I ran away to the Wick, as they say!"

"They don't say that," I said. "I've never heard anyone say that." I came very close to his face. "You are in a lot of danger. Hackney is a very dangerous place for a boy like you. They will get you."

"I don't care! I don't care!" He went hysterical, grabbing at the copper pans hanging from the stove, banging them together. It reminded me of Allegra's performance back in my dorm room all those years ago. Three years ago.

"Sit down!" I commanded.

He sat next to Freddie, who was repeating: "I want a drink. I want a drink."

"I was born to be a DJ!" said Samuel, with passion. "Or a lifestyle—a style consultant."

"Samuel's an Enlightenment polymath," said Freddie, darkly. "I'm going to make him a star."

Samuel turned to Freddie with the light of true love in his eyes. He buried his face in Freddie's neck and said again and again: "I'm sorry, sorry, sorry."

I had agreed to buy the drink, but I had no intention of going all the way to Gerry's because I was due in Soho in two hours anyway to start my shift. I considered trying to find Vic's house after work and using Freddie's drink money to pay him to go out with me. I had £150 in cash in my hand. I had never felt so free. But soon my freedom became a burden again.

I walked around the pond on Clapham Common, eyeing the men in tents. Their fishing rods trailed in the freezing water. A tree bent its gnarled body all the way over so that its branches disappeared in the depths. Yuppies walked their dogs despite the adverse temperature. One mongrel bounded toward a collie of some kind; they yelped at each other and then sniffed each other's backsides in a circular dance of mysterious sweetness before their owners appeared in running gear and ruined the friendship. I passed the fenced-off zone where feral cats and feral children roamed. Like voyeurs at a peep show, young couples stared at sumptuous images of semidetached houses in the real estate agent's window. The public housing buildings soared to the right, wrecking the dream. I passed the local crazy woman, parked outside Specsavers. She wore her hair in bunches and she carried a mangy Cabbage Patch doll. Her whole ensemble was bricolage.

I stopped and counted out fifty pounds. I gave it to her.

"I'll tell you a secret," she said. "It's something I didn't put in my memoir because they made me censor it when I had Betty." She gestured to the doll.

I waited.

"Soon the snow will come. The snow will cover us."

"Do you mean as in global warming?"

She shook her head. "No. I said *snow*. Not sun. It will freeze."

"Do you mean the world or just in London?"

Her teeth were black. She rocked her baby and told me that I was a good girl, really.

"What do you mean, really?"

"Really," she said. "Really you are."

I headed to the only vintage shop in Clapham, which was also a coffee shop. Yuppies were sitting around with their iPads and their real babies. I decided not to use the money to pay Vic to go out with me. Instead, I bought a cream satin blouse with a pussy bow and a black pencil skirt, perfect for work, then headed over to Sainsbury's and stocked up on Bio-Oil to counteract the aging effects of smoking. I bought a bulk pack of Golden Virginia too. I threw the rest of the money—seventeen quid—down the drain outside Snappy Snaps.

I had to go back to the apartment; I needed to get my ballet flats for work.

I tried to discern a sign in the clouds that meant Vic would definitely Skype me. But there was nothing. I saw a black cat cowering behind a trash can but it didn't cross my path. I counted seven crowlike birds fighting over a scrap of food. But then another crow appeared. Eight is fucking useless to me. The grand old doors of the church where William Wilberforce had once preached against slavery were being shut and locked at just the moment that I tried to enter. I wanted to pray for Vic to text me. I got really excited when I passed the pond again and saw two white swans, their necks gracefully arched together, swimming in perfect symmetry. They looked utterly in love.

When I got closer, I realized that they weren't swans at all—just two white plastic bags, floating aimlessly across the freezing water.

"Yah 'cause it's a gay thing," Jasper was saying, spread-eagled on the chaise longue, fondling one of Freddie's uncle's bejeweled daggers. "That's why he wrote it. 'Cause he wanted this guy in, like, Copenhagen in the 1830s or something ridiculous. And the guy was like, *no*. I'm not a homo. I'm getting married. So Hans Christian Andersen was like, fine. I'm going to write a story about it instead and make, like, a shit load of money."

"Who let Jasper in?" I demanded.

They were all dead drunk. Two empty bottles of champagne were standing on the painting of my face. The bust of Freddie's uncle seemed to shake its head in horror. Samuel was as alabaster as Allegra now; he looked like he was going to be sick.

"Jasper," I said. "Get out."

"Ann-Marie, charmed to see you as always," said Jasper. He tried to kiss me on the mouth but I blocked him. He stank of musk.

"I'm allowed to have friends over," slurred Freddie. "We don't have to live like fucking hermits in a cave anymore. Exams are over."

"Yeah, so over. Hey." Jasper had a widow's peak. He had the frigid elegance of the international technocratic elite. "I'm so sorry to hear that you didn't get your degree." He tried to get his arm around my waist; again, I blocked him.

"It was a gesture," I said. "Of emancipation."

"Yeah right," said Freddie.

"You only got a third!" I shouted at him. "Tell that to your fucking father, then see if he lets you curate a bloody show!"

"I think it's fabulous," said Jasper. "Artists shouldn't have degrees. They should be renegades."

"I'm not an artist," I said.

"Yeah, what are you again?" asked Freddie.

"Oh, shut your mouth," I told him.

Jasper collapsed onto the chaise longue. "So actually that cartoon is like a gay allegory. Because Hans was dreaming of being a human née heterosexual instead of a mermaid née queer in order to be, like, part of their world." He swigged from his flute. "It's about yearning."

"I know about yearning," said Samuel.

"So do I, so do I," said Jasper. "I was yearning to smash Sebastian's fucking face in last night when he started doing that preposterous whirling dervish dance."

My heart stopped.

"Yeah, and she was there, clapping and shit." Jasper looked at Samuel. "Your sister."

"Shouldn't hold a grudge, old man," said Freddie.

"Was it a party?" I said.

"Yah." Jasper grinned. "Ann-Marie, I'm surprised you weren't invited."

Freddie laughed.

"It was their going-away bash," Jasper went on.

"Where are they going?" I said.

"Sebastian and Allegra are going to Mexico for six months to do some theater thing about Aztec sacrifice," said Samuel in a rush. "Allegra's going to rip out someone's heart at the top of a pyramid and eat it."

"Yeah, while Seb waits to ask her permission to use the toilet," said Freddie.

The cigarette smoke in the room seemed to move inside my brain, fogging all thought.

Then I was striding over to the mantelpiece and crushing the seven brittle wishbones that I had saved and dried every time Freddie and I cooked Nigella's roast chicken.

FOUR

MICHEL THE SOUS-CHEF was simulating an ecstatic kind of anal sex with a skinned rabbit on the stainless steel cooker in the kitchen downstairs at William's, the Soho restaurant where I'd worked for the last five months. The rabbit's eyes were agog and aware like a human. It looked mortified. Michel held the hind legs with the force of a man about to come and banged the livid red pelvis into his own again and again. The rabbit's body was long and muscular. Only the fluffy tail remained, which Michel squeezed, and he shut his eyes and hollered something about monogamy before he performed a vicious orgasm and collapsed on top of the rabbit's slender back so that we all heard the ribs crunch.

The rest of the kitchen slaves cheered and whistled and looked genuinely happy for once. A pile of rabbits awaited their violation to the left.

This was why I chose the hospitality and catering industry after I failed my degree. I had read Marco Pierre White's memoir *White Slave*, later more tastefully retitled

The Devil in the Kitchen. All that protein and aggression appealed to me—I wanted to experience it for myself.

Now I made an espresso and returned upstairs.

The reception was my domain. I was the reigning door bitch, crowned in the summer, when I had answered William the manager's ad and made my way to Soho shaking like a horse in a thunderstorm. The aftershocks of finals were intense. I lied about my degree; I said that I'd left school at sixteen. William looked at my legs throughout the interview. He told me that my skirt was too short. I said thanks, it was a dress. William said that he'd give me the job if I gave him a blow job. I said no fucking way and stood up, but he said fine and gave me the job anyway, which undermined his authority forever in my eyes.

I had assumed that William owned the restaurant because it was his name above the door, but later Michel told me that no, William had applied for the job as manager because someone with the same name had owned the restaurant back in the 50s, when Muriel Belcher's The Colony Room was at its height just around the corner and Soho was a *place*. William desperately wanted Soho to be a *place* again. The real owner was a man called Bob who never appeared, but oversaw the accounts. He oversaw the renovation of the upstairs into a private members' club, complete with a pianist and a team of mixologists, a billiard room, and something called the Snatch, a cushioned cell where everyone was encouraged to lie down. The iPod nailed to the wall only played songs that encouraged sexual healing.

Everything was going downhill in any case. William's attempt to source reliable foragers in rural areas of the West Country proved bogus; there was a bad write-up in the *Guardian* that used the word "gimmick" three times. But the single most powerful factor that impeded the restaurant's success was William's coke habit, which had soured his soul. He would have been a nice person without it. He was damaged. And damaged people constantly damage everyone else around them, as Madeline the Australian headwaitress had told me often and sadly.

Madeline had left a copy of *Eat, Pray, Love* in the reception drawer. I read it, checking my phone every thirty seconds, then every twenty seconds, then every ten seconds, in the hope that Vic had texted me.

Nothing.

"He's just not that into you," came Madeline's sing-song voice, as she counted the number of covers for the evening. She reeked of a celebrity-endorsed perfume. She was square like a tank but she had a smiley face. She told me about Cirque du Soleil, which she had gone to see the night before with her sister. I told her that I hated musical theater. She said she was amazed that I didn't want to take advantage of all the wonderful entertainment here in London. I said I didn't have the time or money or inclination. She laughed and told me that sarcasm was the lowest form of wit. I said that I wasn't being sarcastic, that I really hated musical theater. I didn't see anything good about it at all. She went to give the waiters their briefing.

My job was to be nice at all times, to stand up when

a guest appeared, to not merely point him or her in the direction of the toilet, but to accompany him or her all the way into the toilet if necessary and even wipe his or her ass for him or her if he or she should so request it because he or she is paying a fuck load of money to be here, and I can get another girl who looks fucking grateful to be working, William had told me. I was paid a lucky seven quid an hour, which was why I took this job as opposed to the door bitch job at Ronnie Scott's, which paid an unlucky eight quid an hour.

William appeared just before the first guests were due to arrive and informed me that I was going to get slammed hard from all directions tonight so I better fucking enjoy it.

Paparazzi on motorbikes arrived just before the pop star, her tall, bald, much older boyfriend, and his parents. The paps seemed to balance like a circus pyramid. Their flashes dazzled me through the glass. The pop star was going for the Patti Smith look but without the courage to be truly haggard like Patti. Her hair was dyed black with a blunt fringe. She tried to hide behind it, but I could see her drugged eyes. Her movements were languid and paranoid. William ushered her to table twenty.

The first sitting was nearly full and there was a lull at reception. The cloakroom was stuffed with mink. Umbrella tickets were scattered on the floor. I never would be able to figure it out. William emerged from the toilet looking jaundiced and told me to wipe the mirrored surface of the coffee table and straighten the orchids. Instead, I read about Elizabeth Gilbert falling to her knees in the middle of the night while her soon-to-be-ex-husband slept, unaware that his wife was praying to God for a divorce so she could embark on a mystical quest of self-exploration. I put the book down and exited the restaurant through the revolving doors.

I was wearing the pussy bow and pencil skirt that I had bought with Freddie's money. I stood in front of the paps and posed. I waited for their bulbs to start popping—would they pop?—but there was nothing.

William came outside. "What the fuck do you think you're doing?" he shouted.

"You said when I started here that it would be a good opportunity to network."

He hauled me back inside.

He threw me in the cloakroom and shut the door.

Now I was alone.

I waited.

There was a knock on the door. I opened it.

An old man who looked like a toad was standing in reception. He was wearing a cravat. He handed me his cane and camel-hair coat.

"Reservation for Douglas at nine," he said.

"Certainly, sir."

The old man was looking at me with shameless hunger. I led him to table twenty-two in the far corner of the restaurant—set for one—and wished him a pleasant evening.

"I hope it *will* be pleasant," he said.

I saw a violently pink tongue dart over thin lips. He ordered the house apricot bellini.

The pop star was crying on table twenty.

I checked my phone. There was a text!

Please call. Love Mum X

"Fuck." I threw the phone at the vase of orchids, but it landed on the leather banquette, and bounced.

A man walked in and shouted: "Taxi!"

All the lights in the restaurant went out.

The taxi driver and I looked at each other in the darkness.

One scented candle flickered.

"Vic?" I said.

There was silence.

Soon the guests started murmuring, and then screaming their complaints. William ordered waiters to get more candles, apologizing, but then he got angry and threw at least three tables out.

"It is my lot in life to search for black umbrellas in the dark," I told the taxi driver.

"Taxi?" he said again.

"Oh my god!" I said. "Vic had a poster of *Taxi Driver* on his wall. I left his room only this morning. This must be a sign." I hugged *Eat, Pray, Love*, then waved it at the taxi driver, but he ignored me and cut out of the restaurant.

Madeline appeared and told me that she didn't know

why the crying pop star had a reputation in the press for being a sweet girl next door because she was a fucking diva and didn't even say thank you for the complimentary amuse-bouches that William had sent over.

The lights came back on.

Freddie and Jasper turned up at the restaurant at ten to ten, fucked. Samuel lagged behind. He was wearing a onesie with the words "Please Snort Me" emblazoned across it. The letters looked appliquéd on. He wasn't wearing a coat and his thin, ginger arms were trembling. Freddie and Jasper were bundled up.

"Go away," I told them. "I'm busy."

"No," said Jasper. His hair was slicked back Lost Generation style, and he wore a white silk scarf around his throat that added to the impression that he was Count Dracula and had come to drink my blood. "We want a table for two."

"Three," said Samuel, glumly. "Freddie, I really don't have any money."

"Nonsense," said Freddie. "We don't need money."

"You do," I said.

Jasper glided into the dining room. He pounced on table fourteen, which had yet to be reset. The tablecloth was a mess of rabbit juice and bread crumbs.

They sat down.

I was returning to reception, when the toad gentleman at table twenty-two said: "Miss. Miss. If you please."

I went over and smiled my door-bitch smile, explaining that only the waiters took orders, but he shook his head. He was looking very intently into my eyes. He held aloft a white wire which trailed somewhere under the table. I saw that he'd gone for the salmon: good choice. At least the salmon hadn't been raped. I put the earbud in and waited. Rising voices of some kind of choral music competed with the din in the restaurant.

"*Spem in Alium*," said the man. "Thomas Tallis."

I pulled the earbud out. "That's lovely. Thanks. I hope you enjoyed the salmon."

He looked disappointed.

I overheard Jasper ordering the most expensive bottle of wine on the menu. "And a cloudy lemonade for the child," he said, nodding to Samuel.

Jasper and Freddie laughed.

A woman was waiting at reception with a girl about thirteen.

"Marge Perez," she said. She was American. Her hair was red and spiraled in massive whorls around her head.

The girl looked like a ballerina. Her hair was done up in a chignon. She yawned: "Mommy, but I'm not hungry."

"Quiet, honey," said Marge. "I'm sorry the sitter got sick, but you know Auntie Steph will be so pleased to see you."

I led them to table eight.

Auntie Steph appeared. Auntie Steph was in fact Stephanie Haight.

I was speechless.

She was wearing a long duffel coat and, beneath that, gray tracksuit bottoms. I led her to table eight. I couldn't walk away. I wanted to tell her all about my botched sex with Vic the war criminal. I wanted to ask her how I could put that in a social and political context. But instead I said: "Why are men such fucking bastards?"

The ballerina looked at me with contempt. So did her mother.

Stephanie didn't seem abashed at all. After a moment she smiled. Her eyes remained sad. Her face seemed burdened with wisdom. She was undeniably beautiful.

Stephanie and I continued to stare at each other.

I felt an acute sense of recognition. Maybe this was the coup de foudre?

Finally she said: "It's not the men's fault. It's the Symbolic."

"Capital S," said Marge, with bitterness.

The scent of Madeline's perfume engulfed me from behind and I had to leave.

"Kill the pig! Kill the pig!"

Freddie and Jasper were banging their forks on the table. Russian linen napkins were tucked into their collars. The restaurant's signature dish sat at the center. It was plagiarized from St. John: a whole pig's head, sawed in half and braised, the brain transformed into beige glue. The pig grinned.

Samuel was trying to talk: "Yeah 'cause there are five ways of saying 'getting money from your parents' in Williamsburg because it's like an informal economy. Because it's based on love not money."

"Do you mean privilege?" said Freddie.

"It's a privilege to be loved," said Samuel, confused.

"I'm not sure you know what your value system is," said Jasper, slurping up the head cheese. A gland spilled down his shirt. "I know what mine is. Do you know what yours is, Fred?"

"Naturally," said Freddie. "It's zero. Zero degree. Start from nothing. Nihilism."

"You know," said Jasper, his mouth full. "Baudrillard said dandyism is an aesthetic form of nihilism. That must be why you're such an effortless dandy, Fred."

Freddie put down his knife and fork. "Jasp. Dandies are painful."

Samuel was ticking the terms off on his fingers. He wasn't eating the pig. "Getting the kush, picking the berries, waxing Oedipal, getting the patrimony, changing the diaper." He paused. "I'm not sure about the last one because surely it's like your *parents* are changing your diaper if you're getting their money?"

The pop star was still crying when I was called on to get her out of the restaurant via the kitchen slave exit. She wanted to avoid the cameras.

"They are *monsters*," said her boyfriend's mother.

I was reminded of one of the pop star's early videos, in which she had cried nonstop for the duration of the song. In a twist on the miracle of the saint crying milk, her neo-goth eye makeup had made her look as though she were crying black crude oil. She had been done up in a saint's outfit, sitting on an oil rig. The North Sea had raged in the background.

The kitchen slaves sodomized the pop star with their eyes when we went downstairs. The pile of skinned rabbits had diminished almost to nothing.

The reception was quiet.

Stephanie Haight was eating a lemon posset. The ballerina was eating a chocolate fondant. The Marge woman was saying: "I'm not getting mad. I'm not getting mad. I just don't know how you can defend that woman."

Madeline was eating rabbit scraps off guests' plates in the cloakroom.

I moved closer to Stephanie.

"Oh, but I do," Marge went on. "I do know how you can defend her. You defend Gabriella because you created Gabriella. How many times, Stephanie, are you going to root out a fine young thing and turn her into a *whatever you want* and then cry yourself to sleep at night when she takes what you taught her and turns her back on you?"

"She hasn't turned her back." Stephanie halted. "She always picks up the phone when I call her. Sometimes. Her work is very demanding."

"Yes, I imagine that ritualistic self-harming is quite demanding."

"And Gabriella was not *fine*," said Stephanie. "She had a natural body, sure. She had a supple, Rabelaisian body. A body of excess. Oh, the monstrous feminine excess!" She laughed. "But she was just a nude model. She would have been a nude model all her life if I hadn't pulled her out of that phallocentric head space and turned her into an artist in her own right."

"Yeah," said Marge. "I remember. You were writing that piece on nude models—right?"

"Right." Stephanie ate another spoonful of posset. "For the *LRB*. Or was it *Spare Rib*?"

Marge shrugged.

"Gabriella stood out right away," said Stephanie. "She looked so sorrowful, the standing female nude. And when she opened her mouth and I heard that she was *common* like me, I couldn't resist. I couldn't resist any single one of my prodigies, Marge. Like you, Marge."

Marge smiled. "Yes, I remember when I first walked into your class on feminist rereadings of the Hegelian unhappy consciousness at Harvard. You looked so beautiful in that African robe. I was so impressed by you—we all were. When was that?"

"Seventy-eight. Must have been. I was in my third year of grad school. And the Kappa Alpha Theta initiations—such fun!" Stephanie finished her posset.

"Gabriella's from a later world," said Marge. "She's from a later, more disenchanted world. She's third wave." She bent her fingers in quotes. "If that is a thing at all."

"Maybe she doesn't wanna be part of any *wave*, Marge," said Steph, expressively. "Have you ever considered that? Maybe she's not into *waves*. Listen. Gabriella's just doing what we did. She's just using what she's got. Her own experience."

"Bullshit." Marge put her fork down. "She's using her cunt."

The ballerina looked at Marge, who said: "Don't worry, honey. It's not a pejorative." Marge went on:

"Gabriella wants a new cunt. And new eyes—better to see out of. Better to see herself out of. She's just like a . . . she's a paradigm of selfish fucking neoliberal individualism, Stephanie."

"We all wanted to be individuals, Marge, remember? We all wanted to be *ourselves*. That's why we got involved. We didn't want to be what our mothers—"

"Yes, but we sought solidarity!"

"But Gabriella is a visual *artist*," said Stephanie. "She's not a sociologist like you—"

"Do artists have the right to disavow their foremothers? To pretend that second wave feminism never happened? That they owe us *nothing*?"

Stephanie sat back and laughed. "Oh, I get it. So you want her to defer to *us*. The great wall of us. You want her to pay homage to our grand narrative—"

"Grand narrative?!" spat Marge. "You're the one constructing the big, macho, monolithic grand narrative, lady. Going around on your book tour. With your fancy agent—"

"Not all of us wanted to stay in the academy, Marge."

"I entered the academy because of *you*, Stephanie. I became an academic because *you* inspired me. *You* told me that that was my path."

"Well," said Stephanie. "It's not my path. The academy is not necessarily the best way to communicate—"

"Communicate what exactly?!" Marge grabbed her glass of wine and chugged it. "That romantic love is structurally akin to the subliminal power dynamics of sadomasochistic relationships? That domination and submission inform the way we treat each other? Ha! Shulie Firestone, Jess Benjamin were talking about that thirty, forty years ago." Marge closed her eyes and became still.

"Mommy?" said the ballerina.

Marge opened her eyes. "You're a *populist*, Stephanie."

There was silence.

"Bite me," said Stephanie.

An alarm started across the street.

Stephanie grabbed her handbag.

The alarm got louder until guests were covering their ears and lowering their heads as though intending to hide under the tables from the noise.

William emerged from the toilets, his eyes googly like a cartoon. He demanded that I check what the fuck—and what the fuck was I doing here anyway loitering near people trying to eat.

I went outside.

The town house across the street was on fire. Its roof burned against the black night, smoking out the stars. Great gusts of red were rising, getting bigger and bigger. I saw arms reaching out of three top-floor windows. The paps had started taking pictures. There were sirens. Fire engines screeched around the corner of Frith Street and firemen leaped out and operated their neon machinery as the smoke curled higher still. Despite the fact that I knew he was nowhere near at all, I wanted to run into the building and save Vic's life.

William was telling the guests to leave their minks behind.

Marge was gripping the hand of her child ballerina, who looked excited. Her eyes were gleaming in a satanic way. Stephanie had disappeared. Samuel, Jasper, and Freddie had disappeared. There was the sound of glass shattering; glass rained down, shattering more on the pavement. From a door on the right of the burning building, people were sprinting into the frozen air, holding hands and pushing each other out of the way. They were men, well-heeled and mostly middle-aged, some younger, mostly bankers and lawyers, slick, clean-shaven, too terrified to look guilty. There were women too, all young, pretty, or at least women who had cemented a mask that could pass for prettiness over their plain or aging faces. Women in short red skirts and patent-leather, thigh-high boots, women with topknots out of which sprouted synthetic hair, women who were accustomed to being tired. The men and their prostitutes shared neon blankets tossed over their shoulders by firemen.

Soon the power of the hoses had beaten the fire into submission and the area was cordoned off. The guests filed back inside to pay their bills.

The toad gentleman remained seated at table twenty-two while I matched guest to mink. There was a lot of shouting about lost items; William was called, but the fire seemed to have endowed him with an ancient kind of Zen and even his verbal abuse was tranquil.

The toad gentleman caught my eye as I said thank you so much for coming, we do apologize for the disruption—a thousand times or more. He was holding up his iPad for me to see. I squinted at it. He beckoned me closer.

On the screen, a mauve heart was efflorescing with digital emotion: it was spurting something. His tongue darted out again; it was the same color as the heart.

"Your fucking friends have left without paying again," said Madeline, bulldozing into reception. "It's coming out of your paycheck." She looked at the receipt. "£790."

I tried to call Freddie, but he didn't answer.

Reluctantly, I called Jasper.

"Come and play," he giggled. "We're playing."

"Where?"

"Upstairs. Up."

I went back through the restaurant toward the slanting stairs that spiraled up the interior of the building.

The toad man shot out a toad hand as I passed. He held my wrist. He was wearing red-and-gold cuff links. "Please," he said in a gentle voice.

I stopped.

His pond eyes looked up into mine.

"The restaurant's closed now, sir. If you wouldn't—"

"Sit with me for just one moment."

I did.

We were alone, side-by-side, on the leather banquette. He plucked the single white orchid out of the vase on the table and gave it to me.

"Thanks," I said. "But that's restaurant property. They get put in the fridge overnight. There are cameras everywhere."

His comb-over fell into his face. His scalp was slick.

There were brown speckles on his forehead and veiny networks on his cheeks.

"My wife died last year," he said. "Breast cancer."

I frowned.

"Yes, it was a terrible, irreplaceable loss. We'd been married for thirty years." He looked down. "I've been waiting for a woman like you. I've been waiting to impart jouissance to a woman like you. Do you know what jouissance is?"

I shook my head.

"It is the extreme of pleasure," he said. "Where pleasure meets nonpleasure and life, existence, the cosmos becomes a black hole. It is the threshold of pleasure and pain, of sanity and insanity." He paused. "Of Eros and Thanatos."

I stood up and gave a sunny, American smile. "I do hope you enjoyed the salmon."

"Where are you from?" he asked me.

"France," I lied. "Paris."

That tongue again. It was actually the color of beetroot. He extended it to maximum length, as though trying to catch a fly. He waggled it around. Then he put it back in his mouth. "Please come to the ASH Hotel bar after your shift." He slid a business card toward me. "I will be waiting for you from midnight onward. I will wait all night."

Jasper was shooting balls off the end of the billiard table in the private members' club upstairs. Samuel had been ordered to stand at the end and catch the balls on the premise that the ball boy was an esteemed and essential figure in any game. "Play up and play the game," Freddie was repeating, stupidly.

"You're not supposed to be in here," I said. "This is members only. Get out."

"Why are you always telling people to get out?" said Jasper, sipping his negroni.

"And I want my money," I said.

"What money?" said Freddie.

"For dinner," I said.

Freddie laughed. "I want my money for the booze earlier this afternoon. Think I'd forgotten about that, did you? Nice little outfit you came home with."

"I'll call the police," I said.

Now they all laughed—even Samuel.

"Tell Ann-Marie where you got that babygro, Samuel." Freddie chalked his cue.

"It's a onesie," said Samuel. "I made it! Yeah 'cause I read this article on *VICE* that had the coolest headline ever—'Please Snort Me!'" He gestured to his chest. "So I, like, copied it!"

"What was the article about, though?" said Jasper.

"I don't know." Samuel looked ashamed. "I didn't read it."

Now Freddie and Jasper nearly killed themselves laughing.

"I'm calling William," I said.

"Ann-Marie." Jasper tried to slink one well-moisturized arm around my shoulders, but I punched him.

"Ow!" He rubbed his gut. "You can take it as payment for all the times you fucked me and then left me and went back to your whirling dervish of a boyfriend. Like what about that time in Vietnam in the Agent Orange forest, where there were just stumps. That was fucking romantic. When Sebastian was supposed to be chugging that fucking dreadful cod trawler around the Thanet coast but he was off poking Allegra in Paris. Wasn't she doing a summer school at Lecoq?"

"Yeah," said Freddie.

"For that one night at least," said Jasper. "You didn't think about Sebastian. You didn't care about Sebastian at all. Did you, Ann-Marie?"

"I always cared," I said.

"But you fucking loved it. Didn't you?"

"Can we talk about something else for once?" said Freddie.

Jasper positioned himself over the billiard table and fired at empty space; no balls clicked. He turned to Samuel. "You know, one thing I will say. The problem with your big sister Allegra as a lay was that she was too damn pliable."

Samuel looked at Freddie.

"Jasper," said Freddie. "Dude. Don't."

"Yah," Jasper went on. "I mean, when I was fucking Allegra and I had her perfect fucking porcelain behind in my hands and I was squeezing her cunt, it was like trying to get blood out of a stone—"

"You're disgusting," I said.

"Wait," said Jasper. "There's a compliment for you."

I waited.

"She was never really *there*, you know what I mean?" Jasper went on. "I felt like she could just be anything I wanted her to be like, like her buttocks were made out of melting wax and I could fashion them into anything I chose. I felt like I was crafting a woman!"

Samuel left the room.

Freddie followed him.

Jasper stared at me.

I stared at Jasper.

"But with you at least I felt like you were with me," he said.

FIVE

What does it mean for a woman to submit?

To submit is to lose oneself. To want to submit is to want to lose oneself. I'm talking about consent. We can lose ourselves through religion, alcohol, sex, drugs, political fanaticism, or love.

Why would a woman want to lose herself in love?

In short, why would she want to fall?

Because it's fun? Oh yes, it's fun.

Or because it offers her respite from the pressures of the meritocracy?

The meritocracy demands that she alone is responsible—for her successes, yes. But also for her failures. Falling is a way of avoiding failure—or success.

Falling is a form of submission.

The modern woman senses that in order to win a man's love, she must deny her capability and regress.

Marge had left her copy of Stephanie's book under the table. It was signed:

Dear Marge,

Sending you love from my (rightful?) place of exile. It's cold here but the sistahood can't get me from all the way across the Atlantic. I'm sorry again—if it's right for me to say sorry?

In solidarity, as ever,
Steph

I stroked the dust jacket, hoping to absorb the gravitas contained in those pages by the power of touch alone.

I was sitting on the front step of the closed Barclays next to Leicester Square station, working my way through a family-size bucket of fried chicken, which I had purchased from the fake KFC across the road.

A bachelorette party wearing angel wings and devil horns staggered out of the all-night pizza place, clutching a long train of torn white netting. *Fiona! Fiona!* they chanted. Fiona grabbed a man wearing a pin-striped shirt who seemed to be attached to the bachelorette party and shoved her clenched fist down the front of his trousers. He groped under her tube top. Her friends began to sing: *Puuuuuurrrrfect!* The old Eddi Reader song. The man walked away.

Rickshaws carrying cargos of people fucked out of their brains swerved dangerously close to the night buses that swelled with yet more people cramming kebabs into their mouths, letting their sleeping heads knock against the windows on the upper deck, missing the view of this splendid city.

"Do you know, there is no direct translation for jouissance in English?" Toad Man was saying to me over martinis in the bar.

I had taken a night bus from Leicester Square to the ASH Hotel, which was situated between the City and the East district, combining money with creativity in an ideal cocktail of dynamic penthouse suites, stellar service, and conceptual art, according to the brochure that I was reading intently.

"I like to think of myself as French in spirit," he went on. "Even though I'm English with only the faintest tinge of Scot." He chortled and rubbed his belly. "So to sit with a French woman in the flesh is something of a minor miracle for me."

"Minor?"

"Oh, they are hard to find in London. The French tend to stick together and close ranks. Unless I were to lurk outside the gates of the Lycée!"

"No, I mean why is it only a minor miracle? To find me?"

"Do forgive me! A major one! *Salud!*"

We clinked glasses; mine was already empty.

I sucked the olive on its stick. I stopped sucking it when I saw what Toad Man's eyes were doing to my mouth. That tongue appeared. I crossed my legs. Then I uncrossed them. I rattled the cocktail stick against my teeth.

There was a long silence.

"But we don't even know each other's names!" I said with a laugh. I let my eyelids droop, seductively.

"Are you sleepy, dear?"

I opened my eyes as wide as possible. "No."

"James." He extended his hand. It was warm and soft.

"I'm Camille."

"How erotic."

"Yeah. My mother named me after my father's courtesan. She was a chorus girl at the Moulin Rouge. She could kick her legs up extremely high."

"And what does your mother do?"

"She . . . bakes croissants. But she was, like, photographed by Man Ray and all the surrealists back in the day."

"Back in the day? As in the 1920s day?"

"Yeah," I said. "She's very old." I gestured to the bartender for another drink. He was about my age. There was a dish of spicy green balls on the bar; I was crunching them at record speed. "Hm," I said. "Japanese, I think. Try one?"

James shook his head. "What do you look for in a man?"

New drinks arrived. I said thanks to the bartender but he averted his eyes.

"I don't look for anything." I paused. "Do you know the song 'I'll Be Your Mirror' by Velvet Underground? Yeah, I'm looking for that. The lyric goes something like, 'when you think the night has taken over your mind and inside you're unkind and twisted, I'll show you that you're not.' I mean,

I'm looking for a man who can see that I'm not horrible even if I act horrible sometimes."

"So you're looking for a punching bag?"

"No. That's not what I meant."

"Some men are very threatened by female strength." He stared at my thighs.

"I know."

"Some men are appalled by the idea of performing cunnilingus ad nauseam. They regard the vulva as a Venus flytrap, designed to eat them alive."

I downed the martini. Now I was getting really drunk. I put my hand on James's shoulder and said: "What I love about you is that you've got a lot of progressive ideas about women. I love that about you." I gave him a kiss on the cheek.

He acted quickly; his face jerked to the left and he tried to get that tongue in my mouth. I pulled back.

He looked sad, so I said: "But how rude of me! I haven't asked you what you do?"

"I am in the pussy business."

"Oh? That's not what I meant." I was slurring. "I mean—this is for free." I opened my arms wide. "I am here for free. Because I like you."

"Why, thank you, my wild orchid." He touched the tip of my nose. "I like you too."

"And I'm lonely."

He pulled a BlackBerry out of his waistcoat pocket. "Look." He showed me a picture. It was a cat with orange eyes and blue-gray fur.

"That looks like a cute alien!" I cried. I gestured to

the bartender for two more martinis. He was wrapping the spirit bottles in layers of plastic wrap; they looked like silkworm cocoons. I told him so. He ignored me.

I hitched my pencil skirt up shorter.

"That's Lola," said James. "She is a Chartreux. I breed. One is not supposed to breed Chartreux on English shores according to the blasted CFA."

"CFA?"

"Cat Fanciers' Association. But to hell with them!" His face became angry. "They are the most sumptuous pussies in all the world as far as I'm concerned! In all of Europe. I've been obsessed with them ever since I came across one while backpacking through the Chartreuse Mountains, from whence they derive their name." He stared into my eyes. "I was a young man then. That was before I met Margaret."

I reached for the tiny green balls but they had all gone.

"There, the mountains are blue," said James. "The monks make blue liqueur. Everything is blue."

"I want to go there," I said.

A white statue wearing nothing but a pair of jazzy Speedos and Ray-Bans was standing in the corner of the elevator, reflected a million times in the mirrors that fenced us in. James and I were reflected too: we looked hideous together. The statue was made of porcelain, not marble. Its hair was slicked back, *American Psycho* style.

"He reminds me of my father," I slurred, pointing to the statue. We were heading up to the seventh floor: good luck. "'Cept my father was taller and looks more like Tom Cruise in *Risky Business*. Have you seen that film?"

James shook his head.

"Me neither. But I've seen the posters. There's a photo of my mother and father on a cruise ship in 1984. That was the year they met. Actually, they met *on* the cruise ship. Because my father was making a noise in cruises. A big noise. And my mother was just . . . there. It was sailing from Portsmouth to Bilbao." I looked at my million weathered faces in the mirrors. "They fell in love."

There was a ding. The doors opened. The hallway was long and pale and candy colored. It was making me seasick. I touched the wall, and found that it was made of leather.

"Was your mother selling croissants on the cruise?"

"No," I said. "That was in her muffin phase. She was selling muffins."

James laughed heartily and grabbed my hand. He kissed my knuckles. I balled my fist. He pried my hand open and put my index finger in his mouth. He sucked it very slowly. I watched him, fascinated.

"I love a girl with imagination," he said to my finger.

"But that bit about the cruise ship was true," I told him.

James was in the bathroom grooming. The bathroom door was closed. I sat on the end of the king-size bed and stared at the cupboard containing the TV for a long while. Then I shouted loud enough for him to hear: "I love you!"

"I love you too!" he shouted back.

I opened the cupboard and stared at the blank TV screen inside. I opened the minibar and uncorked a bottle of champagne. It hissed. I filled two flutes.

A collage of insects hung over the candy-colored leather sofa, which matched all the cushions and all the curtains and all the sheets. On closer inspection, I saw that the insects were cutouts of vintage porn. This was confirmed by the framed text next to the picture. There was a stack of magazines on the coffee table: *Frieze*, *Monocle*, *Dazed and Confused*.

I turned on the TV. *Come Dine with Me*. A brunette was laughing and pointing at a mound of collapsed cream and banana.

James appeared, full of the joys of spring. I was full of something; not spring. The champagne had failed to go to my head. He looked about twenty years younger than he had in the bar. His comb-over was freshly oiled.

Now he opened the box of truffles on the pillow and pushed one into my mouth. It tasted too sweet. He unfastened my pencil skirt and rolled it over my legs. He rolled down my tights too. He rolled down my underpants. He was squatting in front of me like a toad.

I shifted away from him and turned the volume up loud. "I think it's the voice-over," I said. "That's what makes this show so funny."

The brunette was leading a conga line around her front room. A man who looked like an accountant was circling his hips, unevenly. The song changed to "Macarena."

James pawed at me.

I said in a loud, assertive voice: "Sebastian's parents would never let their kids watch TV. That's why they grew up so creative. When Sebastian first came to my school, I'd only ever read *The Baby-Sitters Club* and *Sweet Valley High*."

"Who's Sebastian?" said James.

"But then he introduced me to all these books. Henry Miller and Anaïs Nin." I turned to James. "Have you read them?"

He shook his head.

"I thought Sebastian was a genius like Miller," I went on. "He said he wanted to make my ovaries incandescent like Miller. But when we did it the first time, they didn't go incandescent. So Sebastian." I laughed. "Got really angry and started punching the wall and going insane. It was funny. Because he wasn't really like that—he wasn't insane."

James lay back on the bed. Then he sat up again.

"He wasn't really a genius either," I said. "When we were about thirteen he told me that I wasn't in love with him—I was in love with love itself. He said it was a privileged form of mania because apparently a lot of artists and writers had it. He said he didn't have it, and he seemed really angry about that. But I was sure it was a curse—whatever he said I had. It must have been a curse because it meant my heart didn't belong to—myself. It belonged to someone other than myself. It belonged to him."

"So you like being owned?" purred James.

"No," I said. "That's not what I meant." I laughed.

"We ran away to Paris after our SATs. When we were fourteen. We left in the middle of the night and got the bus to Dover. Sebastian had stolen the money from his parents. Then we got the ferry. It was amazing—we went out on the deck in the pitch-black darkness and you couldn't see the horizon. Everything looked black. We got wet from the water." I laughed again. "Obviously. It was the sea. We stayed away for three days. My mother went fucking crazy but his parents didn't even notice that he'd gone. They thought he was on a school trip that they'd forgotten about."

"Hmm."

"When we came back, there was this awful meeting with my mother and his parents. His mother said that we should give our children roots and wings, but my mother said that ambition is the best form of contraception and the French are notoriously sex mad."

"Yes, you are."

"She said that France is a sex mad country, but Sebastian's father said: 'But a lovely place for a romantic weekend away at this time of year.' Sebastian said his father wanted him to die because he was too tall. My mother tried to stop me from seeing Sebastian, so I ran away to his house and lived there. I used to always feel so safe in his house. I only went back home when she said I could carry on seeing him, but she threw all the party invitations from his parents straight in the trash. She hated the whole family after that—because they were louche. His parents were always having parties."

James was tugging at the ends of my pussy bow. He

realized that it was stitched in place. He unzipped the blouse at the back. My hair got caught in the zip. I lifted my hair up and he told me that the nape of my neck was exquisite. I felt like I would cry—the way he was touching me was so gentle.

"Get off," I said.

He paused. "All right." He paced the room. The carpet was salmon pink. "I know you're young," he said. "I mean, I know I'm old."

"You're not that old."

He had unzipped his trousers. I could see a swarm of Bart Simpson faces on his boxer shorts.

He knelt down before me and clutched my hands. "You've talked about your lost love," he said. "Now let me talk about mine."

I yawned. "All right."

"When Margaret died, I thought I could never love again. I thought I would never see another woman's face who I would know, just know. That familiarity is." He closed his eyes. "What I miss the most." His eyelashes were gray. "I know you were only joking when you said you loved me before, because you can't love me, because we only just met." He released my hands. "Why would you love an old man like me?" He stood up and fiddled with the iPod on the wall. He turned the TV off.

The song began: "I'll Be Your Mirror."

"Turn it off," I said. "Please."

We lay next to each other on the bed for a long time.

"It's a coincidence that you like pussies," I said, eventually. I had my back to him. "Because I once rescued some pussies from a refuge."

"Where are they now?"

"Oh. I don't know. I had to take them back to the refuge."

An hour passed.

James heaved himself on top of me. He whispered in my ear: "I was always faithful to Margaret, right to the end. I cared for her for eight years. But she always said to me: 'After I've gone, James, please feel free to impart jouissance to whomsoever you do wish. Otherwise it is a crime against women.'"

"A crime?"

"Yes. And let me tell you, there was crime *in* her jouissance too. The way she howled when she came. It reminded me of an animal caught in a trap." He rolled off me. "It was the same sound that she made in the hospital bed during her last moments on earth. She howled like she was coming. She howled because she wanted more of life."

His tongue slid into my mouth; I pulled away. He sucked on my nipple like an energetic little baby and I let him for as long as I could. Then I sat up and lit a cigarette. Out of the window, I watched the traffic circling around something in the distance.

"This is a nonsmoking room," he said.

I put my cigarette out on the lid of the truffle box. "Would you say that Margaret was your muse, James?"

"Perhaps. I never thought of it before."

"Because there was this one time that Sebastian and I were sitting on a bench outside Finsbury Park station and he was like: 'I never believed in the concept of the muse until I met you.' We were about eighteen. I had no idea what a muse was. He said a muse was a mythic woman who inspired men to make great literature. The men extracted her feminine essence. She couldn't create anything herself. Sebastian said he was going to extract my essence. He sounded really mean when he said that. I got up and I was like—I remember that he was smoking a Marlboro Menthol—*I'm not your fucking muse*. Then I ran off. He caught up with me. He said that being a muse could be really sexy like *Betty Blue*. We had watched that film recently. I said: 'But the woman goes crazy. She gouges out her own eye.' And he said: 'But the man writes a novel about it, so it's worth it.' And I was like: 'It's worth her losing an eye?'"

James stuck his finger inside of me.

"Yeah," I went on. "So like a couple of months later, our teacher entered us both for this writing competition. We both got short-listed. We had to go to the Royal Festival Hall. It was really boring. The man who was a poet or something was going on and on and then he announced the winner of the prose category. Sebastian won it for 'The Reluctant Muse.' He went up to the stage like a fighting cock and read a bit of it—something like: "'I'm not your fucking muse," she shouted into the biting North London wind.'" I laughed. "I was shaking because I was so nervous but it turned out I won the poetry category. So it was fine. Otherwise, I wouldn't be able to look at him. My poem was called 'I'm Not Your Fucking Muse,' and there was a line in it which said: 'I'll fuck you up.'"

"That's charming," said James.

"On the way home, the teacher was going on about how Sebastian and I were going to be like Ted and Sylvia. 'But Ted cheated on her,' I said. 'And Sylvia killed herself.' The teacher said: 'Well, you can be like Ted and Sylvia without the cheating and killing yourself parts,' and Sebastian was like: 'Don't worry, Miss. Ann-Marie and I will be together forever.'" I stopped.

There was a long silence.

Finally James said: "Who's Ann-Marie? I thought your name was Camille?"

"Oh—yeah. That was before I changed my name. Camille is my stage name. But I changed it legally, so it's real."

"So you're an aspiring actress?"

"Yeah."

James held my breasts from behind and murmured: "What really turns you on?"

I paused. "Offal."

"Offal?"

"Yeah. Tripe in cream and onions and . . . hearts. Big, bouncy hearts that crunch like an apple when you bite into them and stuff kind of spews out. And kidneys, smelling of piss."

"Piss?"

"Yeah," I said with passion. "*Piss*." I jumped off the bed. "Play, boy!"

James looked startled.

"Play!" My voice was imperious. "Why don't you play?" I went back to my normal voice. "That's what Miss Havisham says to Pip in *Great Expectations*."

"Have you done a lot of community theater?"

"Yes. And professional stuff. RSC stuff. I played Miss Havisham—at Cambridge."

"I can just imagine you in rotting white lace," he said, lurching forward and grabbing me with both hands. His face looked full of hate for a moment. Then he pushed me backward on the bed and I couldn't see his face anymore, but I could feel his mouth latch onto my Venus flytrap and eat it out like a little boy who's terrified his plate will be snatched away at any moment. He ate and ate and ate. My heart was banging. I tried to push his head away, but his scalp was too well-oiled and my hands kept slipping off. He was good at it. I began to moan. I tried to sit up, but he pushed me back down. I had a terrible feeling of losing, as though he were taking the most precious thing I owned.

And then I came.

I lay there, limp and blank.

It seemed to blot out something there in the darkness. It seemed to blot out the darkness itself.

James's face appeared, wet and triumphant.

I said thank you like a good little girl leaving a friend's birthday party, dressed, and ran down leather hallways until I was alone again in the blue light of dawn. I staggered to the nearest trash can and was violently sick.

SIX

THE FORCE OF love was acting on me as I made my way back, groping blindly and ecstatically to a place that I could call home.

It would have to do.

I walked all the way from the ASH Hotel to Russell Square. Then I got a bus to Chalk Farm. The pub where Vic and I had fallen in love stood empty and dark in the dawn. The last hedonists of that Saturday night were slouched around Camden Lock, staring at their own shattered reflections in the water. Men and women wearing rainbow-colored wool were splashing Red Stripe onto the tongues of their panting dogs. The Wetherspoon's was closed; it was too early to get a breakfast meal deal. The bongs and Che Guevara berets and sets of rubber underwear looked terrifyingly sticky, as though nothing had ever been wiped down anywhere in the world.

Finally, I found Vic's terraced house. It was dark inside.

I picked up a stone from a nearby water feature and threw it at a first floor window. It rebounded.

There was silence.

I called Vic's phone; he didn't pick up. I called seven more times.

Then I texted:

I'm outside.

A light came on.

Vic opened the door, thumbing his eyes farther into his face. He was wearing a pair of crisp khaki pajamas. "What are you doing here, Ann-Marie?"

"You remembered my name," I swooned.

"Yes."

"Can I come in?"

"No."

I barged in anyway and shut the door behind me. "Why didn't you reply to any of my emails, Vic?"

"You're a bunny boiler, that's why."

"Those were fucking messages in a bottle, Vic," I said. "Do you know what a message in a bottle is? It's sent in *faith*, Vic, *faith*. Do you know what *faith* is?"

"Quiet," he said. "You'll wake the operators."

Light fell through the front door and illuminated his ghastly feet. I got down on my knees and tried to kiss them.

"Get off." He kicked my cheek by accident.

I gripped my cheek and stood up. I made my eyes look

stricken. Then I slid down the wall until I was squatting on the floor.

"Hey." Vic knelt down in front of me. "Sorry." He tried to move my hand away, but I wouldn't let him.

"So you're a woman beater as well as a war criminal?" I said. "Goes with the territory does it, using women as a weapon of war?"

He stood up again.

I pulled down his khaki pajama bottoms. He tried to pull them back up, but I was already sucking his flaccid penis. He pushed my head back but I made my mouth into a black hole of suction.

"Stop it," Vic was saying. "Stop it." His penis rose, in spite of himself.

I sucked more vigorously.

Vic pulled my hair hard until I couldn't take the pain anymore; I let his penis go. He came, volcanically, all over my face. His semen felt like warm rain.

When I opened my eyes, he was staring down at me in disgust.

"Because I love you," I said.

He released my hair and disappeared down the hall into the kitchen.

I followed him.

Three tampons were laid out on the draining board.

"Whose are those?" I demanded.

Vic threw me a wad of kitchen towel, but I didn't wipe my face. "The operator's," he said. "I'm going back to bed now. It's the middle of the night."

"No, Vic, no." I pointed to the sky beyond their sorry substitute for a conservatory. It was split with hot yellow light. "It's early. It's now, Vic! Now!"

I tried to corner him beside the fridge, but he slipped around me. I picked up one of the tampons and demanded: "What kind of woman leaves their private business right here for all the world to see?"

"It's for the guinea fowl." Vic was washing his hands with the same government-certified antiseptic gel that we use in the restaurant.

"Is that your pet name for her?"

Now I dropped the tampon and drew a knife out of the rack; it was serrated.

"Hey," said Vic, moving around to the other side of the breakfast bar. "That's dangerous."

"Where is this *guinea fowl?*" I said in a baby voice. "Sorry it's the time of the month so you won't be able to fuck her like you want to. Or maybe you're not squeamish at all?"

Vic had his hands flat on the counter. "Please, Ann-Marie. Put that down."

I swiped it through the air.

He said very slowly: "The guinea fowl is not a woman. It is for the food blog. Jan read somewhere that food photographers used to put tampons in a bowl of water and then microwave them. They tuck the tampons in the bird's cavity. It means they keep on steaming. It looks good."

"And who the fuck is Jan?" I said.

"The operator who you met. She's the creative director of the blog."

"Sure."

The rising sun behind him made him look worse and worse, illuminating every flaw on his face.

Vic straightened up. "It's a fact. They can't do it on commercial ad campaigns now, but the Internet doesn't have to comply with the Trade Descriptions Act. They can do whatever the fuck they like."

I pulled open the fridge. There was a hump wrapped in tinfoil. I tore at it. Meat. I ripped off a leg.

"Stop!" Vic screamed. "Stop it, please!" He got the broom and jabbed the guinea fowl out of my hands. He hauled me out the front door and slammed it.

I heard the bolts slide.

I was alone in the street again.

I leaned on the bell with all my weight.

Vic wouldn't open the door without the chain on it. He threatened to call the police. I told him that I was dirty and begged for more paper towels. He tried to slide it through the crack, but I said no I was absolutely filthy and needed soap and water and a proper rinse down.

He opened the door.

I forced him against the wall so that his head banged against a photo of Big Ben. I pinned him in place with my pelvis. I grinded him as mechanically as I could. His eyes rolled up in his head. I pushed my tongue into his mouth. He was saying: "No, no, no."

I ripped off my pussy bow and pencil skirt and pushed him inside of me. I hammered.

He screamed.

"Fuck you," I was saying. "Fuck you, fuck you, fuck you."

He tried to push me off but I wouldn't get off.

Finally he threw me across the hall and crawled frantically toward my handbag. He was tossing my shit all over the place: Golden Virginia and *Heidegger: An Intro* and balls of hair from my hairbrush. He found the condoms.

"Don't think I don't know what your game is," he sneered.

"Vic," I said. "I want to do it bareback."

He was tearing at the packet with his teeth.

"I want there to be nothing." I knelt beside him. "I want there to be nothing between us at all, no layer of protection at all, separating you from me."

"Yeah," said Vic. "Then you'll be coming back here next time at the crack of dawn and telling me that it's mine."

"You can withdraw." I took the condom out of his hands.

"I don't want to withdraw. What about precum?"

"That's a myth," I said.

"What about disease?"

"I want your disease, Vic." I chucked the condom down the hall. "I want you to infect me like you said, with everything that you are and everything that you will be. You'll be a great man one day, I know it."

"I don't have many more days," said Vic. "I'm approaching forty."

"Forty is the beginning of life," I said. "That's when you really start to know yourself."

Vic looked doubtful.

His penis was dead.

"We'll get it back, Vic, I swear," I said. "We'll get it back together." I started doing an erotic dance on the stairs, wrapping one leg around the banister and gyrating against it.

Vic ran down the hall and rolled the condom on his penis before I could stop him. It looked like a transparent blue holiday banana boat. He turned me around on the stairs and pushed himself into me. My fingers kept sliding around the carpet.

Jan the operator opened one of the white doors on the first-floor landing. She paused on her way to the toilet and contemplated us.

Vic came, squawking something about a man called Jeremy who didn't deserve to lose his sight.

Amy Winehouse had been reduced to her formal elements on the wall behind the bus stop at the lock. Her graffitied spirit urged me to destroy myself with drink and drugs and heartbreak. "Go on," she snarled. "Death by love is honorable for a woman. Everyone needs a chance to prove themselves."

A bus arrived and I got on without checking where it was going.

I waited for a sign.

It came: *Angel.*

I had the great idea of breaking into Sebastian's parents' house and positioning myself at the head of their wonderful, old, oak kitchen table, the site of so many of our lively debates. I wanted to rest my head on the cool, oak surface for a while, perhaps tracing my fingers over the familiar cracks. I would leave before his family woke up to discover that I'd completely lost my fucking mind.

I walked along Upper Street until I got to Highbury & Islington station. Then I crossed the road. There was the familiar row of Georgian houses.

I would need a brick to smash a window.

But no.

The front door was open. Sebastian's parents were having a party.

Baby boomers were filing into black cabs, talking about how naughty it was to be out after the sun had risen. The street was shining with light. I put my sunglasses on.

A middle-aged woman in a black velvet cape accosted me in the hallway. Wooden parrots swung from her ears. "You've missed all the celebrations!" she said. "You've missed an unforgettable time that is absolutely not to be missed!"

I took my sunglasses off. "What is everyone celebrating?"

"Winter!" She hugged herself and pretended to shiver with cold, then disappeared into the living room.

I followed her.

Couples were swaying to the opening chords of Roberta Flack's heinous swan song, "The First Time Ever I Saw Your Face." It was the song that had propelled my parents to fall in love under a disco ball on a cruise ship in 1984; it was the song that the drunk girls had been singing on Chalk Farm Road when Vic and I got the taxi back to his; it was the song that recurred within me, a dead ideal. I looked for the source of the doom and there she was: my mother. She was standing guard over the iTunes.

The parrot woman attempted to get a look at the screen, but my mother blocked her.

"This is my favorite," my mother was saying.

"But haven't we already heard it?" said the woman.

"There's nothing like hearing things again," said my mother.

Now Sebastian's parents appeared. His mother was at least two feet taller than his father. They'd always reminded me of a Robert Crumb cartoon, the Amazonian woman bearing the man on her back.

His father held up his hands. "Don't worry," he told me. "They've gone."

"They've got a lot of packing to do," said his mother. "Sebastian will leave everything to the last minute. Luckily Allegra is a planner."

"Wait," I said. "Is this party *still* their leaving party? When are they *actually* leaving?"

"No," said his mother. "This isn't their leaving party. They had that at a Mexican-themed bar the night before last called—I can't remember what it was called. This is a completely different party. No one's leaving here!"

"This is just a winter soirée," said his father.

"How come you are friends with my mum now?" I said. "I didn't think you were friends."

"Oh," said my mother. She had the laptop under her arm. "Ann-Marie, I had no idea at all that you were invited, otherwise I could have given you a lift from home." She was jauntier than I'd ever seen her.

"I came from somewhere else," I said. "It wouldn't have worked."

"London sometimes feels like a desert where the best thing to do is just stay put," said my mother. "And send up a flare rather than risk walking when one never does know when one's supply of food and water will run out!"

Empty wine bottles covered the oak table so I couldn't see it. A Clarice Cliff serving platter bore the remains of smoked salmon blinis. An earthenware bowl of crème fraîche had exploded over the oak, seeping into its sagacious cracks like spackling.

"Everything in the world is ruined!" I screamed.

"Watch your mouth," said my mother.

"I didn't swear." I sank into a chair.

My mother assembled a tower of salmon; I ate it. She passed me a bowl of feta-stuffed cherry tomatoes and I ate those too. I picked up a wine bottle and shook it into my mouth but there was nothing.

"You look ill," she said.

"I'm a rapist," I told her.

A man wearing a brown suit wandered into the kitchen. Hair grew out of his ears.

Mother stared at me. "I'm very concerned about you," she said. "I read the Wikipedia page on Nietzsche. I'm concerned that you've become a Nazi. We've always had a lot of Jewish friends." She crossed her arms.

"I'm Jewish," said the man.

"Nietzsche was not a fucking Nazi!" I screamed. "That is a total travesty! It was Lisbeth his sister who gave his sodding walking stick to Hitler! Nietzsche never would have given him that walking stick! He *hated* nationalism."

"But what about fascism?" said the man. "It's not a laughing matter." He turned to my mother. "Some commentators think that the Western world has entered a neofascist phase."

My mother blushed. "Gosh, if only Phillip were here."

"Who's Phillip when he's at home?" I shouted. I swept about four or five bottles off the table in one gesture and laid my head on the oak. Olive oil had spilled; it covered my forehead.

"I think everyone's had a bit too much to drink," said the man, rocking back on his heels and staggering into the door.

People were crouching on the floor in Sebastian's room, smoking weed and listening to Café del Mar chill-out music. I could see their younger faces trapped like ghosts in their older faces. I could see the younger ones straining to get out.

"That's the thing," a woman with straight gray hair wearing a tribal neck ring was saying. "She just woke up one morning after fourteen years and said: *I've had enough*. She packed her bags and left. You can't blame him for being angry."

"Yes, but to drive her car into a wall?" said a man. "That car meant a lot to her. It was her father's car."

"There are too many cars in this city anyway," said the woman.

They all laughed.

"There are too many people," said the man. "I heard he bought a house in Tuscany."

"Yes," said the woman. "And Diane decided she'd made a horrible mistake and bought a house on the other side of the mountain and begged him to take her back, but he'd already shacked up with a local woman! A potter! A local expat Swedish woman who makes pottery in her own kiln!"

"Excuse me," I said. "This is my room. Would you mind if I have just a few moments in here by myself?"

The man pointed to the license plate stuck to the door, which said: SEBASTIAN, and beneath: STATE OF ARIZONA.

"Oh yeah," I said, exhausted. "Olive bought him that when she first eloped. That was a long time ago."

They didn't move.

I climbed over them and lay on the bed. I got under the duvet. It was the same duvet that Sebastian and I had slept under for years. It smelled of him.

There was a lull in conversation.

"I think I need a refill," said the woman. "Shall we?"

They left.

I burrowed all the way down until the world was black and safe. Then I got up and locked the door. I had a look through Sebastian's wardrobe: his collection of old rags. He'd always despised fashion. I found his old, pilly gray school trousers in a drawer and put them on. Then I found an old school shirt and black school sweater and put those on too. There was nothing on the walls except a framed black-and-white photograph of Jorge Luis Borges looking cross-eyed. Sebastian lived in an apartment with Allegra now.

The wait for the toilet downstairs was unbearable.

I banged on the door.

Sebastian's older sister Olive opened it a crack. "Oh, honey!" She pulled me inside.

Her husband Hal was sitting on the floor by the bath smoking a tube of tinfoil.

"Is that heroin?" I said.

"No." She sat on the edge of the bath. "Don't mind us."

Hal sat back, dead eyed. He wore no shirt.

"What is it then?" I said. "Crack?"

"It's just weed," said Olive. She stared at me intently while I pissed. "Are you all right?"

"Yeah," I said. "I'm fine."

"Is that my brother's school uniform?"

There was banging on the door.

"Come in!" murmured Hal, his head against the white tiles. He was American.

"No, baby," said Olive. Like Stephanie, Olive had acquired an American twang. They had been living in Santa Fe for eight years.

She had blonde hair like Sebastian, but hers was shaved off. She was as good-looking as him. She held my hands between both of hers. "You know the awesome thing about mourning is, you know what the lost object is. You can feel, taste, *wear* it." She nodded to my uniform. "The real bastard is melancholia because you don't know what that object is."

"That's what I've got," murmured Hal.

"Honey, you are supremely talented," she said. "Democracy of Sand is gonna get a second shot."

"You should come to one of our gigs," said Hal.

"I'd love to." I got off the toilet.

"Wait," said Olive. "I haven't seen your delicious face for ever such a long time." She pulled me down onto the bathroom floor. She stroked my forearms. "It was because, like, Seb had this oedipal gig going on with Dad," she told Hal.

"That's rough," he mumbled.

"Rough, yeah," she went on.

More banging on the door.

"Hold up!" she hollered. "Because first of all Seb wanted to copy Dad to, like, please him but then the more he copied him, the more he realized that he was in danger of surpassing him."

"When did Sebastian try to copy his dad?" I said. "He hates economists."

"Oh, I mean only in the abstract," said Olive. "Like, to be the big boss guy. Seb was never allowed to win at *anything*." She spread her hands. "For fear of being cast out. Right."

Hal opened his eyes. "You know, I've got big love for your mum for giving you guys the verbal skills to articulate your shit. I still can't figure out why me and my bro Paul got so much beef after all these years."

"The psychoanalytic lexicon must be handled with care," said Olive. "It should come with a warning."

There was silence.

Hal dragged himself into a standing position and stuck his head under the shower. He shook his long brown hair.

"Honey," said Olive.

"Sorry." He produced a spoonful of black fudge and lit it.

I covered my mouth and nose with Sebastian's sweater. "That's one thing I said I'd never do. Smack."

"That's not smack," said Olive. "It's just weed." She stroked my hair. "And Allegra looks like Mum, right? With that long, luscious black hair. Like a black-haired Barbie doll or something. Mum always said to me: 'Remember that when men tell you you're beautiful, they're just talkin' to your wrapper. It's the shiny packaging that conceals the real product.'"

"Why do you use metaphors of the marketplace to, like, criticize the fucking marketplace all the time?" Hal was drooling.

"Oh, honey. You're so smart." Olive crawled over to Hal and kissed him.

Before I left, she said: "Remember that you're welcome in this family."

The woman with the parrot earrings was getting into a cab when I finally staggered into the sunshine. She was telling the driver to go to Balham. I asked her if she could drop me off. Those parrots continued to laugh all the way back to South London.

"Thanks," I told her, getting out.

"It's just such a shame that you missed everything," she said.

"What do you mean?"

"You only got there just at the very end, when everything was nearly over."

SEVEN

Dear Vic,

Thank you for this morning. I really do appreciate your athleticism and best efforts to make me cum, though I'm sure you know as well as I that the female orgasm is more akin to a wave machine than a pistol firing once followed by resounding silence.

When I looked at you lying facedown on the hallway carpet, the light created a kind of halo around your head and made me think that you were given to me by God. I don't believe in Him anymore, since I read Nietzsche. The death of God happened apparently in the nineteenth century or possibly earlier, but He only really died because we all stopped believing in Him. I don't think I ever believed in Him. My mother brought me up an atheist.

But I always believed in love. How does one live without love, Vic?

Luckily you and I don't have to worry about that anymore.

Ann-Marie X

P.S. It's funny that you called me a bunny boiler. You know me so well, even though you don't know me at all. You were almost right. But I boiled a hamster, not a bunny.

It happened the night after the crème de menthe—about two years ago. We'd been playing truth or dare at Hammerton Hall, Freddie's father's country estate. I dared Jasper to fuck Allegra with a bottle of crème de menthe. Allegra wasn't interested, but she went along with it. Sebastian was furious—he thought we'd degraded her.

The next morning, we all got in Jasper's Alfa Romeo and drove to Allegra's parents' house in Buckinghamshire. Her parents were in the Maldives.

It was three in the morning and Sebastian and Jasper got in a fight in her parents' kitchen. They got in a fight because they were both in love with Allegra. Even though Sebastian was still going out with me.

Jasper said to me: "If I were you, I'd be really humiliated that my boyfriend is prepared to fight a duel for another girl." And I said: "Fuck you all."

Allegra was just loving it, crying on the stairs. Freddie was off somewhere with Allegra's younger brother Samuel, who was only about fifteen then. That must have been the first time they met.

I tried to get up the stairs, but Allegra grabbed me by the ankle and said: "Why did you suggest that with the crème de menthe, what the fuck is wrong with you, blah, blah?" And then she said: "I never would have gone out with Jasper in the first place if you hadn't marched me down to Ann Summers on the high street and made me buy that stupid, frilly French maid uniform, and then marched me over to Emmanuel College bar, and found Jasper, and handed me over."

"Allegra," I said. "What are you talking about? You're crazy."

She accused me of orchestrating her whole relationship with Jasper, just to get her away from Sebastian, and I said: "No, Allegra. This might be beyond your understanding but I orchestrated your whole relationship with Jasper *to make Sebastian want you more.*"

"Why?" she said. Her face was stunned and waxy like a teen horror heroine—straight to DVD.

"Because," I said. "Because."

Then I went upstairs and lay down on Allegra's bed, which was covered with all her cuddly toys. The walls were covered with her certificates and the mantelpiece was groaning under the weight of all those trophies. She'd been head girl and hockey captain and Desdemona, Cordelia, Juliet in all her school plays. There was a poster of Molly Ringwald above her dressing table. Her pet hamster Vera was scampering inside its cage, spinning inside its fluffy wheel. It was driving me nuts. Vera just did whatever the hell she felt like regardless of the people she hurt.

I fell asleep.

When I woke up, it was about four in the morning. The house was silent. It was a terrible house, like anyone who attempted to live there would immediately die, but Allegra always got so touchy when Jasper said anything bad about it. He likes to think of himself as a cruel libertine. His father owns every car in the world, or something like that. He's very rich. That's what he and Freddie have in common.

I went into Allegra's parents' bedroom. She and Sebastian were lying on the bed on top of the covers. They weren't touching, they were fully clothed, but they were next to each other, and I could tell that he had been looking at her before she fell asleep because he was facing her. She was on her back. I wanted to kill myself, and then I wanted to kill him, and then I wanted to kill her, and then I decided to kill that hamster, Vera.

I got it out of the cage and went downstairs to the ranch-style kitchen, which was wrecked. I waited for the water in the pan to reach a rolling boil, then I dropped Vera in, just as though I were making pasta and pesto.

A sonic violation of Ariel the little mermaid was taking place in the living room. Samuel had installed his turntables, and now he was attempting to amalgamate "Part of Your World" with a hellish industrial clanking noise. The dumb purity of Ariel's voice became hysterical and hacked to pieces: *I want to be, be, be where the people are, are, are.*

I closed my laptop, ran down to the living room, and shouted: "Get out. Out."

Samuel turned the music off. Then he sat down and started to cry.

"That is so manipulative," I told him.

He cried more.

Freddie came into the room and kicked over the Victoriana triptych dressing screen in the corner. It was adorned with the face of a little blonde girl wearing a white nightgown, surrounded by cherubs carrying white handkerchiefs.

"Bloody squat-dwelling Samuel," Freddie said to me. "You'll never guess what happened this morning."

"What about the restaurant bill?" I said. "That's £790."

"Relax. Jasp paid it. Over the phone. Or he got someone else to pay it. Over the phone. He said it's a gift for you."

"For me?! It was you and him eating the bloody pig's head. Remember that I'm the only one here with an actual profession."

"Ha!" said Freddie. "Call that a profession? *Serving?* No one I know would serve." He rooted around in his satchel and pulled out the weekend papers. He found his tobacco. "Samuel and I were walking in Hyde Park this morning and who should we see but my bastard uncle and aunt." He gestured to the malformed bust of Professor Frank. "Yeah, and Samuel was wearing that stupid babygro."

"Onesie," said Samuel.

"And holding a transparent bronze parasol, for crying out loud."

"From Japan," said Samuel.

"We were holding hands. My uncle's eyes nearly popped out of his head. He is such a fucking homophobe." Freddie hauled Samuel upward by his onesie, resurrected the dressing screen, and shoved him behind it. "I don't want to look at your face, you fucking faggot!" Freddie screamed. "You have ruined my opportunity to lead an ordinary life with a woman. With her." He looked at me.

I sat on the chaise longue and flicked through a lifestyle magazine. "Freddie, we don't have a life. We're not actually together."

There was a double-page spread of Stephanie Haight standing in a spacious kitchen. She looked radiant in a tan suede jacket and jeans. There were overtones of cowgirl. Cowhide was draped over an armchair. *I got this in Seattle in '92. Grunge had just dropped. Some said that Generation X was shocked and numb. They were shocked by their own numbness. In that case, Generation Y and Generation Z are just numb without the shock. They are used to it.* There was a poster: *I'll Be A Postfeminist In A Postpatriarchy!* There was a mannequin lying on her back with her legs stretched horizontally over her head, so that she was folded in two and flat. She was wearing thigh-high latex boots and a pair of tiny underpants. A black leather cushion was strapped to her backside to make a coffee table. She wore blue eye shadow and a short blond wig. *This is a rip-off of the classic pop art piece by Allen Jones. I bought it in 1988. I don't know if he was being ironic or just straightforwardly offensive, but it gets some laughs. I like watching people's faces as they laugh to see if they secretly approve of it in some dark corner of who they are. That's false consciousness—a retro term these days. There are scant terms now for the forces that make women blind to their own condition, but I'm still fighting.*

Freddie turned to me. "I tried to tell them that Samuel was my intern for *Making A Racket*. That's the group show I'm curating. It all centers around an emerging bee artist who has some issues about bees. He's going to hit them with a racket—plus they make a noise. They buzz. You're invited to the opening. It's Saturday."

"Great."

Freddie seized me. "If they find out I'm a queer, they'll take the apartment away and we'll be homeless." He disappeared behind the screen.

I turned back to the magazine. Stephanie lived in Camden Square. The view from her kitchen showed a tree with torn bits of paper stuck to its trunk. There was a picture of Winehouse next to the tree, looking confrontational in yellow. *I wanted to buy a property as close to Amy as possible. Next door was the closest I could get. I saw it all: the hounding, and then, the final slaying. I saw the preamble and the epilogue of the slaying. I'm not voyeuristic. I just felt so terribly sorry for her. I wanted to protect her. She is an icon of our times. Her pathos and rage exist in the tradition of Billie Holiday. Her aura of tragedy is that of all women who feel more.*

Samuel was gushing something about his mermaid DJ set that evening at a disused peanut factory in Hackney Wick. He begged me to write and perform a spoken-word poem about a mermaid.

"No," I said. "I don't want to do that."

Freddie was smiling at his own reflection in the mirror; Samuel was looking with lovesick eyes at Freddie. I had to get away from these idiots.

I located Stephanie's house on the map and got on the train to Camden.

An hour later, I was standing outside Stephanie's house in Camden Square, reading the torn tributes to Amy stuck on that tree. Someone had left a can of Stella at the base, along with a candle. A polka-dot ribbon had snagged in the branches of a nearby bush.

Nothing was growing.

An Anglo-American voice said behind me: "It's so nice of you to leave those. Most people have stopped."

I was holding a bunch of pink carnations.

Stephanie stood before me.

She had a dog on a leash. She nodded at the flowers. "We welcome mourners."

"Oh," I said. I was nervous. "No. These are for you."

We were sitting at Stephanie's big wooden kitchen table. It was mahogany, she told me. I was dazzled.

There was another mannequin, which had been moved out of the lifestyle photographer's shot. "I wanted to keep her all to myself," Stephanie was saying, sipping her java deluxe. The mannequin was bent down on all fours. A leather cushion was strapped to her back. "I wanted to keep her private, safe. It's silly, really." She scrunched up her nose and shook her head.

I heard myself saying: "No. It's not silly at all. I know exactly what you mean."

"You do?"

The house was cavernous and comfortable. The central heating was turned up high. There was a feeling of calm.

"Well," I said. "Only in my small way. My roommate Freddie and I made a series of films in the summer—of different women writers, committing suicide."

Her eyes widened. "How fascinating. Why?"

"It was Freddie's idea. I think he admires tragic women. He likes to watch women die."

"Is he a queen?"

"Yeah—if that's an empowered word."

"Queens can be just as oppressive as normal men."

I laughed, nervously. "Surely there's no such thing as normal?"

"Oh, but there is." She blew on her coffee. "Go on."

"I guess he got the idea from me because I was always going on about how there are no strong women role models, you know? No one who we want to aspire to." I reddened. "Apart from you, of course."

Now we were wandering around the edge of her swimming pool, downstairs in the basement. Stephanie had commissioned an architect from LA to design the house.

Faint pink light fell over the water from an obscure source. The ladder sparkled in the light. The drains sparkled. The walls were painted chlorine blue to match the water.

Our voices echoed.

"And how did you feel—playing the victim?" she asked me.

"I don't really see those women as victims." I watched our shadows fall across the water. We were the same height. "I just see them as victims of circumstance, I guess. I don't know. I don't really have the words—to say what I mean."

"Without language, the rebels can only eat themselves," said Stephanie. "Or something like that. That's Acker. Have you read her?"

I shook my head.

"Oh, you must. *Blood and Guts in High School* is a classic of the underground. She's much better known in the States than she is over here." Silence. "She had a double mastectomy, you know."

I stared at her.

Stephanie moved to the other side of the pool. There was a door.

We entered a gym.

"The shoulder press is still being put together," she explained.

There was dust everywhere.

"I'm a big fan of the elliptical," I said, dumbly.

Stephanie ran her hand over the levers. "Well, you can use this one whenever you want."

Now we were sitting on her roof terrace, wrapped in matching Afghan rugs, heated by electric suns, or so it seemed to me. We watched the mist rise over Camden Square.

"Maybe I'll move back to North London soon," I said. "I'm from here."

"Oh?" She took out a packet of Gauloises and offered me one.

We smoked together in silence.

"I'm from South London." She exhaled.

I exhaled. I watched her mouth.

"Bermondsey," she said. "I was born above a candy store that later turned into a hardware shop." She laughed. "DIY shop. That comes from years of living in the States."

I waited.

"My family was poor. White trash, they'd be called over there. It was just me, my mother, my father, and brother in two rooms. Man, it was tough. That's why I ate. Yes. I used to be a fatty."

There was a pause, and then we both laughed.

"I ate and ate and ate because I was depressed," she said. "Because I was smart. Clever. And I was a *girl*." She tutted. "Not a good combination. You must have read *Gatsby*."

"A long time ago."

She fetched a Tiffany ashtray. "You know when Daisy has a baby and she finds out it's a girl? She says—'Well then she'd better be a perfect little fool.'"

My heart was thrashing.

"I wasn't a fool," said Stephanie.

We were in her study.

Stephanie had asked me to type *falling* into YouTube. She was leaning over my shoulder and I was sitting in a teak swivel chair, overlooking the garden.

"Now see what we get," she said. "Songs about falling in love. A song called 'Falling' by Florence and the Machine. There!" She pointed to a video titled "Beautiful Girls Falling."

We watched a procession of models with stick-legs attempt to make it down the catwalk. Their shoes towered. Each one tripped, stumbled, fell onto her fragile knees. The shot replayed: trip, stumble, fall.

"Precipices." She reached over me. I could smell her perfume: dead oranges on a hot day. It was too tart. "Here." She found a clip of the glamorous Tallulah Bankhead reading an excerpt from Dorothy Parker's short story "A Telephone Call." We listened to the incantation, the gravelly voice, the rising delirium of a woman who simply waits. She waits by the phone for her lover to call. She waits because she can only wait, because for a woman to be active and just pick up the goddamn phone and call the man herself at the time that Parker wrote the story—1928—was to be deemed a predator.

"Or worse," said Stephanie. She turned the computer off. "I've had that all my life." She stood behind me. "I can see it in your eyes that you're going through the same pain that I went through."

"I'm not fat," I said.

"No," she said, irritably. "I mean when I was older. After I'd graduated. I was thin by then."

I could see her looming in the reflection of the blank screen.

"There was a reason that you came to this house," she said. "There was a reason that you found me."

"What was the reason?"

"Can't you see?" Stephanie laughed joyfully. "Can't you see?"

After a moment, I laughed along with her. Then I said: "See what?"

"*This* is the call. This is the call you've been waiting for."

We were in the bedroom. It was lined with books. The curtains were red velvet, brand new. The walls were a stark, unforgiving white. A rich red rug was spread on the wooden floorboards.

"I wanted a red room," she said. "But I didn't have the courage to go all the way."

"Like Christian's Red Room of Pain in *Fifty Shades*?"

"Have you read it?"

"Yes—well, only because Madeline, the head waitress, left it lying around reception. I read it during my shifts. I never would have read it otherwise."

"Did you like it?"

"No?" I watched her face to see if this was the right answer. "It gave me nightmares. The violence. I hated Anastasia's—submissiveness?"

"Quite." Now she looked angry. "That book is poison. Pure toxic poison. It is fortuitous that *Falling Out of Fate* coincided more or less with that . . . trash." Her face became normal again. "I wanted this room to be like the red room of Jane Eyre's childhood. Where she goes as a little girl—or rather, where she gets locked inside. There she has visions. She has hysteria. Hysteria is the corralling of women's natural jouissance under patriarchy."

"Yeah, I met this guy," I said, excitedly. "In the restaurant last night—"

"*Yes*," she hissed. "*Yes*. That is where I saw you."

I reddened.

"The restaurant that serves the delicious rabbit," she said. "That is where you read *Fifty Shades?*"

I nodded. "I didn't want to say I saw you there. In case you thought . . . I was stalking you. I took this." I pulled her book out of my handbag. "It was meant for your friend?"

We were sitting on the bed.

"Oh. Marge." Stephanie rolled her eyes. "Marge has been through a very bad divorce. Her ex-husband is English, of Chilean descent. And you know what Latin men are like, notoriously." She leaned back and rested on her elbows. "Luckily I have exorcised all the superstition out of myself, Ann-Marie. Otherwise, I would think that you and I meeting was a perfect instance of fate."

Now she led me to the landing on the third floor. The lamp above was a Chinese paper dragon. There was a stone sculpture—a woman sitting in a rocking chair.

"This," said Steph. "Is Penelope."

The stone woman was gripping a stone garment. She was knitting.

"Don't you know who Penelope is?" said Steph.

"I can't remember." I blushed.

"She is the wife of Odysseus! She waits for him for years and years! She waits by the window!" Stephanie gripped the stone woman's shoulder. "She wove and wove to put off her suitors because she *believed* in her heart of hearts against all common sense that Odysseus *would come back for her.* If she finished the thing she was weaving, if she ever dared to complete her labor, she would *have to betray him.* To complete her own work was to betray her man. Do you know what that means?" Steph bowed her head. "So she unraveled every night what she had done every day. She never *owned* it."

"What happened?"

"He came back. They were happy. Then there were other complications—you know, people turning into animals, sleeping with their mothers."

"I'm sorry." I blushed again. "I never had a classical education. I went to a comprehensive."

Stephanie's eyes glimmered. "Me too! They were called secondary moderns in those days!" Now she was twirling me round and round on the landing.

We had returned to the swimming pool.

Steph was slipping into a bright red bikini. She had tossed me a bright green bikini.

I was hoping that she would point me in the direction

of a changing room. To ask for privacy now would be tantamount to a mythological betrayal.

"Oh, screw it," she said, and ripped off her bikini. Her body was smooth. I could detect some incisions under her arms and around her buttocks. She dived into the pool.

I was hoping she would stay underwater for a minute and let me change, but she bobbed, staring at me. I took off my clothes and put on the bikini.

I eased myself into the water.

Steph swam toward me.

"Every woman who wants to come into consciousness of her being must become a mythographer," she was saying. "Every woman who wants to understand why she does what she does. Why she is so fucked up."

"I'm not fucked up," I said.

She laughed.

"No," I said. "I'm really not."

"How could you not be?" She kept laughing. "You are subject to normative femininity, which is a perversion. *You* are a perversion." She ducked underwater.

When she resurfaced, she said: "The antidote to the snakebite is." She ducked again. She was making me chase her down to the other end of the pool. She launched her shimmering body onto the side. "You must make your *own* myth. Make a myth of *yourself*. That's what *I* did."

Later, wrapped in towels, we were sitting on loungers by the pool and drinking double Jamesons on ice because Steph said it reminded her of her New York days. I was telling her about Samuel and how he desperately wanted to be from Williamsburg. "Why?" she groaned. "What's interesting about self-regarding hipsters with nothing to say?"

I told her about Samuel's fixation with *The Little Mermaid*.

She got excited. "Read a chapter called 'The Woman in Love' in *The Second Sex* by de Beauvoir. Have you read it?"

I shook my head.

"You must," she said. "She talks about why love shouldn't be sacrifice. Because the mermaid sacrifices her tail for legs and leaves everything behind. But when she goes on land, she feels there are hot knives stabbing into the soles of her feet with every step that she takes. It is torture."

"But they're happy in the end?" I said, dumbly. "Her and Eric?"

"Who's Eric?" laughed Steph. "I'm talking about the original, the Hans Christian Andersen version. There's no *Eric*. The prince falls in love with someone else. He rejects the mermaid. And then she dies."

Steph and I were back in the kitchen.

The front door opened. There was the sound of a child, an American. The prima ballerina from the restaurant appeared, along with Marge Perez. They were weighed down with bags.

"Oh," said Marge. She held her key aloft, as though ready to open another door. "You have a visitor."

Steph stood up. "Don't be like that, Marge. How was shopping? Get everything you need?"

"Yeah!" chirped the ballerina. She pulled out a packet of marshmallows.

Marge sat down heavily at the breakfast bar and said to me: "So. Are you seduced?"

EIGHT

STEPHANIE HAD PROMISED that I could return, soon.

It was Sunday night. I had relented and gone to Samuel's party at the peanut factory in Hackney Wick. My poetry slot was at eleven thirty.

From the podium, I read to a crowd of fools dressed like creatures from the deep: "I can't love you if you kill me. Lover, I am ransacked."

Freddie and Samuel waited for me to continue.

"That's it," I said into the microphone. It screeched— an amplified gull.

Mirages of mermaids flew across the room. The crowd ignored my poem and continued to dance to no music.

Freddie looked at Samuel, who shrugged. He fiddled with his cards. The noise returned: *Siren, siren, siren SONG.*

I got out of the papier-mâché seashell, climbed down from the podium, and pushed through people and piss-stained hallways until I found an exit. It opened onto a back alley. There was a rotting mattress, a green dreadlock. A giant cartoon peanut waved to me from the roof. Its white-gloved hand looked like a cloud against the black sky.

Freddie appeared. "What the fuck was that?!"

"I'm sorry." I lit a cigarette. "I couldn't think of any mermaid-themed stuff at the last minute so I just used something old. Do you remember when I wrote that poem?"

"Your self-obsession is no longer amusing," said Freddie. "It's become vulgar."

"Freddie, when you've done loads of drugs you look like a frightened horse."

"How sweet." He attempted to run up the brick wall, which didn't work. He crouched before me. "Why don't you write a poem like that for me?"

I stared at him.

He stood up and brushed his harem pants. His face was smeared with blue. "That wasn't even a poem, anyway," he said. "That wasn't even a haiku. That was more like a song lyric. A fucking schmaltzy R&B song lyric that I have to hear whining out from behind your bedroom door every time you fuck some random who never calls you." He shouted in my face: "I always call you!"

"I don't want to be called by you, Freddie," I said. "We live together. You don't have to call me."

"Well, I'm *going* to call you." He pointed to me and staggered against the wall. He snorted something off his key. He offered me some.

I shook my head.

"You know what you are," he said. "*Sentimental*. You

believe in the *soul*. When I told you a million times that there is no such thing as the *soul*."

I looked at the sky; three stars were aligned.

Freddie grabbed the front of my vintage, shoulder-padded, 80s, black leather jacket and sneered: "Life is a constant process of decay."

"No, Freddie. Life is a constant process of becoming. Nietzsche—"

"Oh, fuck Nietzsche!" He disappeared into the peanut factory.

I checked my phone: twenty-eight messages. It was an unknown number.

Hey bunny-boiling bitch, where are you?

You said you wanted to fuck me, now where the fuck are you?

You thought you could turn me on with your hamster-boiling stories and then leave me for dead?

Are you going to leave me?

If you don't tell me where you are, I'll hunt you down and spit roast you like that fucking sow.

Like the sow that you are.

Vic!

I texted him the address of the peanut factory and told him to come right over. I headed to the toilet to freshen up.

It was a sea of shit. Brown footprints ran in circles

on the floor. Hipsters of every subgenre were skating all over the place, grabbing at each other's sewn-on fish scales. The cubicles had no doors. I reapplied my Pleasure Me Red lipstick, fighting for space in front of the broken mirror.

A girl wearing a sheer, blue tube dress buckled in her wedges. She tried to drag me down backward, but I clung onto the grimy sink, supporting her weight as well as my own. Another girl barged into the room wearing a toga the color of a miniature golf course. It was draped over one breast and one shoulder so that her other breast stared out at everyone. This girl was painted green. Her face was green. Her hair was a tangle of green dreadlocks. She hauled the tube-dress girl into a standing position, then leaped onto the sink. She squatted over it and hoisted up her green, billowing skirts to reveal no underwear. "Look!" she shouted.

The room turned to stare.

She pried open the lips of her vagina to reveal a deep, pink interior. "There's an alien waiting to crawl out of me! Yep! That's right! I'm pregnant!"

"Congratulations!" said the room, hugging her.

Samuel ran into one of the cubicles, but he must have changed his mind when he saw all the shit because he ran out again. He flung his ginger arms around my neck. He was crying. His vertical hairstyle had wilted in the heat.

"What's wrong?" I said.

"Why is he trying to punish me?" he sobbed. "I was already punished."

"Punished for what?"

Green Girl shoved Samuel. "Hey man. What the fuck did he do?"

"Do you two know each other?" I said.

"Yeah." She addressed the room: "Who could hurt this cute ginger mermaid boy?"

"Yeah," came the consensus.

"Freddie," said Samuel. "He was getting off with this mixed-race guy right in front of my face. I think he was half-Japanese and half . . . *black*." He was scared of the word. "He's got a flattop."

"Cap?" I said.

"No. Afro."

"I'll kill him!" shouted Green Girl.

"Don't get involved," I said. "These are my friends. Besides, you're pregnant. You shouldn't be doing anything strenuous at all."

"I'll do what I want with my own fucking baby!" she screamed in my face.

Samuel was holding my hand as he explained his love of Ariel: "She has beautiful red hair like mine. I used to get teased at school. Before I learned to love myself as beautiful. The boys used to pull down my pants in the changing room to look at my pubes. I used to collect the characters. I had the whole collection—Flounder the fish and Sebastian the crab. From McDonald's Happy Meals?"

"I used to collect those too. Everyone did."

"But I had to hide them at school. I had to hide them at home too. I had to pretend to my mum that I only wanted the Happy Meals for the cheeseburger. But I never even ate the cheeseburger."

"What?"

"I never ate it."

We were sitting on the dirty mattress in the back alley.

"I watched the film over and over," he went on. "Because the scene where King Neptune finds Ariel's trove of treasures from the human world and destroys her statue of Eric—that was just like my life. My mother found all my shit and destroyed it all up in the place. She told me I wasn't a cronkite."

"Samuel," I said. "Alienated people often develop a rich inner life."

"What does alienated mean?"

"Alienated means . . . feeling like an alien, landed from another planet. I've always felt like an alien. Freddie is an alien too. That's why we became friends." I paused. "I don't know why we're friends now."

"You and Freddie are so deck. You are so sophisticated. Thank you for letting me hang around with you."

"I didn't let you," I said.

Samuel looked like he would cry again, so I said: "I mean I like that you're hanging around with us. It's just a bit weird for me because your face looks like Allegra's."

He put his arm around my shoulders. "There's something hard about Allegra," he said. "Don't ever tell her I said this. She was always hard. Maybe it's the will to win. I never had it." He looked at me. "But you're not hard. You only pretend to be hard. Maybe that's why you're not winning."

"Yeah," I said. "Well. It's a long race."

I was about to tell Samuel the unabridged story of how his sister poleaxed my relationship, but he leaped to his feet and shouted: "I've got to find Freddie."

He was gone.

I got out *Heidegger: An Intro* and scanned the index for F—*Fallen-ness*. I turned to page 18. *One is fallen into the world and one cannot get out.* Then I pulled out Stephanie's book and read from a chapter called "Monomania":

In the nineteenth century, French psychiatrist Pierre Janet identified a condition called "monomania." It was an overwhelming obsession with one person or idea. Janet analyzed a lot of bright young women, confined to a domestic life. This was the Madame Bovary syndrome.

These women devoured books. They existed in their own fantasy worlds. Many of them were obsessed with romantic love. It was love that they exalted above all else. But like Madame Bovary, many were crushed by the failure of reality to live up to their ideals. Many went mad.

In the early 1960s, Betty Friedan identified "the problem that has no name" in her seminal book, *The Feminine Mystique*. "The problem that has no name" was the depression that descended on young, middle-class women who graduated from college and then became housewives and mothers. They never developed careers, although their minds were as alive as their husbands'. To counter their misery, they medicated.

"The problem that has no name" was a modern incarnation of monomania. In both cases, women were stifled to the point of insanity. In the prime of life, their minds and bodies straining to explore the world, they went inside. They went inside the house, they went inside themselves. This introspection intensified their romantic obsessions.

They wanted to fall in love with gods, not men. They fantasized about men other than their husbands—the pseudo-Heathcliffs of cheap romance novels. They wanted to lose themselves in a higher being that would pall the sense that life was not worth living.

Romantic love—idolatrous, based on distance—was itself a form of self-medication. It made them feel like they were flying when in fact they were going nowhere. When in fact they didn't need to fly at all. They needed to stand up on their own two feet and walk. To figure out a practical way to survive. To get their heads out of the goddamn clouds! That would be a good start.

Both monomania and "the problem that has no name" were caused by claustrophobia, by limited space. Today, our fixation with love is caused by the opposite—it is caused by agoraphobia, by too much space.

I closed my eyes and tried to sleep through the time it would take Vic to get from Chalk Farm to Hackney Wick.

I opened my eyes to find the Incredible Hulk ramming something wet and fragile into my mouth. "Toke," Green Girl was saying. "Toke it."

I did. "Should you really be smoking that?" I looked at her stomach.

"Sure. Why not?" She tried to ram a pill in my mouth, but I spat it out.

"I'm clean," I told her.

"Were you a junkie?"

"No, I just did too much ketamine at university."

"Your friend Freddie is fucked on K right now."

"Great." I checked my phone: fourteen messages.

Where the fuck are you, Vera?

Who are all these peanut eaters?

If you've led me up the garden path, I'll fucking gut you, cock-tease slag.

What do you want to drink?

Hackney is v friendly :)

Everyone on the dance floor seemed to be suffering a simultaneous epileptic fit. And there, by the bar, was Vic. I could tell that he had been enjoying himself in my absence.

He was trembling with excitement. The formlessness of his spine appalled me all over again. He looked like a string of saliva.

I approached him from behind and clamped my hands over his eyes.

He wriggled like a worm on a hook. His arms were full of Red Stripes.

"Guess who?" I shouted into his ear.

"This is wicked!" he shouted back. "You're wicked . . ." He turned around to kiss me.

I gagged. But I let him.

Two boys in drainpipe trousers came over.

Vic gave them each a Red Stripe.

"Thanks Vic, man," said one.

They walked away.

"Vic," I said. "You shouldn't let people take advantage of you."

"What do you want to drink?"

"A double vodka tonic, please."

"They only serve Red Stripe."

"You were supposed to hunt me down and kill me, not buy me a fucking beer."

He threw me against the wall and gripped my neck so that I couldn't breathe.

"Stop," I croaked.

He loosened his grip.

"No!" I screamed. "Tighter!"

He tightened his grip.

"You're not supposed to do what I say," I rasped.

I tried to get my leg around his waist, but now he was really cutting off the oxygen supply to my brain. I managed to slide down the wall.

"Stupid little rich girl." He faltered. "Rich bitch."

"Vic, do I look rich to you?"

He stared at me for a long time. "No."

The mermaid mirages flew harder and faster. Samuel was crouched next to Freddie, who was sitting in the middle of the dance floor with his legs drawn up beneath him, saying: "Don't touch me. Don't ever touch me. If you touch me, I'll die."

A very good-looking, mixed-race guy with a flat-top afro was having a screaming argument with a very good-looking girl with an undercut to the left. "What the fuck?!" she was saying, over and over.

I pushed through the crowd and said to Freddie: "What have you taken?"

"Nothing," he said. "I've taken nothing."

"K-hole," said Samuel.

"Don't talk to me." Freddie looked shocking; he had aged forty years.

"Don't you even talk to me, though!" said Samuel. "Seeing as you got off with that flavorless guy right in front of my face."

"Is that a racial slur?" said Freddie. "Fucking public school boys."

"Freddie," I said. "You are a public school boy."

"Flavorless means *straight* in Brooklyn," said Samuel. "I'm not racist."

Freddie looked up at me. "Scarlet woman. You have turned me against all women. You have turned me gay."

"You were gay to begin with," I said.

I called a taxi; the man said we'd have to wait around the corner because he didn't pick up from illegal raves and if we vomited in his car, we were paying for it.

Vic and I returned to the bar to stock up on beers.

"Let me get it," I told him. "I don't like to be indebted."

There was a voice behind me. It was saying: "Yeah, a bottle of water too, please. Thanks so much."

I turned around.

The voice belonged to Allegra. She was standing in front of me, a vision of sweat: her glorious black hair was stuck to her forehead with sweat, her luminous skin was streaming with sweat, her black rags were heavy with sweat. They were clinging to her. They were his black rags. She was wearing his clothes.

"Oh," she said. "Hi!"

"Hi!" I said.

"Hi!" said Vic.

We both ignored him.

There was a silence.

"Sorry to miss you at, er—his parents' party," she said. "We didn't know you were coming."

"Well, I didn't know I was going," I said. "Until I got there."

"Hm," she said. "So how are you?"

"How are you, Allegra?"

"Oh, you know! Packing."

Another silence.

Then she said: "I know Sebastian would love to see you."

"Vic," I said. "Let's go."

The barman leaned toward her and shouted: "Sorry, what else was it, love?"

"She'll have a crème de menthe," I shouted back.

"Ann-Marie," she said. "That's a bit inappropriate, don't you think?"

I started to laugh. I was laughing so hard that I had to bend over to get my breath. Vic slammed me on the back. When I stood up again, she was gone.

The song on the radio was promising that sometimes the sun went around the moon and sometimes the snow came down in June. I looked out of the window and saw that the snow had started to fall on the streets of Hackney. But it was November, not June. It was supposed to fall.

Vic snaked his arm backward and I held his hand. He was sitting in the front next to the driver. Freddie was squashed between Samuel and me in the back.

Freddie was gray. He was saying: "Foucault was right. We *are* made of the power that oppresses us." He laughed bitterly into his own sick-covered T-shirt. "It's *better* than the panopticon! It's much, much better! One no longer has to even *stand* in the middle of a circle of windows to be constantly watched! One need only to *be*! To *be* is to be watched! Because the eyes are within us! They are fucking swarming within us!"

"Are you sure he didn't take acid?" I asked Samuel.

"Don't you people work?" said the taxi driver. "In my day, Sunday night was for resting. Ironing shirts and having a roast and watching TV."

"Things have changed in the postwar period," said Freddie.

"Watch it," said the driver.

"Are you watching me too, mister?" Freddie screeched.

"March me to the guillotine, mister! With a hood over my head before all the townspeople because I will take their jeers, I will take their caterwauls." He turned to Samuel: "But we are not losing that apartment, Ann-Marie."

"She's Ann-Marie," said Samuel, pointing at me.

Freddie jerked forward; his head got trapped between his knees. "I love you," he said to the floor.

"Who?" asked Vic.

Vic and I were lying fully clothed on the detritus of my bed. Nietzsche quotes were scrawled in my rabid hand over rolls and rolls of white revision wallpaper. I had been trying to find a particular quote the week before from *The Birth of Tragedy*. It was something about super-abundance leading to explosion. I put on TLC's "Creep." Vic asked to see my Facebook profile. I told him that I wasn't on Facebook or Twitter or anything. He said he'd searched for me but he couldn't find me.

"Vic, that's so sweet," I said. "I've been searching for you. I've been searching for you all my life."

We watched the snow fall outside the window, cuddling. He kicked a soiled sanitary pad off the bed and said: "Christ, this room is like what's-her-face. Tracey Ermine."

I didn't bother to correct him.

There were screams from Freddie's room, then silence.

"Vic, it was so funny that we were in a taxi just now," I

said. "Because when I was working in the restaurant last night, the lights went out at exactly the same time that a taxi driver came in. I thought that you must love me because you had a poster of *Taxi Driver* on your wall." I turned to him in the dark. "Do you love me now?"

"What is it with you and your mate, Freddie? Always asking people if they love you."

"Freddie and I are both incredibly needy." I paused. "Do you, though?"

Vic shifted away from me. "I'm scared of love."

I squeezed him as hard as possible, wrapping my arms and legs around him like a boa constrictor. He let me do that for a couple of seconds and then he leaped off the bed and shouted: "How the fuck can I love you if you don't know what I've done?" He crashed around the room. "If you knew what I'd done, you wouldn't love me."

I sat up and lit a cigarette. "Tell me then."

"All three bridges were bombed." He scraped back his hair. "Cluster bombs were coming out of the sky and all the city people were running to the countryside because they thought they'd be safe in the countryside."

I could see his open pores in the glare of the street light.

"Don't look at me when I'm talking to you," he shouted.

I faced the wall.

"And don't turn on any of the lights." He marched across the room, tripping over my new black leather duffle bag from Topshop, and pulled the curtains closed. They fell off the rail; I had never bothered to hook them.

He stared down at the cheap lilac fabric and said: "I don't want any light. I'm too guilty for light." Several minutes passed while Vic tried to hook the curtains. Eventually, he just left them on the floor.

I waited.

"No," he said. "I need to be away from you. I need to not have you in my line of sight." He got in the wardrobe. The door wouldn't close. He got out and sat on the floor at the end of the bed.

I couldn't see him at all.

"We set up as quick as we could," he said. "There was a tent. The villagers had killed a pig in the morning."

"So, like, you didn't kill a pig yourself?" I said.

He raised his hand above the bed and fired an imaginary gun at me.

"I had this fantasy of you killing a pig, that's all," I said.

He lowered his hand. "They hadn't drained the carcass properly. It was running all over the instructions manual for the contractible deep fat fryer. It was Jeremy's job to man the deep fat fryer. We needed an accompaniment for the pork. It got cold at night. I could hear the planes coming, more bombs. A tree caught fire. People were screaming. Children. Children were screaming. Through the trees, I could see the river on fire."

"Wow."

His voice became vague. "Because I knew in my heart of hearts that it was wrong that we were there."

"So were you like antiwar?"

"We got an old woman from the village to help us chop the potatoes. No time for peeling. The fat had run into the gutter." He paused. "It was a special kind of gutter. Jeremy tossed the first batch of potatoes in the fat."

There was silence.

"And then the whole damn thing exploded." Vic crawled up the bed and lay his head on my stomach like a child.

"The whole village?"

"*No.* The whole deep fat fryer."

"Oh."

"Jeremy was only eighteen years old, an apprentice from Yorkshire. He was engaged to a beautiful young girl called Melanie, but now he will never again see how beautiful she is." He raised his head. "What gets me the most is that it was a *British* design. Manufactured in Sheffield."

"The bombs?"

"*No.* The fryer. Haven't you been listening to a word I've said?"

"Yes, Vic, yes. But so—you were . . . ? What was your role?"

"I was the supervisor."

"But you weren't a soldier?"

"I was a military caterer."

"So you weren't even fighting?"

"Cooking for fighting men is fighting."

"But you're not a war criminal?"

"I'm a criminal." Vic slithered off the bed. "I belong down here," he said.

NINE

"SAMUEL." I KNOCKED on Freddie's door. It was Monday morning. "Samuel." I wanted to tell him what Stephanie had told me about the mermaid sacrificing everything for love and then suffering excruciating pains in her feet with every step that she took, but when I entered Freddie's room, Samuel had gone. Freddie was alone.

Clapham Common was covered with snow.

On the train, I read Steph's book:

> Women use the weapons of the weak. We are coquettish; we preen. We are less than ourselves in order to get more for ourselves. What some scoundrel "feminist" academic recently called erotic capital.

I skipped to a chapter called "Free Love?"

> I remember reading an article about a beautiful young blonde girl with flowers in her hair and the

words "FREE LOVE" painted in red on her forehead. She was a hip girl in Greenwich Village. This was the late 60s. She was having fun. She was far-out. I can't recall the details exactly but I know that she was high and she was naked and she was dancing. The crowd was far-out too. They were nice. Everyone was in love with everyone else because the old bonds had been destroyed. All bonds were oppressive so they were all destroyed. So there was no duty, no restraint.

The party turned against the girl. It happened in the street. She was gang-raped by men who were flower children. Everyone watched. No one helped. I can't remember if she was murdered or if she simply sustained horrendous injuries, but those words remained printed on her forehead: "FREE LOVE."

A woman opposite was reading the *Metro*: there was a picture of a man with his face bandaged. He was ironing, grinning at the camera.

When the woman got off, I picked up the paper. The bandaged man lived in a twenty-first-century household; he did the housework while his wife earned the money. He had been ironing like a bitch when the phone rang. Because men's brains aren't programmed to multitask, he had absent mindedly picked up the searing-hot iron and stuck it to the side of his face. He hadn't had time to say "Hello?" before the iron branded his skin with the mark of his emasculation.

I was late for work by an hour. I went around the back

and said good morning to the slaves in the kitchen. There was a treacherous trail of ice leading up the stairs to the offices on the top floor. I could hear William screaming: "They could come at any moment! Any moment, they could come!"

"Who?" I said.

William was bent over his desk, scrabbling through picked over animal remains. It was mostly bones, fine and delicate. Not cow or pig, too big to be chicken. "Rabbit!" he ranted. "Rabbit is for eating, okay?" He brandished a skull. "In this country, we do not fuck rabbits."

Michel the sous-chef was leaning against a crate of gin, his arms folded. "I was just trying to show her a good time. She should think herself lucky." He laughed. "I fucked all of them just the same. Even the fat ones. She should be grateful."

The rabbit remains were making a terrible mess on the desk. Invoices were covered in bone jelly. William's hands were glistening with fat. "It was rape," he was saying. "I'm going to find the evidence."

Michel laughed some more. "William, you English are the fucking crazy bastards! How are you going to find evidence of rape in stock bones? We only saved it for stock."

William was opening and closing desk drawers. He found a battered pair of glasses. "I haven't put these on for a long time," he said. "But now I'm going to put them on." He inspected each bone, turning it over.

"I admit," said Michel. "I did it. Everyone saw it. Everyone laughed." He pointed to me. "She saw it."

"But I didn't laugh," I said.

William registered my presence for the first time. "You saw the rape?"

"It wasn't really rape," I said. "Because the rabbits were dead."

"So it's necromancy," said William.

"Necrophilia, do you mean?" I said. "And bestiality, yeah."

"Don't listen to her," said Michel. "She's just the door bitch. She don't have no skills except looking nice."

"Thanks," I said. "Actually I hang the coats up too."

William picked up a handful of bones and then rained them down on the desk. "The people could come at any moment."

"What people?" said Michel. "Customers?"

"We call them *guests*," screeched William. "Not the *customers*. The TV people, asking if one of their contestants can have a *trial*."

Michel made a face at me.

I laughed.

"This is a trial," said William.

"No, it isn't," said Michel. "You're an asshole. What about that time you stuck that oyster up your asshole? We served that."

William almost smiled. "That was before I became a professional."

"That was last week," I said.

There was a poster of a baby peeking out of a flowerpot over William's desk.

"Let me put it to you very simply." William swung his desk chair backward and straddled it like a mobster. "I had a call from immigration."

The atmosphere in the room changed.

"You're not French," said William. "And your name isn't Michel. And you've got no papers." He paused, sadistically. "You've got no papers so you've got no right to be working in my establishment."

"But I've been working here for nearly a month," said Michel. "Payday is Friday."

William stood up. He said, breezily: "Yes, well, *Mihaita*."

Michel went white.

"You are a Romanian national. We can't pay you for your work so far and if you don't make a fuss and go quietly then we won't make a fuss about the rabbit rape."

"You have to pay him!" I said. "He works about fourteen hours a day for you!"

William threw a handful of bones at my head; they hit me.

"If he goes, I go," I said.

"I'm not going," said Michel.

"Okay then!" I shouted. "I quit." I paced across the room and grabbed the lost-and-found box. It was full of the designer clothes that all the private members forgot when they got fucked in the club.

The brothel opposite had been boarded up. The walls were black with smoke damage. I sprinted around Soho for a while, nearly breaking my neck on the ice, dazzled by freedom.

There was one bar open. It had a sign in the window: *What is your future?*

I went downstairs.

"Running Up That Hill" by Kate Bush was playing. The bar was empty. There was a picture of Shirley Temple stenciled onto a mirror: her ringlets, her angelic, fake face, puckered in a look of surprise. There was a map of the human chakras and a smell of incense, burned out.

I rang the bell on the bar.

A rottweiler growled at me, then barked. A woman appeared and castigated it. She had pendulous breasts. A gold silhouette of Queen Nefertiti bounced on a chain between them. She looked old and perceptive. "We're closed," she said.

"Please. Can I at least have a drink?"

She stared at me. "What do you want?"

"Double Jameson on the rocks?"

She poured it slowly.

Time had slowed.

"I can't pay you," I said. "I'm unemployed."

"What do you have?"

"This." I rooted through the lost-and-found box. There was a pashmina from Oscar de la Renta. I tossed it to her.

She smelled it.

"You can sell it on eBay," I said.

"Okay." She sat down behind the bar and produced a pack of tarot cards. She got a whiskey for herself. It was still only ten in the morning. She lit a cigar; it was laced with something—hibiscus, perhaps. I asked her for one; she obliged. The smoke curled around us. The song changed to "Wuthering Heights."

"Greatest Hits." Her voice was rough. She turned the first card over. It showed an unsmiling sun and a circle of broken columns. "You have been cursed," she said.

"I knew it."

"Yes. Some witches have put a curse on you." She paused, thoughtful. "They must have got your photo from somewhere."

"When?" I said.

"Maybe they took it on their phone when you weren't looking." She turned over another card. It showed a man hanging upside down by a noose tied around his neck.

"But death means rebirth, right?" I said.

She shook her head. "Death means death. You play near the gallows."

I tried to think. "No. But Allegra was always going up to Castle Mound in Cambridge, where the gallows used to be. She said thousands of people were hung there. It looks over the whole of the countryside. One night she went up there when there was a storm. It was raining, and there was thunder and lightning and everything. She said she wanted to feel the charge of the dead. She tried to go into a kind of bacchic trance. She had had a very classical education. But when she came back, she was drenched and she said she felt nothing. She couldn't feel the charge. She couldn't feel the dead. She said she felt stupid. She sat on the radiator and then she just kind of looked at me and said: 'You've got the charge, Ann-Marie. Naturally. I haven't got it.' She seemed really resentful. That was before anything happened with Sebastian. Freddie said the charge meant being evil. Then Allegra said: 'My housemistress always told us that achievement is 99 percent effort and only 1 percent natural ability. So all I have to do is, like, work really hard.' Freddie laughed and said: 'To become evil? What are you talking about, Allegra?' But I knew what she was talking about."

The woman contemplated me through her shroud of smoke. She turned over another card. It showed a naked man and a woman, bound by a black snake. "The Lovers," she said. "You lost your twin. Your mirror. Your best friend."

I went cold. "I mean, I guess that was implicit in the story I just told you," I said. "You could have gauged that from my story."

She shook her head. "No. You have suffered a fracture of the soul. You are cut in half. One part of you is woman, the other part is striving to be man."

"I don't want to be a man!" I said.

"You want to be tough and alone like a man. Sleep with men like a man sleeps with women."

"No," I said.

"Yes," she said.

"No." I stood up.

"You lost him because you wanted to be like him. To be better than him."

"I wanted to be equal to him," I shouted.

"You wanted to be the same as him."

"No!" I shouted. "Equal!"

The rottweiler barked. "Men and women can never be equal," said the woman. "It's not written in the stars. There is one more card."

I sat down again.

She turned it over. "The Empress." It showed a woman in an orange dress in a meadow. "Fertility," she said. "You have three sons?"

"No."

"Two sons?"

"No."

"One daughter?"

"I haven't got any kids."

"The witches drowned your kids in a river."

I stood up and walked out. "Babooshka" was playing.

"I want my old job back," I told Madeline.

She was manning the reception.

"Look, I'm dressed for it and everything," I said. I gestured to the pussy bow.

The phone rang; she took a reservation.

When she hung up, I said: "I was really excited at first, but now I'm scared. Really, really scared." I was sweating. "I'm scared of freedom."

She stared at me.

"Where's William?" I said.

"He's gone to the emergency room. He had a fight with Michel."

"Well, I need to talk to him. I'll call him on his cell."

"You can't," she said. "He's unconscious. And he told

me that if you came and asked for your job back, I was to say no, absolutely not, fuck off."

"Well, that's not very nice. How did he say that if he was unconscious?"

"He said that before. And oh—this came for you." She went into the cloakroom and returned with a white box.

I sat on a bench in Soho Square and opened it. There was a blue, fluffy toy cat inside, wearing a pair of crotchless, decayed, white lace underpants. The underpants weren't stitched onto the cat; they had been added.

There was a note:

i hear your sighs of ecstasy recur throughout my dreams against a background rhythm of a million purring pussies. i await. yours, james X

I walked along Oxford Street without a purpose. To my left, a man was selling fake celebrity-endorsed perfumes to a crowd of tourists, who spritzed themselves liberally with the testers so that the toxically sweet scent conspired with the pollution to make the air unbearable. That must have been where Madeline bought hers. Another man was watching out for the police. The snow had stopped, but the gutters were lined with it. The white had turned to black, not quite black. There were cars and cars. A bus swung to a stop and a woman carrying ten Liberty bags and a dog got off. The dog got trapped inside the automatic doors; its paws skidded everywhere as the bus began to move again. The dog was being strangled by the leash. A man in a suit banged on the bus driver's window. The dog was saved. I could feel the onset of an existential crisis. The crowd was bombing toward me but there was no face that I recognized. I wanted to see Sebastian. I wanted so badly to see him that I tried by the power of my will to turn these strangers' faces into his. I wanted to see his blond hair and his absurd, rugged beard. I wanted to see his tall shape. I wanted to tell him that I would forgive him for everything but then I remembered that I was guilty as well. I wanted to ask his forgiveness. I wanted to say I'm sorry for boiling Allegra's hamster but she really had it coming. I wanted to say I'm sorry for that night at the dreadful May Ball, when I made you dance with me on a very slippery floor, surrounded by all those Cambridge girls, dressed up like catalog princesses in two-tone gauze. And all the men in top hats and tails. The band was playing "Big Spender." The princesses tried to roll their hips in a pseudolesbian way for all the men who watched with contempt. Or was it lust? Jasper was there. That was the night he and Allegra met. I told him to ask her to dance, and he did, and I told him that she wanted to sleep with him, and then she did. But before that I was watching your eyes the whole time because your eyes were watching her and I was sick with jealousy. Freddie spilled champagne on the floor. And then I made you push me away and twirl me back toward you, holding my hand all the time. I was holding your hand. And then you fell. You broke your leg.

I had reached Oxford Circus station. The God squad

man was pacing in his usual spot, blasting the crowd with capitalist revisions of the Bible: "Do you want to be a sinner or a winner?"

"Can I borrow your megaphone for just one moment?" I asked him.

He moved his mouth away from it. "No."

"Please," I said. "I want to tell everyone that love is a chimera."

"I don't know what that word means."

"Love?"

"No," he said. "Chimera."

I followed the crowd down the steps to the train. I couldn't decide whether to go left or right. I stared at the list of stops for a long time. I could hear the scream of a train approaching, northbound. The dead air lifted my hair. It was warm. I ran at the tracks as the scream turned into a thunderous wail, but my decision to die came just a second too late. The train was already in the station. I got on it. A woman was knitting to my right. I watched her fingers loop and curl the wool over the needles, clicking happily away. She was making a red scarf. I wanted to throw my arms around her so badly, but I decided to get off instead and found myself at Euston, power walking to a place where Sebastian and I had spent days and years together.

The guard at the British Library checked my bag and then I went down to the locker room and left my stuff. I took the elevator up to the first floor and scanned the faces of the people along the aisle, but no one was Sebastian. A couple were leaning in for a kiss against the railing around the glass tower of books that ran through the center of the building.

The guards in Rare Books were happy to see me. They asked me why I never came anymore and I told them that I had finished my exams. I decided not to tell them that I'd got a double-starred first. "You lost so much weight," they said. "We were worried about you." They asked me where my fella was and I said I didn't know. I said I was looking for him—had they seen him? They couldn't remember.

I sat down opposite an octogenarian who had fallen asleep with his head on a pile of books. I got out my copy of *Falling Out of Fate*, and read at random:

> Telos was Aristotle's word for an overarching goal or guiding spirit in life. It was a guiding light, a thing to move toward. A meaning. A telos is what all humans need in order to make life meaningful. The point of philosophy was to learn how to live the good life—not a life of limitless pleasure, but a life of balance. Ethics and pleasure were not dissociable.

The octogenarian grunted.

> Now we have lost our telos. There is no spirit to guide us. Or rather, we have been left free to invent or choose our own. I say "left" free. We have been abandoned by God in our freedom. Although He, in the form of the church, the family, and, in wom-

en's case, the patriarchy, oppressed us, controlled us, He also watched over us. He told us what to do. He told us the difference between right and wrong. And when we did wrong, we were punished. Now the rules are hazy.

Love is the telos of the modern world. It is a modern idea. We reach for the One as a means to construct a whole ethical and pleasurable universe. In short, to give life meaning.

The purveyors of love—the love songs, romantic comedies, ads, dating sites—promote love as a route to solving the meaning of life. These products are for the most part directed at women. The job of loving remains feminine. This is what University of Chicago academic Lauren Berlant calls "the female complaint." Turn on any TV in any country in the Western world and you will find a channel on which a woman is complaining that her man doesn't love her enough, doesn't need her enough, isn't emotionally available or faithful or honest or committed enough. The whine goes on; but it is not natural. It is—

The octogenarian sat up. He wiped his mouth with the back of his hand.

Our eyes met.

He got up and exited the reading room. I followed. He looked over his shoulder, unnerved. I smiled. I followed him onto the smoking terrace. He lit a pipe. I lit a cigarette. The statue of Mr. Punch bowed to us, grimacing.

"What are you in for?" I asked the octogenarian.

"Botany," he said, grimly.

I followed him back through the cafeteria and that's when I saw Sebastian.

He was sliding a dirty tray of food into the rack. He didn't see me. My heart started pounding. I followed him to the water fountain and hung back while he filled his cup. He drank three cups. Then he went into the men's toilets. I must have been in a trance because I followed him in there. Men were pissing against the wall. They stared at me and started proclaiming that I was a girl. Sebastian had disappeared into one of the cubicles. I ignored the men. I waited for him.

And waited.

I felt a hand on my arm. Someone was trying to get me out.

"No," I said.

When the cubicle door did finally open, I saw that it wasn't Sebastian at all.

TEN

I WAS STANDING outside Elephant & Castle station. The snow had started again. The hideous pink shopping center had been painted blue, but the elephant impaled on a spike persisted in its lurid pinkness. The merry-go-round roared in the blizzard. I called Freddie.

"I need Sebastian and Allegra's address," I told him.

"No."

"Come on."

"No." He sounded fucked. "Samuel's gone."

"I know."

"But Vic's still here. He showed me his medal."

"Please, Freddie."

There was a pause.

"I'll give you their address if you promise to come to my uncle's for cream tea and pretend to be my girlfriend," he said.

"No way."

"Okay, I won't give you their address then."

I could smell the lamb cooking before Allegra answered my knock on her bright green door. There was no bell. They lived in a low-rise block of council apartments.

"This place is no way near as nice as mine and Freddie's," I told her. "Literally, how can you bring yourself?"

"Oh, hi," she said. Her voice was rough. Her glorious black hair was clumped in a knot at the back. She was wearing Sebastian's old T-shirt: "I Wanna Start A Revolution From My Bed!" "He's not here. If that's what you want."

"No." I hesitated. "I don't want—that."

"What do you want then?" Her legs were bare.

Behind her, I could see backpacks open and books in piles. One corner of the living room was covered with newspaper and splattered with red paint.

"Tea?" She turned and wandered back down the hall, leaving the door open.

After a few moments, I followed her. I closed the door behind me.

The TV was on: *Nighty Night*, series two. Julia Davis in red lace was being chased over Cornish hills to the soundtrack of Dolly Parton's "Jolene."

Allegra turned it off.

"I love that show," I said.

She boiled the kettle. "I know."

"That's my show. I introduced you to that show."

"I know. Seb doesn't like it. He doesn't think it's funny."

"It is funny."

The living room was small.

"My god, Allegra. You can't swing a cat in here."

She poured the tea. "Has my brother moved in with you?"

"No—I don't know. He's a nice boy."

"Yeah," she said. "But Mum and Dad are so angry with him. More angry than they are at me."

"Why?"

"Because I'm not doing the Bar Professional Training Course."

"Why not?"

She looked stern. "Because if I become a lawyer, I'll die."

I laughed.

She handed me the tea.

"Have you poisoned this, Allegra?" I said. "Because Freddie knows where I am. Plenty of people know where I am."

She studied my face. "Are you okay? You seem a bit . . . mentally unstable."

I laughed. "Yeah! 'Cause I've just been to the library. It's a mentally unstable kind of place."

The window looked onto another window. I watched a woman watching TV; she got up, left the room, and returned with a banana.

"It's the overachiever thing," Allegra was saying. "Like the J. D. Salinger thing. The Glass family. Because my parents had this thing that geniuses—genii." She laughed.

I didn't laugh.

"Are made, not born," she went on. "So they pushed Samuel like really hard. With the whole chess thing. He became anthropophobic for a while."

There was a silence.

"It means being scared of people," she said.

"I know what it means."

"He just used to cower in the corner of the room between moves during competitions and stuff. From when he was about thirteen—he was fine before that. Mum and Dad said something happened to him at school because he wouldn't go. He had CBT but it didn't work." She sighed. "And now he's dropped out. I was hoping he would be the good one so I could be the bad one!" She smiled; I wanted to put my sunglasses on. "But I'm, like, not talking to Mum and Dad at all now and I hate them."

"That's not very nice."

"No," she said. "It's not very nice. I'm not prepared to be a simulacrum of a human being." She became angry. "I mean, why don't I just make a façade of myself—like the kind of façades they put on buildings when they're being renovated. The façade looks like the building but it isn't actually—"

"I know what a simulacrum is, Allegra."

"So when they come to London for dinner, I can just, like, send the façade of myself out to have dinner with them instead of me and operate it by remote control while the real me just sits on the sofa. Here. I can make it say all the right things at all the right times."

"I don't know what you're talking about," I said.

Silence.

"Do you want to know where Sebastian is?" she said.

We were sitting on the arms of opposite sofas.

"No," I said.

"He's gone fishing!" She laughed. "He's at the Walthamstow Reservoirs. Well, really it's in Tottenham. He spends days and days there."

"In this weather? Allegra—you've pushed him over the edge. He's trying to freeze himself to death to get away from you."

"That's not a very dignified thing to say."

I stood up.

She stood up too. Then she sat down again. She extracted a hairbrush from her bag and started brushing that long, stringy hair. The brush snagged at the back. Her hair transformed from dull black to inconceivably luscious black, like an advertisement. It shone and shone and seemed to absorb all the light in the room so that I began to wither like one of Ursula the Sea Witch's poor unfortunate souls. A curtain of black fell over her face. "Can't we just let bygones be bygones?" she said.

I stared at her.

"I mean." She flipped the curtain of hair back and her face appeared. "What you and Seb had was sweet."

Lights had started to pop in my vision.

"But you have to admit that you blocked him," she said.

"Blocked what?"

"You blocked him. His talent. Men like Sebastian come along once in a generation."

I laughed. "Are you joking?!"

She considered me, sadly. "I'm sorry he doesn't want you anymore. I really am."

I ran at her and managed to get a fistful of that hair. She grabbed my hand. I pulled and pulled, waving her head around the room. She was screaming. When she loosened her grip on my hand, I yanked, hard. Strands of black hair came away from her scalp. There was blood. I staggered backward. She clutched her head. Her face was wrecked and flushed—more beautiful.

"Get out," she said.

"No." I stormed into the first room that I saw. It was their bedroom. There was Sebastian's Goya print on the wall. It showed Saturn the old man with hollow, hunted eyes eating his baby son. Saturn had the baby's head in his mouth; he looked caught in the act, furtive and guilty and disgusting.

She was panting behind me.

"Oh, when is he going to let those bloody daddy issues go?" I shouted.

"He can't let it go!" she screamed. "That's the fuel of his art!"

"What art?!"

"Art!" she cried, crazily. "His life is a work of art! He is a work of art!"

Suddenly I was exhausted. I sat on the end of their bed. "Can I smoke in here?"

She stared at me.

"Well, can I?"

"If you must. I always tell Seb to go outside." She sat down beside me. "But I guess it's okay."

We sat for a long time.

I was looking at Saturn.

Finally, she said: "I'm sorry about what happened."

More silence.

Then I said: "I think I walked out of my finals to make Sebastian love me again. I never thought of it before. But I think I thought maybe, if I failed my exams then maybe he would love me."

"But I got a first and he still loves *me*," said Allegra.

Freddie had told me to meet him outside the fish and chip shop on Endell Street in Covent Garden. There were three fish and chip shops on Endell Street.

I walked up and down for a while.

Then I caught sight of that stooped, devastated form. Vic.

"Hey," I said, punching Vic too hard on the arm. "What are you doing here?"

Freddie came out of the shop, his face in a bag of chips. He looked ill. "Said he wanted to see you." Freddie's mouth was full. "Said he couldn't stand not to see you."

"Ann-Marie," said Vic. "I've taken the day off work. I don't want to go to work anymore. I don't want to operate anymore." He took my hand. "I want to be with you."

I pulled my hand away.

"I want to be a bohemian," he said.

"Come on, Freddie," I said. "Let's go."

We left Vic waiting in the snow across the road from Freddie's uncle's apartment.

Freddie and I were sitting in a bamboo, minimalist paradise. Professor Timothy Frank, retired, was leaning backward in his bamboo throne as though a gale force wind were blowing in his face. To his left, there was a taxidermy seal. Its tail was raised and its fur was sparse and yellow. There was a weird, happy smile on its face.

Professor Frank saw me looking at it. "Do you know why it is smiling like that?"

Despite being made out of bits of car, the conceptual bust in our living room had captured something of the old man's thunderous authority.

I shook my head.

"Because it has been got by the Mahaha." He laughed.

The professor's wife scuttled in with a tray of scones, strawberry jam, double, single, whipped, and clotted cream, and tea. Her hair was short like a boy's. Her face was delicate and rotten. She was a rotten peach. She whispered instead of talking.

They both looked about one hundred years old.

Freddie and I smiled and said thank you very much.

"Well, do you know who the Mahaha is?" said the professor.

"No, Uncle," said Freddie. "I'm afraid I do not."

"Did I not tell you to read arch and anth?" he hollered.

"Yes, Uncle," said Freddie. "But it's all paid off now—studying history of art. I'm a curator. And a video artist. Thanks to your kind patronage. Letting us use your space."

"My *space?*" said the professor. "It is not a *space*. It is an apartment." He slathered his scone with both clotted and whipped cream. "When Freddie was a little boy, he loved nothing better than to hear my tales of the Arctic. For a long time Greenland was my area."

"You owned it?" I said.

"Don't be ridiculous," he said. "I am against colonialism of all kinds. Besides." He looked at his wife. "We couldn't afford it on an academic pension!"

She mimed laughing.

"The Mahaha are demons of the cold. They wear no clothes whatsoever." He chuckled. "Despite the endless ice, as far as the eye can see. They are very strong and very sinewy and they leap about. Do you know how they kill their victims?"

I shook my head.

"They tickle them to death!"

I laughed politely.

Freddie laughed—too late.

"They have very long fingernails. And they are always giggling. That's how you can hear them coming." He looked at the seal. "They leave a frozen, twisted smile on the face of their victims."

"Do the Eskimos believe in them, though, or is it just a myth?" said Freddie.

"*Eskimos* is a pejorative term, nephew," said the professor. "The Inuit people have not suffered genocides of disease and now this cretinous global warming to be reduced to an igloo animated picture by you."

There was a photograph on the wall of the uncle standing next to a hole in the ice, raising a type of spear above his head. There was also a photo of him with an

Inuit woman, bundled in matching furs, standing by an igloo with a gaggle of what looked like half-Inuit, half-Western children.

"That's Aguta," said the professor.

There was silence.

Then Freddie said: "I've brought this girl here to tell you that she is my girlfriend."

The professor squinted. "But what about that chap wearing that . . . romper suit? Whom we saw in the park. I've got your number, boy. I was at Cambridge in the 30s. Yes, it was all the rage then—homosexuality. There were the communist poets with whom I sympathized on political grounds."

"Uncle Timothy fought for the International Brigade in the Spanish Civil War," said Freddie.

"But I did not sympathize with the likes of Auden, Spender, etc., on the grounds of their sexual preferences," the professor went on. "When I was a youth, it was a crime. Crimes were punished for the sake of the community. It is against the laws of reproduction, this." He searched for the word.

The wife croaked something.

"*Decadence*," said the professor.

"Oh, I'm not decadent," said Freddie. "Oh, no. Ann-Marie and I are very much in love."

"Why?" thundered the professor.

"Why are we in love?" Freddie looked at me. "Er."

"Because we've got a lot in common," I said.

"I intend to marry her," said Freddie. "Once I've established myself on the circuit."

"And of what does this circuit consist?" said the professor.

"Oh," said Freddie. "Parties."

The professor's face contorted.

"And business," said Freddie. "Lots and lots of business."

"Like father, like son," said the professor. "Your father was like that, riding the wave, back in the 60s. Pop art. What is pop art, may I ask you? Replicas of advertisements? For soup? And you call that a contribution to humanity?"

"I don't think Father would put it in such highfalutin terms, Uncle."

"No," said the professor. "He wouldn't. He'd laugh. If he can laugh, now that he's had a face-lift. Living in *California*."

"Part-time," said Freddie.

"Living in Switzerland."

"Part-time. He's still got Hammerton Hall in Suffolk."

The professor lurched to his feet. The wife handed him a cane. He got an object off a shelf, and handed it to me. It was a tiny white carving of a whale.

"*That* is art," said the professor. "They put it in the baby's mouth when it is born. To bring good luck." He passed me a dagger. "That is walrus ivory. Look at the intricacy of the handle. Look at the craftsmanship." He sat down. "Butterflies being murdered before the very eyes of the spectator is not art."

"Father hasn't bought any Hirsts since '97, I think," said Freddie.

"What about those," I said, pointing to two glass cases hanging on the wall. One contained a psychedelic array of butterflies, their wings spread and pinned. The other contained petrol-blue birds, perched in their own compartments. Their beaks were open.

The professor stared at me. "I like you," he said. "You are honest."

Freddie laughed.

"In this late industrial capitalist inferno, honesty is a rare quality," said the professor. "It entails a kind of brutality. I've been saying that since the 50s, when the mixed economy and the welfare state were not a phantasm."

There was silence.

"You are not a rower, Freddie," said the professor. "All the men in our family were rowers. Even your father was a rower. Get up early, bracing cold. Row!"

The wife croaked.

"She wants to know how you two met," said the professor.

"At a garden party," said Freddie.

"Yes," I said. "I was there all alone. I always do feel so alone at parties."

"I too have often felt alone at parties," said the professor. "Continue."

"I was standing by the oyster tent, at the back of the queue." I nodded. "And then the fireworks began at the far end of the field. By the river. It was nighttime. They were the college colors, whatever college it was. I can't remember now. Blue, and yellow, and white. The fireworks looked like a stab in the dark to me." I paused. "They made it worse—the sadness. The explosion of light made it worse. Everyone got terribly excited and ran off to see them better and so there was no line for the oysters anymore. So I took the opportunity to eat as many oysters as possible. I do adore oysters, don't I, darling?"

Freddie looked angry.

"There were three different types: tabasco, shallots and sherry vinegar, or plain, old lemon." I looked at the professor with emotion. "Sometimes plain, old lemon is the best."

He nodded.

"So the silver service catering staff in their black suits and bow ties were shucking as fast as they possibly could for me. The food was all included in the price of the ticket. For a hundred quid one wants to get one's money's worth!" My voice had become posh. "I remember the deftness with which they gripped the shells in a napkin and inserted the knife and twisted it, whetting my appetite further. I could feel my appetite becoming demonic. The way they wrenched the shell open with a flick of the wrist to reveal that gray, creamy mollusk." Now I looked at the range of creams on the table. "The way they squeezed that lemon for me with such fortitude, never for one moment stopping to say: 'Aren't you sure you've had enough, dear?'"

Freddie dug his nails into my hand.

"But I never did have enough. I could never, ever have enough. I wanted more, so much more. I wanted everything, all of it, all of the time. I wanted to keep eating until I was dead."

There was silence.

"I must have downed about twenty or thirty, knocking my head back, letting the juice run down my chin. I was sweating. The salt was making me thirsty. I reached for the champagne and downed that too. Soon the iodine was overwhelming me. Overwhelming my sense of reason. I was lost in the sea, in the rock pools."

"Oysters are farmed," said the professor.

"I was lost in the farms, then," I said. "Deep down underwater and drowning. I felt as though someone had me by the back of the head and was forcing my face down in salt water and I couldn't breathe." I closed my eyes. "But no one told me to stop. Not one of the catering staff said: 'Careful, love. You know those are aphrodisiacs.' So a surging feeling of love was starting to rise within me. I was turned inside out with it. I felt as though I had a vortex in my chest of monumental emotion that was spiraling upward and upward and out of my mouth." I stopped. "And then I saw Freddie."

They waited.

"The fireworks ended. The crowd cheered. But that was all in the background because my vision had narrowed and my world had narrowed and now there was only him."

They waited some more.

"Can you tell me where I can use the toilet?" I said.

There was a taxidermied crow on a fake branch on the cistern. It held some kind of stick in its beak. The plaque said that it was a native of New Caledonia, one of the few nonprimates to be able to make and use tools. Lévi-Strauss's culinary triangle was framed above the sink. The points of the triangle were marked: Raw, Cooked, Rotten.

I looked out of the window. Vic was standing in a phone booth. He'd taken his shoes off. The snow continued to fall. He was looking up at the apartment. He didn't see me.

Down the street, kids were making a snowman, its face adorned with a horizontal brick, which may have been a nose or a mouth.

"I was just saying how rare it is to find a young person who is attuned to the unseen spiritual forces that govern our fates," the professor said when I returned to the living room. "It is a given in all indigenous cultures around the world. It is only the imbecile white man who has spoiled all that, who has expunged the human reverence for mystery from the world."

"Ann-Marie doesn't know anything about indigenous cultures," said Freddie. "She's barely been out of England."

"Shut up," I said. "Sebastian and I went to Morocco. That's my ex-boyfriend," I told the professor. "We were looking for Paul and Jane Bowles's house. That's where Sebastian learned to do whirling dervish dancing." I laughed. "Now he's going to Mexico with Allegra."

The professor tapped the cases of butterflies and birds with his cane. "Those are from Mexico. The hummingbirds are sacrificed to the plumed serpent, Quetzalcoatl. It is purification. These are merely tourist trinkets, of course. Although I saw footage of a human sacrifice from the early part of the twentieth century while I was doing fieldwork. It was remarkable." He leaned forward; the bamboo groaned beneath him. "Five priests on top of a pyramid, hidden—somewhere in the jungle. It contravened all rights, all modern laws. The Spaniards had done away with most of the old practices. I recall a man, not screaming, not running for his life. Just waiting. Waiting. One of the priests stabs him in the gut." He thrust his fist. "And twists—just like shucking an oyster—and pulls out the heart. It's still beating. They put it in a bowl, held by a statue of the god they are worshipping. It is a great honor to be killed like that." He sat back and said to me: "I wish my nephew were interested in my stories."

"I am interested, Uncle," said Freddie.

"The Inuit elders are the storehouse of all the knowledge in the community," he went on. "It is a pernicious myth that they are slain by their children when they are no longer useful. Why would you kill a living library?"

The wife croaked.

"There is an Inuit saying, which I think you will appreciate, Ann-Marie: 'The great peril of our existence lies in the fact that our diet consists entirely of souls.'"

I smiled.

"Because they eat 90 percent meat. And if they don't kill respectfully, the animal spirits can return and avenge themselves on the eaters."

The wife croaked her agreement.

The professor shut his eyes. "I wanted a nice girl with a bell on her bike and not too much up here." He tapped his head. "But my wife was a Magdalene scholar. I was a research fellow and a fully assigned apostle. She was doing her thesis on Julian of Norwich." He turned his eyes on me.

There was silence.

The wife raised a scone right up to my face, but I shook my head. She moved it closer until she was almost mashing the scone into my mouth. I shook my head again. She smeared the scone with clotted cream, then jam, then squirted whipped cream on top. She shoved it near my face again. I batted her away with my hand. She dropped the scone facedown on my empty plate and looked at me with malice. I picked up the jam jar and scooped out a handful. I shoved it in my mouth like an animal.

Freddie snatched the jar from me.

I snatched it back. I threw it against the wall; it smashed. Red jam exploded over white. The base of the jar had remained intact and now I knelt beside it, pawing the jam into my mouth.

"Freddie *is* gay," I said.

Vic ran toward me through the snow when I came out of the building. His feet were dark purple, almost black. He was shaking uncontrollably.

"Ann-Marie," he said. "I've been waiting for you."

"So wait," I said.

"What's that stuff around your mouth. Is it—blood?"

I looked up: the sky was white and blank.

"But we've been to each other's houses," Vic was saying, desperately. "I've met your friends. Freddie made me an affogato this morning. It means *drowned* in Italian. I learned something new! I'm learning new things every day with you! I feel like I'm looking at the world like new!"

He tried to take my hands but I pulled away and walked in the direction of the train.

He scrabbled along beside me. "This is love," he said.

I turned to him. "Vic. That's a dream. It's a nice dream. I'll call you."

ELEVEN

Dear James,

Thanks so much for the pussy. I'm not working at that restaurant anymore. Please send any future presents to 29 Camden Square, London. I don't know the postcode yet.

Camille X

It was Tuesday. I was staying with Stephanie. She had been understanding when I'd turned up at her door with nowhere else to go. I couldn't go back to the apartment in Clapham after all that chaos at Freddie's uncle's.

The child ballerina was doing cartwheels around the cross-trainer as I broke through my personal pain threshold. I was wearing a leotard that belonged to Stephanie. Lana del Rey's "Video Games" was playing on the screen: faded footage of the Chateau Marmont coalesced with the percussionless music and the golden light of serotonin in my veins to lull me into an oceanic state.

The ballerina stopped cartwheeling and stood by the

machine. "I saw you," she said. "In the restaurant. You were *working*."

"Yes," I panted.

"Are you working here now?"

"No. I don't know."

"Then what are you doing here?"

"Auntie Steph said I could use her gym. Mine's out of order."

"She's not your actual aunt."

"She's not your aunt either."

"Are you going to stay here for, like, ever?"

I started on the weights.

That satanic look returned to her face: "Are you like *going out* with Auntie Steph?"

Auntie Steph was waiting for me in the kitchen with a glass of iced tea. She wiped the sweat off my face then led me upstairs to the walk-in shower. She watched while I exfoliated. I smiled at her uneasily through the glass and she smiled back. She handed me a fluffy towel. Then she handed me a paper heart, colored in with red felt-tip. A safety pin had been stuck to the back.

"I give all of my guests one of these," she explained. "It's a goofy little thing. My friend Gabriella is an artist and she makes them. Their spirit is deliberately crude and cute, even childish. They are actually very valuable—limited edition—but she gives them to me in bulk because I helped her out when she was on the way up." She brushed a strand of my wet hair behind my ear. "Like you."

I thanked her.

"Gabriella is really a force of nature," she went on. "She was horribly shy when I met her. Like you."

I said nothing.

"Now she is unrecognizable. She does a lot of work on *Das Ding*. Do you know what that is?"

"I can't remember?"

"It's the Thing. The Thing called It."

"Like in *The Addams Family*—the thing called It with all the hair hanging over its face?"

Steph laughed. "No, no. It's the Thing called It that is Unnameable, Unspeakable, Unwritable, Unrepresentable. It's very Žižek. Gabriella is immensely influenced by Žižek but I just can't get on with his interpretation of Lacan through a Hegelian lens."

I was dripping on her carpet. "We weren't allowed to study Žižek at Cambridge."

"Oh," said Stephanie. "You went to Cambridge?"

"The real Cambridge," I said. "Not the ex-polytechnic."

"Why would I doubt it? You are phenomenally intelligent."

"Am I?"

"You are an Ivy League girl, through and through. You have that look of frustration."

I wrapped the towel tighter around myself. "My director of studies, Dr. Kyle, said that Žižek was too alive. He thought that was a funny joke. We only studied men who are dead. Although I didn't really study anything because I was always drunk or high."

"That's a conspiracy." Stephanie combed my wet hair with her fingers. "To get young people *wasted* just at the moment when they have access to the knowledge, not to mention the time, to really learn hard and topple the system. The drinking culture is urged on by the institution."

"Really?"

"Covertly."

I sat down on the edge of the bath. "I remember one time we were studying *Utopia* by Thomas More?"

She sat down beside me. "Go on."

"All the public school boys and girls in the class were laughing about utopia, saying it couldn't possibly exist. They kept saying that the name itself meant 'no place.' Like that was a brilliant thing to know."

She waited.

"So I put up my hand, which I never normally did, and Dr. Kyle pointed to me and I asked: 'Why can't it exist?' And he said: 'Because it can't.'"

Stephanie was staring at the bathroom floor.

"I never put my hand up again," I said.

She was still staring at the floor.

Eventually, I said: "Why does Gabriella make hearts?"

Steph took the heart brooch out of my hands and pinned it carefully to my towel. She stood up and stroked my shoulders. "Because hearts are everywhere, yes, but they remain the great Unrepresentable. The heart is only a symbol. It is an inadequate symbol. It points to the greatest of Unrepresentable darknesses."

We were standing in a room painted pale blue. It had white curtains and a narrow single bed. "I keep it for him," she was explaining.

There was a toy lion on the bed, and a pile of *New Yorker*s on the mantelpiece. Dried flowers stood around the room in jars. They had the same prickly scent as Steph's perfume.

"Florida Water," she said. "I spritz everything I can with the stuff. I simply love it. These are—were—orange blossom."

"Lovely," I said.

"I keep this room because it keeps me thinking that one day he'll come home, but I know he's never coming home."

"Your husband?"

She laughed. "God, no. I never want to see any of *those* again. No—my son."

"Where's he gone?"

"Oh, Snowdonia now. He lives in a yurt. He's got his botanicals and his druid friends. They're a closed community up there."

The black trash bag of clothes that I had hauled over from Freddie's was stuffed in the walk-in wardrobe.

"He was very sensitive," said Steph. "Maybe too sensitive for this world." She touched the curtains. "He enrolled at film school in New York but then he got into bad things, starting running with a bad crowd."

"The druids?"

"No, this was way before. He could have been the next Hal Hartley, but he became a taxi driver."

"That's wonderful!" I said. "I've got a thing about taxi drivers!"

"You shouldn't. Sure, you get a lot of great conversations, but what's the use of that if all you do when you come home at night is worship the devil." She touched the desk, the chair, the unplugged printer. "He was very angry with me." She turned to me: "You can burn the nights in here in complete and unrelenting solitude, if you like."

Stephanie was showing me a framed tabloid picture of Amy Winehouse. There was a red heart nestled in Amy's mountainous black hair. The heart was pierced by Cupid's arrow and "Blake" was written across it.

We were in Steph's study.

"This is what inspired Gabriella's heart phase," she was saying. "Amy used to wear that heart in her hair all the time. I used to see her around Camden all the time, reeking like an alcoholic and desperate. It was unbelievably sad. Her love for that terrible man had implanted itself in her brain, at the center of her soul, to the extent that she had no thoughts beyond him. But he was just a *him*, you know? He could have been anybody. The point was that she was an addict. A love addict. Like you. Now look." She pulled an art book about Frida Kahlo off the shelf. She showed me a picture of Frida done up in a virginal gown, tight and high at the neck. An image of Diego Rivera was emblazoned on her forehead. "Like a third eye," said Steph. "He became her sight. He slept with her sister, you know? She was tragic but she was great." She closed the book. "Amy was tragic and great but she couldn't make it. This culture killed her. The Symbolic killed her."

I was shivering.

"It will kill you too if you let it," said Steph.

We were in the den. I was wearing a voluminous dunga-ree dress that belonged to Stephanie. It was frayed and comfortable. "For loafing!" she said.

Stephanie produced a ball of hot-pink mohair wool and two sets of knitting needles. "This is likewise a Gabriella creation," she explained. "Of course Gabri-ella has always borrowed a lot of her concepts from me because you see conceptual artists are trained in *art*, not philosophy. Even though *the idea* is supposed to take pre-cedence over *the execution*. Many conceptual artists are in fact conceptually barren."

"Was Gabriella the artist you were talking about in the restaurant?"

"Now, now." Steph frowned. "Were you eavesdrop-ping?"

I blushed.

"It's okay if you were." She laughed. "Eavesdropping is the best bad habit going for a writer."

"But I'm not a writer," I said. "I mean, I used to write some really bad, really corny poems about my ex-boy-friend sometimes, but that was just like therapy mainly. Sebastian, my ex, he's the writer."

Stephanie tossed the ball of wool at me. "*You* are the writer," she said. "You *will* be a writer. I saw it in you right away."

"You did?"

"Don't ever let me hear you put yourself down again or I'll throw you out on the street."

She showed me how to loop the wool and work the needles until our clicking became synchronized. Gabriella had provided a knitting pattern. Steph explained that it was a Project. It was an intervention into the genealogy of the Penelope myth. By imitating the conventions of traditional femininity—knitting—we were actually subverting those conventions. Our hot-pink blanket was already growing. Eventually we would send it to Gabriella and she would photograph it and possibly include it in the British Pavilion at the Venice Biennale next year.

As we got through jug after jug of iced tea, chatting and laughing, Steph explained her plan for me: she had conceptualized a course of action through which I could achieve transcendence over my demons.

"Oh, you don't have to do that!" I said. "I don't have any demons!"

Steph gave me a look.

"I mean, I do, but—they're fine."

"It's best to get started as soon as possible." She said that when we had finished knitting for the day, Marge would escort me to a location in Hoxton, where I would audition. She wouldn't tell me what I was auditioning for.

Marge drove in dead silence, her mouth a line. She stopped on the edge of Hoxton Square and pointed me down a one-way street. There was a club called Sparkle

Hard. She threw me a packet of baby wipes, then drove off.

The line of girls extended down the street and spiraled in on itself so that I had to get to the middle to stand at the back. They wore fishnets with black seams that vanished under petticoats. Beauty spots were stuck on their cheeks. Their hair was set in waves. The girl in front of me wore a Lurex choker so red and wet looking that it appeared her throat had been slit. The lips of her friend were glossed a flamingo pink and when she opened her black coat I saw that she was in fact dressed as a flamingo, albeit a highly pornographic one. Pink feathers hung from her nipples. Her skin looked thin and blue; too thin to protect her from anything. The cold was lacerating.

"I heard that they were gonna, like, film this," said the flamingo girl to her friend.

"Really? Oh my god, who is?" said the friend.

"I don't know, some kind of crazy fashion blogging thing. Or art thing. Definitely not a sex thing."

"No, this is definitely not a sex thing." The friend paused. "But Chloe, I don't want my mum to see this. You said no one would see this."

"No one's gonna see it, Milly," said Chloe.

"Yeah, except on the *Internet*," said Milly. "And what if it, like, goes viral."

"Your mum just wishes she had your tits," said Chloe.

They both laughed.

I tapped Chloe the flamingo on the shoulder.

She turned eyes flicked with black on me.

"What exactly is this place?" I said.

Chloe looked at her friend and laughed. "What do you mean, what is this?"

"What are we auditioning for?"

"Erm, it's like a neo-burlesque social innovation start-up? It's a pop-up?"

"Oh great."

"It's not like stripping," said Chloe. "It's beautiful. It's like art. It celebrates a woman's curves even if she's got no curves."

"Yeah," said Milly.

"Shouldn't you be at school?" I said. "Or are you going for the whole Jodie Foster in *Taxi Driver* thing?"

They looked at me blankly.

Then Chloe said: "We're on our gap year."

The line moved through a door and down a flight of stairs. Red light washed us out. We went through another door. The girls cooed and tittered like well-tamed doves. Their mouths looked like internal organs in the red light. There seemed to be no end to it, this slow walking. The girls checked their reflections in antique-looking compacts incessantly until I was forced to check my own reflection.

"You haven't done yourself up at all," Chloe told me.

I was still wearing Steph's dungaree dress.

"Didn't you get the thing about the rules?" said Milly.

"The rules," echoed Chloe.

We were approaching the end of a hallway. It smelled of wet concrete. A piano started and a woman's rich, kittenish voice began: "You Better Go Now" by Billie Holiday. We entered a room. There was a circular stage in the center and a pole. Cardboard cutouts of retro hourglass starlets winked at us. The music swelled. The singer was wearing a red rose behind her ear and a white dress. Her eyes closed. Another woman got on the stage and clapped her hands three times, very loudly.

The song stopped.

The woman was holding an iPad. She wore a headset. Her hair was curled like a wartime pinup but otherwise she was plain. She wore a pair of jeans and a T-shirt that said: "Sparkle Hard . . . er."

"Right, guys," she said. "My name is Sarah and I'm the captain of your ship today!"

Everyone whooped.

Her voice was bureaucratic, a drone. "Now we're all so glad here at Sparkle Hard that you have been *lured*."

Another whoop.

"Into this net of female entitlement. That is the word we use here. *Entitlement*. Because for too long men have been entitled but we haven't."

People clapped.

"Men are the eyes that see. But women are the bodies that make the eyes see. So the sexes need each other, like yin and yang."

A cheer.

"Unlike yesteryear when us girls could sparkle soft, we're now fully entitled to sparkle as hard as we possibly can! As though our lives depend on it!" She became serious. "Because our lives do depend on it." There was silence. "To fulfill our potential as women and as human beings. Let's do a show of hands. Who here is dying to fulfill their potential?"

All the hands went up.

"But who has felt inhibited from doing it 110 percent in the past?"

Most of the hands went up. Milly's went up, but Chloe's didn't.

"Wicked!" shouted Sarah. "Now—this side of the room, I wanna hear you say: *Sparkle*."

"*Sparkle!*" roared the crowd.

"And this side . . ."

The chanting assumed the intensity of a fascist rally.

Sarah the captain was interrogating me in a back room.

"Are you claustrophobic?" she said.

"Depends what you mean," I said. "I don't want my head shut in a box of any kind."

"Okay." She put a line through something.

There were no mirrors framed with lightbulbs. There was no girly camaraderie now. The furniture seemed to have been borrowed from a primary school. Only rows of very small tables, and girls on very small chairs.

"And I don't want snakes," I said.

She looked at me with hatred. "Do you pole?"

I stared at her.

She put a line through something else. "Upper body strength?"

"Good," I said. "I go to the gym religiously."

"What's your greatest ambition?" she said.

"To be a stripper."

She put down her iPad. "Sultriness is fine. Even brooding, mean, and moody smouldering enigma to an extent. But sarcasm is out. Our guests want to feel that you are loving every minute of your life."

I did the door-bitch smile.

She looked convinced. "Think sunny times. California."

"Ah!" I said. "The orange groves. The mythic destination."

She looked at me like I was crazy and said: "You're gonna have to take what we give you, costume-wise. Your lack of costume might count against you. Plus you're older than our average performer." She called the next girl.

The doves had been disabused of their dark winter coats. They showed their plumage in clash over clash of color. I wished they'd made the purples stand next to the purples, or at least next to the complimentary yellows. I was yellow. They had decked me out in a Big Bird ensemble minus the puppet head. Yellow feathers sprouted from my hips. In the mirrored ceiling, I looked like a big ball of sunshine. A makeup woman had stuck her latexed finger in my mouth and smeared Vaseline on my teeth.

The girls shook against the circular wall, watching each other. Many seemed to be performing a striptease for a camera in their heads. Their faces transitioned from innocence to experience and back again. There was a real camera, slung around the neck of a man. A blonde woman holding a microphone appeared to the left. She made some frantic introductory comment that had to be reshot. She seemed more nervous than the girls. I didn't catch what website they were from.

Sarah the captain told the camera that it was time to introduce the competition winners.

Two men appeared.

One was muscular and metrosexual. The other had a shaving rash. He pumped his fist in the air. The girls clapped but they laughed as well, and soon the man stopped pumping his fist. Two screens were positioned in front of the crotches of the men. The screens seemed to function as magnifying glasses.

"Okay, drop your drawers," said Sarah.

The metrosexual complied immediately. The rash man complied, less enthusiastically. He pumped his fist again, but then he clawed at his spine.

The girls jeered.

"All of it," said Sarah. "Now get behind it properly so that we can see you. And come into the light."

The room darkened. A spotlight roamed, then found the men. Their penises were obscenely enlarged on the screens.

"Quiet now, ladies." Sarah's voice seemed to come from everywhere, all at once. "Remember these lads are the lucky ones. The ultimate test of a woman's nature is to make a man hard. Let's give them what they want." She turned to the men. "You wanted this?"

The man's rash got worse.

"Did you want this?" boomed Sarah.

"Yes," they said.

Chloe the flamingo was first. She had managed to push her way to the front of the queue and now a giant pink balloon made out of something thicker than normal balloon material was being rolled onto the stage. The pole had contracted into the floor.

She did some fetching arm movements, biting the tips of her gloved fingers before dragging the gloves off with her teeth. She got the arm-length gloves between her legs and pulled them back and forth. Next she did a mime of chewing gum and pretending that the giant pink balloon was in fact a bubble that she had blown by mistake. The men looked enthralled. She fastened her flamingo-pink mouth onto the balloon's concealed airhole and by some trick of neo-burlesque flexibility managed to get her whole hand inside it. The balloon was bigger than her, but lighter. She waved it around.

The process of getting out of her costume was halted to the point of agony. There were aborted attempts to unzip this and that, but the truth was that Chloe possessed no grace. She was too self-conscious to be sexy.

Suddenly she got her whole head inside the balloon so that now she looked like a circus balloon woman—born with a balloon instead of a head. Her face was barely discernible inside the opaque plastic. Then she managed to wiggle her whole body into the balloon. She did the splits inside it. There had been no music throughout her act. A ripple of laughter could be heard from within her plastic death trap. Finally she popped the balloon and emerged with another ripple of laughter.

There were balloon tatters all over the stage.

The men were hard.

"Next," said Sarah.

Milly appeared on the stage in a flesh-colored ensemble which outlined her sex organs in diamanté. Her body was toned and open and swamped by the spotlight, as though there were no part of her that wasn't disclosed. Flesh-colored feathers were draped over her legs. The pole zoomed upward. She smiled with sincerity. She fixed one leg around the pole and swung her body in circles. The piano started and the woman began to sing "That Ole Devil Called Love." Milly revolved and revolved. Then she got off the pole and did a few cursory undulations. She whipped off her costume and spun her nipple tassels.

The men were hard again.

"Next, next, next."

Girls performed, one after the other, accompanied by that mournful music, which turned their sex into elegy and made me feel suicidal. I went and sat by myself for a long time in the toilet.

When I returned, there were only about three girls left in the line. The rest had been divided into the saved and the drowned. The singer had slipped into some self-induced miasma of heartache.

Sarah pointed at me and said: "Next."

The men looked exhausted.

"This is the girl who hasn't had time to rehearse," said Sarah.

The camera crew moved closer.

A giant martini glass was wheeled out, filled with frothy liquid that smelled of magnolia. A giant plastic olive bobbed on the surface. The stage became a ramp. Some of the liquid spilled over the sides.

Girls wearing "Sparkle Hard . . . er" T-shirts hoisted me into the glass.

The music started. It was Flack's funereal "The First Time Ever I Saw Your Face."

I was drowning, already. "This is destiny!" I shouted.

"Why?" said the blonde presenter, coming closer. She pushed the microphone in my face.

"This was my parents' song," I gasped.

The stage started to revolve; the glass started to revolve. My yellow feathers were destroyed.

"*What about finesse?*" boomed Sarah.

I was clutching the edge of the glass like a dying dog, while the singer sung about a captive bird, and a trembling heart, and a—someone was demanding something. Now I could feel the onset of a panic attack. I managed to get a look at the screens before I went under and stopped breathing.

The men were hard!

Then the world went black.

Marge wasn't there to pick me up so I had to get the train home. I didn't feel like reading Stephanie's book.

I got out *Heidegger: An Intro* instead and read about the concept of finitude: "Things must end in order to have any meaning at all."

Stephanie laughed like a hyena when she saw my yellow face. She stirred a few of the satanic ballerina's marshmallows into my hot chocolate.

I didn't want it.

"Do you mind if I go and lie down on my own for a while?" I said.

"What do you mean?" She looked hurt. "You're so jacked up with insight right now. Suffering is *juice*. You must squeeze it out right away."

"I'm really tired."

She laughed. "This is a crisis of healing! I should have warned you about it." She drank the hot chocolate herself. "Depression is really just buried anger." She stood up. "I know what we'll do!" She led me into the living room.

The fire was on. There was the beginning of our hot-pink blanket, trailing yarns.

"Stephanie," I said. "I'm not in the mood for knitting."

"No." She shook her head. "No. Not knit. Destroy." Her eyes looked mad. "We must punish ourselves for performing this hyperfeminine task." Her voice became soft, cloying. "Like Penelope. Like this." She tore at the blanket. Holes appeared. The ball of wool fell, unraveling. "Now you."

I watched her face while she tore at the wool some more. She looked old.

"No," I said.

TWELVE

I WOKE UP to the sound of crying. It was midday.

They were in the kitchen.

"I'm sorry, Ilka," Steph was saying. Steph wasn't the one crying.

"But she can't clean like I can," cried Ilka. She was changing out of fluffy dinosaur slippers into a pair of high, cheap pumps. "I am a professional." Her accent was Eastern European.

"I said I'd pay you for today, didn't I?" Steph saw me. "Good morning." Her voice was flat. "The early bird arises." She turned back to Ilka. "I paid for your fairy-princess wedding on Lake Balaton, didn't I? That was very expensive. Those swans were very expensive. I let you record a few songs in the studio, didn't I? I helped you achieve your dreams of becoming a singer."

"But I'm not a singer," said Ilka. "I'm a cleaner."

"You're not my cleaner anymore, unfortunately," said Steph. "Look, I've loved having you around."

I reached for the French press, but Steph gripped my arm so hard that I couldn't move.

"No," she said.

Ilka left.

"No coffee for you," said Steph. "No stimulants. I want you to be clean for tonight."

"What's happening tonight?"

"There." She pointed at a plate of half-eaten pancakes and syrup that had been left on the table. It had congealed. "That."

I stared at it.

Steph crossed her arms. Today she was wearing a loose-fitting Indian smock. "I told Raegan deliberately not to clean up after herself this morning. She was up early."

"Who's Raegan?" I said.

"Raegan is Marge's daughter who you've met like a gazillion times! So don't just stand there! Clean it up!"

"Why should I do it?"

"Because I've fired my gorgeous cleaning champion Ilka now, and she was *good*. She was real good. The first lesson of feminism is that there's no such thing as a free lunch." She laughed. "Did you think you could stay here for nothing?"

I didn't move.

"Don't you like cleaning?" she said.

"No," I said. "I hate it."

"Excellent," said Stephanie, and went outside to smoke.

Raegan the satanic ballerina had been enlisted to make a mess of the toilet. Now I was on my hands and knees, cleaning that shit up. Steph had bought me a brand new bottle of power bleach. She hadn't bought me a pair of rubber gloves, however. The bleach was burning my knuckles, burning me all the way up to the wrist. My hair trailed over the toilet bowl. I was still wearing my pajamas. Steph was sitting on the edge of the bath, watching me.

Marge was spraying her curls in the mirror. "You know this reminds me so much of all the superb days I spent in the ashram in Rishikesh back in '79," she was saying. "That was the summer after my first year at Harvard." She seemed a hell of a lot happier than usual.

There were undigested marshmallows in the shit.

"Yeah," said Steph. "It's a Buddhist thing."

"It's a Hindu karma thing," said Marge. "We did five hours of selfless service every morning at dawn, before chanting and prayer. I was hesitant at first—me being the little Waspy sorority girl with only a sense . . ." Marge touched her heart, "that I was looking for something."

"Whatever I'm looking for I don't think I'm going to find it down the toilet," I said.

"That's precisely where you *will* find it." Marge kneeled beside me. "I didn't wanna scrub those steps at the height of the monsoon—in the *rain*—either. But gradually, as I was doing it, day after day, month after month, I found peace. I found humility." She stood up. "I realized for the first time in my white-ass little life that I was no better than any one of the peasants or monkeys." She put a bobby pin between her teeth. "God! The monkeys were everywhere! Clambering all over that goddamn bridge! It was wild. If you're lucky, maybe Aunt Steph will take you to the Ganges one day."

"She's gotta pass the test first," said Steph.

They left the room.

I texted Freddie:

I'm sorry for what happened. Can we keep the apartment?

I got the toilet as clean as possible. I looked out the window: the snow had melted overnight. Steph was manically gathering armfuls of dead leaves in Camden Square and stuffing them into a trash bag, held open by Marge. I ran a scalding hot bath and wallowed in it, contemplating murder.

Soon Steph was banging on the door. "Open up, open up."

I ignored her.

"Open up or we'll kick the goddamn door down," came Marge's jokey voice. "Little pig," she added.

I let them go on banging and shouting for a while until I heard the buzz of an electric drill. I pulled a towel around myself and opened the door.

Steph was wielding the drill and wearing a pair of safety goggles. She snapped them off. "I hope you weren't using my Crème de la Mer," she said. "Come."

I followed them downstairs to the swimming pool.

Raegan was sitting on the tiled floor, reading *Antigone*.

Steph grabbed the trash bag from Marge and emptied the dead leaves into the water, walking the length of the pool as she did so, making sure that they were well and truly scattered. Bits of soil and twig and a potato chip bag floated on the surface too. The serenity of that luminous blue was ruined.

"Get them out," said Steph.

"Go on," said Marge. "We all had to do it."

"When did you have to do it?" I said.

"We all *rushed*," said Marge. "We all did the rites of spring, the rites of passage."

"Kappa Alpha Theta wasn't officially recognized by the university but we certainly took our responsibilities seriously," said Steph.

"But I don't want to join a sorority," I said.

All three pairs of eyes turned on me.

"You don't *what?*" said Raegan.

"Can I have a net?" I said.

"Oh no," said Marge.

Steph beckoned me to the shallow end and then pulled my hands roughly behind my back. My towel dropped. She tied my wrists with garden twine.

"Lucky I had some of this hanging around," she said. "To make sure my roses grow erect."

She pushed me into the pool.

"With your mouth," said Steph. "Your teeth. Use your whole mouth."

"Yeah," said Raegan, standing on the side. "With your face!"

I hesitated. "But is this instead of rent?"

"If you must think of things in such base materialist terms," said Steph.

I gulped at the leaves, carrying them to the side of the pool, spitting them into the trash bag that Steph held open.

Now I was standing naked and wet, looking at the toilet that I had just scoured.

"Do you think that's clean?" said Steph.

Marge and Raegan were standing behind her.

"Yeah," I said.

"But do you think it's *really* clean?" said Steph.

"Yeah, I do."

"Well, it doesn't look that clean to me," said Raegan. She was holding a Bratz doll.

"Well, it looks sparkly and fresh to me," I said.

"Think about the worst thing you've ever done," said Steph.

"Yeah," said Marge. "Close your eyes and think about it."

I did so.

"Now tell us what it is," said Steph.

"Why?" I said.

"Because the personal is political," said Steph, exasperated.

"Okay. Let me think. It might be the first time I slept

with Jasper. Sebastian stayed in London that weekend. He was at UCL."

They nodded.

"There was a house party. There were all these girls everywhere—like girls from *Heathers*. You know the film?"

They nodded furtively.

"All perfect and private school and Allegra knew all of them, of course. She had sworn to disavow all of them but she never really did. They came to this performance she did. But that was later. We were all sitting on someone's bed. I'd done some MDMA. I felt like I was going to kill myself out of love for the whole world. I looked at Allegra and she looked like an angel. All my vision was lurching up and down—the whole fucking room. Then her face changed. Her face looked like a bad omen. Her hair was a bad sign. She was a bat. Suddenly I didn't believe in her at all, and then Jasper came in and sat on the bed between us and put an arm around each of us. He looked at me and then he looked at her and then he unhooked this mirror off the wall—it was warped, like convex."

They nodded.

"It was like the kind of security mirror they have in shops to check if anyone's stealing. And it was surrounded by gold-painted brambles and thorns—like, baroque or something."

Raegan was agog.

"And then Jasper said: 'Right ladies, who wants a line?'

And he made loads of fat lines on the mirror. And then he passed the note and the mirror to Allegra first. Not to me."

They waited.

"Her first," I reiterated. "So we did all this—whatever it was. And I could tell that he liked her. Well, yeah, because they were actually going out at the time. She was his girlfriend. So when she went to the toilet, I must have been high as a kite because I said to him: 'Do you want to fuck me?' His face was mean like marble. Like there was nothing in his eyes—only the whites of his eyes, no iris, and no pupil. For a moment, I felt sure that he was the devil himself, that I had done a pact with the devil and there was no going back, but then Jasper just opened his mouth and laughed and laughed. He said: 'Who is your family, anyway?'"

"Asshole," said Marge.

"I had never cheated on Sebastian before. I had never tried to cheat on him. Jasper got up and left the room. Allegra never did come back from the toilet. I was alone. I tried to call Sebastian but he didn't answer his phone so then I went into the living room where loads of rich hippies wearing stupid outfits were doing stupid hippy dances and I found Jasper squashed between two other members of the international technocratic elite wearing polo shirts. I wanted him more then, so much more, because he had rejected me."

"So then what happened?" asked Raegan.

"We went and fucked in the toilet."

Marge covered Raegan's ears. "Baby, I'm not sure you should be listening to this."

"Nonsense," said Steph. "She needs to learn about this Sadeian generation, reared on Internet pornography. They are just ahead of her."

"I did wrong," I said. "Not Jasper."

"He humiliated you." Steph's voice became harsh. "Get down and prove to me that it's clean, if it's as clean as you say it is."

"What?"

"Get down on your hands and knees, lift up the lid, and lick the goddamn toilet bowl!"

I stared at her.

"Do it!" said Marge.

I got down on my knees, lifted the lid, and licked the bowl.

I heard the door slam; Raegan had gone.

A few hours later, Marge and Stephanie were having a screaming argument in the recording studio, which, according to Raegan, was the best place to have a screaming argument because it was soundproof. It was in the basement, next to the swimming pool. Stephanie had never shown it to me.

I had been ordered to look after Raegan. We did some drawings at the kitchen table—mainly of Miley Cyrus's on-off boyfriend. Stephanie had bought her a Winsor & Newton pinewood box of art materials.

"Did you know that Aunt Steph introduced my mum to my dad?" Raegan addressed her sketch pad.

"Really?"

"Yeah." She paused. "And Aunt Steph helped Mum to *heal*—after."

"After what?"

"After what happened between all of them." She turned the page. "The Lord hath giveth and the Lord hath taketh away." She drew a detailed and highly accomplished pencil portrait of Miley Cyrus. She bit her lip in concentration as she shaded. Then she scrawled over the whole thing so that the paper tore. Over Miley's face she drew two stick people in thick, aggressive oil pastel. A female stick person with giant red curls spiraling out of her head was strangling a male stick person with red glasses and black hair.

"Look." She showed me a photo of a man on her phone. "That's my dad." He did have red glasses. He was Hispanic-looking, bookish.

"He looks nice," I said.

Now she drew a floating entity above the stick people: it was a pink scribble that might have been a rain cloud or a ball of wool. In case there was any doubt, she wrote in spiked black letters across it: *Aunt Steph*.

Night was falling when Stephanie appeared in the kitchen, composed. She had changed into what appeared to be a Little Bo Peep outfit. Or maybe it was an old bridesmaid dress? It was satin pink with a puffball skirt. The edges were trimmed with white lace and she wore a white lace veil over her face. She had doused herself in so much tangy Florida Water that I was forced to cover my nose with my sleeve.

"Auntie Steph," said Raegan. "You look pretty."

"Why, thank you," said Steph. Her accent had switched to Deep South. "Now will you two ladies please join the good and long-suffering Marge and I in the den. But, oh—wait." She pointed at the red turtleneck that I was wearing; it was hers. "You have to please take that off." She pointed to Raegan's black jeggings. "And those. No red or black."

We did as we were told.

A corner of the den had been transformed into some kind of pink ceremonial altar. Everything matched Steph's outfit.

Marge was sitting on the sofa, stone-faced. She looked like she'd been crying. A large picture of a goddess was propped in the center of the altar, surrounded by looping French writing and the name *Erzulie Freda*. The goddess wore a more grandiloquent version of Steph's outfit, and she was black. Two paintings flanked her: One showed a horse, crying. The other showed a horse with wild eyes, gagged. There were other things on the table: A white candle and a pink candle, unlit. Some iced buns, an open tin of rice pudding, a goblet of water, a packet of Virginia Slims cigarettes, and a frosted pink Rimmel lipstick. Three gold rings had been laid out on a white doily. There was the bottle of Florida Water.

Steph put on The Crystals' "He Hit Me (And It Felt Like A Kiss)."

"This was Amy's favorite song," she said. "It inspired her."

"Erzulie Freda is the voodoo Iwa spirit of love," explained Marge. "Aunt Steph worked with and observed a lot of houngan priests and priestesses when she was in Haiti."

"Back in '86," Steph said to me over her shoulder. She was busy sprinkling the Florida Water over the altar. She lay a pink cloth over the coffee table.

"Erzulie is a very complex goddess," said Marge, looking pointedly at Steph. "She is very flirtatious and full of love and affection. She is one of the most powerful goddesses going. But she wants you to spoil her—and you mustn't spoil her."

"And she sees other women as rivals," said Steph, lighting the candles. "She greets women by waving her little pinkie at them but she greets men with a lot of hugs and kisses. Now." She gave us each a printout from the Internet. "Let's say together: 'Maîtresse Mambo Erzulie Freda Dahomey! Beautiful woman! Woman of luck! Woman of my house! Come here, I beg you, and accept these offerings!'" Steph repeated the lines several times; the rest of us trailed off.

Steph began to sway. She danced over to me and put her hand on my head. Marge lifted Raegan off her lap and put her hand on my head too.

"Free this child, please, Erzulie," said Steph. Her speech was cracked and warped. "Free this child from the spell of love cast by the Symbolic. Free her from the neo-liberal patriarchal web of incitements to fall in love." I could feel the animal heat of their hands pulsing into my brain. "Free her from the masochistic need to wait. Free her from false consciousness and awaken her and make her see that true freedom does not consist in happiness which too often means being at rest. No!"

Steph reeled back as though struck by lightning.

Marge gripped Steph's hand and put it back on my head. "Go on!" shouted Marge.

Raegan had backed to the far end of the room.

"True freedom consists in overcoming one's fallen state, not to fall some more, true freedom—" Steph fell back. She whacked her head on the corner of the coffee table.

The fire continued to roar behind her.

She was out cold.

Marge threw the goblet of water over her face. Steph woke up and castigated Marge for expending a gift to Erzulie so disrespectfully.

The music had stopped.

Steph staggered upward, her veil askew, and opened a bottle of pink champagne; likewise a gift to Erzulie. She became frantic when she thought one of the candles had blown out. She cupped it, desperately. The candle burned back to life. "Thank god," she breathed.

There was stillness.

"Those horse paintings are done by Gabriella," she told me. "Can you feel the transition?"

"What transition?" I said.

"I can," said Marge.

Steph lifted the painting of Erzulie and revealed

another painting behind it. This one was Catholic. It showed a saint, crying. There was a sword through the saint's exposed and bleeding heart.

Now Steph seemed properly drugged. She pointed one woozy hand at the saint and fluttered her fingers. Her smile was inexact. "When you've given Erzulie all you've got and you don't have any more to give her, she changes into Mater Dolorosa," she slurred. "Erzulie always leaves crying. She is the spirit who can never achieve her desires, that is her tragedy." Steph traced the outline of the sword with her finger. "Mater Dolorosa holds the weapon calmly in place with her own hands. She accepts her fate." She shook her head, muddled. "That's why things can never go forward." Now Stephanie looked like she would cry. She was talking to herself. "That's why things haven't gone forward enough." She turned to me. "For you. For your generation. You're caught between the housewife and the whore." She shook her head savagely. The veil fell off. She twisted it between her fingers. "That bloody Nigella Lawson has got a lot to answer for."

Steph slumped on the floor by the fire. I went over and put my arm around her.

We sat like that for a long time.

Eventually, she said: "We must wait until the candles have burned all the way down, on their own." Her eyes looked young. "Did you feel something, Ann-Marie?"

"Kind of."

"What did you feel?"

"I felt—better."

"I'm doing it for you." She gripped my hand. "You must believe that. I'm doing this to help you."

I got up and lay down on the sofa facing the fire.

"I want you to go through all the stages." Steph was talking to the fire. "Knitting, stripping, cleaning, gathering, degradation, child caring—hyperfeminine actions." She seemed unsure of herself. "To see."

"I don't know what you wanted me to see," I said.

The fire roared and roared.

"To see that you're strong," said Stephanie.

THIRTEEN

Dear Ann-Marie,

I can't pretend that what you said the other day about it being a nice dream didn't cut me like a knife. I told myself to man up Victor, and remember that you're a victor in life.

Love is eternal. I knew you were a slut but when I watched every single one of my pornos, you weren't there on the screen. None of the actresses had your face.

The sound of thunder that's not thunder. It's only what man is doing to man. Yes, I've become deep.

But when I went over to yours and Freddie's apartment in the night, you and he weren't there. No one was there. I waited for you to ring my bell at the crack of dawn like you did right before you humiliated me yet again but I hear only silence. I've quit my job.

If you don't show yourself to me soon in a film

or a message on the Internet or even the stars, I
want to do it.

Vic

Steph had finally granted me Internet access so I was
able to read the deluge of emails from Vic. A pair of pink
pajamas scented with that nauseating Florida Water had
been left on my bed after the possession.

I heard groaning and banging in the night.

Marge shook me awake at seven thirty. She was wearing the same pink pajamas as me. She said. She said that
Stephanie had gone into a trance and wouldn't come out
of it. Apparently Erzulie Freda had accused Stephanie of
sleeping with one of her three husbands. Erzulie threatened to turn into a red-eye. Marge's hands were shaking.

The curtains were closed against the cold sun.

Steph looked like a Victorian hysteric. She had soaked
the bed with sweat. Her teeth were chattering. Her eyes
were rolling all over the place. Her skin was a sick yellow. She was wheeling around the mattress in a circular
motion, thrashing her legs. Great handfuls of books had
been torn from the shelves.

Marge tried to make Steph take Xanax but Steph
screeched about Marge working in the service of the
Symbolic, drugging her to nullify the radical implica-
tions of her insight. She screamed about Marge wanting revenge. She screamed about the sistahood wanting
revenge. She screamed that guilt was just a neurosis
concocted by Christians and mainstream psychoana-
lysts to punish people who wanted to self-actualize. She

screeched about the Symbolic being like a whirlpool that one must never look directly at. Like the sun. She whimpered that if one stares into the abyss for too long one becomes part of it. Then she seemed to fall asleep but her eyes remained open.

When Raegan appeared in the same pink pajamas, Steph arched her back like a cobra and lunged. She got a fistful of Raegan's pajama shirt.

Raegan screamed, but Steph wouldn't let her go. Steph seemed to be hugging her and hurting her at once.

"I'm sorry," said Steph. "I'm so, so sorry."

Raegan seemed to know what Steph was talking about. "Sorry for what?" she said, sarcastically.

"Sorry for what happened with your mum and dad. Sorry for what I did. For hurting you, baby."

Then Steph curled up like a satisfied kitten.

Marge decided that some chicken soup for the soul was in order so would I mind popping over to the Hampstead Butcher where I could pick out a nice, well brought-up, corn-fed bird for the pot? She only had a fifty-pound note.

"Will you run away?" she asked me.

"Do you want me to run away, Marge?"

"Steph doesn't."

I told her that I'd bring back the change.

Then I headed over to Tottenham Hale, where the chickens were cheaper.

I couldn't see any butchers in the vicinity of the train but I had already checked the route to the Walthamstow

Reservoirs online. I walked up a highway that inclined into a frigid blue sky. A white cloud hung, broken. I passed a street cleaner in an orange vest and she told me that yes, I was going in the right direction but it wasn't the season for chub. She said her friend's husband had caught a mirror carp that weighed forty-five pounds. I asked her if she'd seen a man who looked like a German idealist with a savage blond beard and piercing, Nordic-esque blue eyes but she said no. I went through an opening in a fence and entered a vast marshland. There was nothing and no one. The tourist information board listed the names of birds for birdwatching but nothing flew above. There was supposed to be "various insect life, meaning stocked fish very quickly turn into firm-fleshed, fighting wild fish," but I couldn't see any water, let alone fish, let alone insects. There was a parking lot. A man with a brown leather brief-case who wasn't Sebastian was hurrying into the bushes. I followed him. He turned right onto a canal. There were houseboats, laden with smashed furniture and flowerpots. The windows were close to the water. The water ruffled against itself. The wind blew. The man turned right again. There was a river, shielded by trees, but no one was fishing. Warnings of electrocution and toxic shock. The river ran the wrong color. The surface reflected the white sky. Birds flew up but no one was watching. There was nothing to watch. There was nothing here. There was nothing.

I was in another wasteland.

I climbed over a turnstile.

There was a white swan in another canal. Its head was underwater.

I found him.

He was standing on a small hill, tangled on all sides by weeds. He was wearing a long dark coat and it was open and blowing in the wind. He had his back to me. His stance was wide legged and proud. He was holding a fishing rod.

I circled the hill until I could get a look at his face.

Yes. It was definitely Sebastian.

His expression was that of a man contemplating the sublime power of nature. But he was overlooking an empty children's playground. One swing had been unhooked from its frame. The seesaw was smashed in two. When he saw me, his frown got more metaphysical.

Then he smiled.

Now he was running down the hill. "Do you know that stalking is an offense?" he was shouting.

"Were you trying to look like Caspar David Friedrich, posing like that?" I said.

He tried to give me a kiss on the cheek, but I folded my arms.

Lurid images of bacon and eggs ran above the counter. The man frying the eggs looked depressed. All the customers looked depressed. Sebastian was saying how much he loved the café because it was real.

"My god," I said. "She's put words in your mouth."

Our coffees arrived; they were weak and instant.

A woman with a purple rinse dropped all her change on the floor.

"I've become a lesbian," I told him. "Yep. That's right. I'm gay now."

He made a face.

"You've made me gay," I added.

There was a silence.

"Lucky Allegra never found out about that time in the ball pit," I said.

"It wasn't in the ball pit."

"Okay. In Jasper's father's apartment after we bumped into each other in the ball pit."

It had happened just after my nongraduation, last summer. I hadn't seen Sebastian for nearly a year. Freddie had forced me to go to a festival called A La Merced in Andalusia. Jasper invited us to stay in his father's holiday apartment. It was unfurnished. Of course he had purchased a king-size bed for himself that he was intending to abandon on departure. He invited me to get in it with him, but I said no. The three of us went to a restaurant and watched hedonists flow like an English dragon toward the main stage, wrecking the tranquillity of the mountains. Teenage girls with vacant eyes were handcuffed and marched out by police. Jasper said he couldn't wait because the Prodigy was headlining and "Smack My Bitch Up" was his favorite song. We made a human chain but then someone stamped on my heel and I lost my flip-flop. I lost Freddie and Jasper. Then I lost my other flip-flop. I ran around barefoot for a long time. Bits of glass and stones got stuck in the soles of my feet, but I didn't feel it because I was high. Next thing I knew I was on a bouncy castle. I went down a slide. I landed in a ball pit. Sebastian was in the ball pit. I had no idea that he was at the festival and he had no idea that I was at the festival. I thought it was fate.

He asked me what I was doing there and I said I was attending a conference on EU subsidized export laws and he said no, what are you really doing here? He was there because Olive's husband Hal was playing. Democracy of Sand was getting quite big then—before the lead singer had a schizoid episode. Allegra was at the Edinburgh Festival with Sue. I was coming down. My feet started to throb. They were bleeding. Sebastian offered to get a first-aid kit from his VIP tent but I said no, I'd rather suffer than let you help me at all. He said: "You always refused to come to a festival with me, I thought you didn't like loud music." And I said: "Yeah, but it's different with Freddie." And he said: "Different how?" And I said: "Different because I'm not in love with Freddie."

Sebastian came back to the apartment with me. I didn't tell him that it was Jasper's father's apartment because he never would have come. I said it was Freddie's father's. He pulled the glass and stones out of my feet with my tweezers and poured Jasper's sherry from Jerez over the cuts. It was agony. He wanted to get in Jasper's king-size bed but I said no fucking way. I wouldn't tell him why not. We found a deflated air mattress in the cupboard. It was dusty and stank of rubber. After two hours, he managed to pump it up. We lay together for a long time without talking. We must have fallen asleep because when we woke up there was no air left in the bed and we were on the floor and drowning in black rubber. It covered my face. All I could see was black and all I could breathe was rubber and the person lying next to me was a stranger. I tried to stand up but my feet had swollen in the night. I screamed in pain and fell backward and then he had me, anyway.

Now his cheeseburger and chips arrived.

"I don't believe in fate anymore," I was saying. "Since I moved in with Stephanie—my girlfriend."

Sebastian was shoving the burger in his mouth.

"She's famous," I said. "She's like a famous intellectual."

"Yeah right." Ketchup ran down his wrist.

I wiped it for him.

"Get off," he said. "You're right. It's not fate or coincidence. Because you stalked me into the ball pit like you stalked me today. Like you stalked me yesterday coming over to the apartment and the day before that, coming over to my parents' house. Problem with you is that you don't even know anymore what's real and what's fake because you're so much in your own fantasy world."

"What's real and what's true, don't you mean."

Sebastian laughed.

"The real is what everyone thinks is there," I said. I didn't feel like eating my hot dog. "But the true is what's really there. But it's not always visible, or logical. But it is true."

"You pulled Allegra's hair out of her head."

"Fuck off," I said. "I hate you. Leave me alone. Don't even talk to me. Don't even try and come near me."

The depressed chef cleared away our plates.

"Do you ever actually catch any fish in that lake?" I said.

"It's a reservoir. No."

"Then why do you sit there all day?"

"Because it lets me think," he said. "Because. I like to think that one day I might catch a fish, if I sit there long enough."

"Just sitting doesn't get you anywhere," I said. "That's what I love about my girlfriend, Stephanie. She's spent her whole life realizing her ambitions. Just realizing and realizing them. She's a doer." I picked up the salt.

Sebastian took the salt out of my hands. "I am doing," he said. "I'm planning my novel in my head."

"And what's that going to be about?"

"It's a monumental work. About modernity, set in Mexico. Yeah. I'm using Mexico as a paradigm for modernity."

"Please."

"It's for posterity," he said.

I laughed.

He sat back. "This is why," he said. "This is why. She doesn't laugh at me. She doesn't laugh."

"Yeah, because she's got no fucking sense of humor!" I shouted.

The hairy man came over. "Hey," he said. "Quiet down."

I apologized.

We went out for a cigarette. We were on Seven Sisters Road. The shop on the left sold plastic baskets and AA batteries. The place on the right was a loan shark's.

"Can I ask how you're living?" I said. "How can you afford to sit not catching any fish all day?"

"She's supporting me."

I was speechless.

"Yeah!" he shouted. "That's right! And I don't feel guilty! She says all artists need patronage! She says I'm doing her a favor by letting her be a patron of the arts!"

"And who patronizes her? Her parents?"

"No," he said, ferociously. "She works."

"Where?"

"In the library. In Southwark Local Library."

"She's a librarian?"

"Yeah! Bataille was a librarian. She's supporting public services. It's important."

Some kids got off the bus. One spat on the floor. Then another one spat on the floor. Then two of them got in a fight. They drifted off, fighting.

We went back inside.

"I'm going to have to go soon," he said.

"Me too. I have to go now in fact." I didn't stand up.

Sebastian stood up. "I have to go."

He paid, with her money.

Outside the café, he told me he was sorry.

He got on the bus, which came straight away.

I walked toward Seven Sisters station, feeling like I was going to kill myself.

His bus got stuck in traffic. I ran for it, and jumped on at the next stop. He wasn't on the bottom deck. I ran up to the top deck, but he wasn't there either. I looked out the window: he'd got off the bus. He looked like he was looking for me, but when I ran downstairs again, the driver wouldn't let me off until the stop after the station. I ran back toward where I had seen him, but he was gone.

I could have run away from Stephanie's then, but I didn't. She seemed to be the only person in the world who cared about me. I returned to Camden Square.

Marge opened the door. She went absolutely nuts when she saw that I'd bought a halal chicken instead of a Hampstead chicken. She asked me for the change and I handed over two quid. I tried to explain that it was very expensive these days to drain the birds of blood prior to slaughter but she told me that I was a common thief. I let her shout for a while.

Steph was swinging around and around in the teak swivel chair in her study. Her hair had been combed back but her eyes were still glazed. She was playing with something white and frilly. She stared past me. "What's this?" She held up the frilly thing.

I turned around as though she might be addressing someone behind me, but there was no one in the hall. "I don't know," I said. "A garter?"

She stretched the garter like a cat's cradle. "It came for you." She kicked a box on the floor. Ribbon lay around it. "From your lover." She held out a card, which read:

Dearest Miss Havisham. I'm glad you liked the pussy. Thou shalt not be jilted again. X

"Oh," I said. "That's from James."

Steph threw the garter at me.

It was antique and beautiful. The lace was rotting.

"Who's James?" she said.

"James is just this old guy who I let eat me out the other day. I got really sick afterward. He's nice though." I paused. "He's like a sugar daddy."

"Sugar daddy?" Her eyes seemed to focus. "Have you not been listening to a word I've *said*?" She got up and shook me by the shoulders. I tried to push her off, but she had developed an Übermensch strength.

Finally, she staggered back. "It hasn't worked," she said. "The ceremony didn't work. It must be. It must be because Erzulie is still angry with me."

"What did you do?"

"Exile, exile," said Steph. "Subjugation in exile." She took my arm. "Come with me."

We were in the basement. The swimming pool shone before us but Steph pulled out a ring of jailer's keys and led me down a hallway to the left. It was carpeted with leopard print.

"Like Graceland." Her head whipped round. "You know what kitsch is?"

"Erm. Kind of tacky stuff?"

"No. Kitsch is the aftermath of a true experience."

"Yeah." I nodded. "I keep having these aftermath experiences of love. They're not real experiences—like with James. I don't love him. It's nothing really." I paused. "We don't have to do this, Stephanie."

"Do what?" She jangled her keys.

"Whatever it is, what it is you're going to do to me. Yesterday was enough. I get it. I need to repent. I need to sort my life out and maybe do an internship at a women's domestic violence charity or something."

Her smile was dark. "You don't get it," she said quietly. "You really don't get it at all."

"What don't I get?" I said, desperately.

"Liberation means a rejection of all that came before."

"Not necessarily?"

She snapped her fingers. "Erm, hello? Man was woman's *god*. He only got knocked off his pedestal—metaphorically died, if you will—back in the 60s and 70s when the sistahood, in which I played a key part . . ."

"Yes," I said.

"After the death of the patriarchal god, a void opened up. It is harrowing to think about that void. Male writers had to think about it back in the nineteenth century when *their* god died. Like Dostoyevsky. He had to think about it. We have to think about it *now*." She opened a leopard-print door.

It was the recording studio.

She locked the door behind us. "This place is completely soundproof," she said. "It's like a panic room but better. It's like a torture chamber but where healing happens."

She positioned me inside a large glass box. It was slightly bigger than a coffin. She planted some headphones on my head and pointed to a microphone.

"I really can't sing," I said.

She said something back, but I couldn't hear it.

I took the headphones off.

"I said, *but can you scream?*" she said. "Because no one can hear you in here, anyways." To demonstrate, she screamed—loud. She kept screaming. Then she started grunting from the back of her throat.

Eventually she left the box, locking me inside it. She moved behind a glass wall. A bank of a million buttons lit up. She gestured for me to put the headphones back on.

We were facing each other.

Her voice boomed loud in my ears: "The sirens ensnared Odysseus by singing their deadly song. He couldn't resist. They say a way to a man's heart is through his stomach. Well, a way to a woman's heart is through her ears." She slid up the buttons on the mixing desk. "I've taken the liberty of consulting your personal effects."

"My what?" I shouted, but my voice was muffled.

"Your laptop," boomed Stephanie. "Your top three most played *tunes* on *iTunes*. Whimsies you can't stop listening to. Candy you can't stop eating. First, I'll play the original. Then it's your turn. You sing along. I want feeling. This is catharsis. This is your chance to get it out once and for all. To expunge those saccharine lyrics until they are dead to you. Until you realize you have been aping sentiment all along. In descending order."

The celestial chords of Beyoncé's "Halo" began to play. Her voice was like an injection of honey, emptying the world of reality and replacing it with happiness. A large monitor outside my box showed Beyoncé bathed in quasi-religious light, makeup free, admiring her lover as he slept. She sung that she was addicted to his light. The song was arresting and lulling at once. It was an ecstatic dream, a way to return. "*Halo, halo, halo.*" It ended.

"Now your turn," boomed Steph.

An instrumental version began.

"I can't sing," I said into the microphone.

"Try!" screeched Steph. "You've got to try!"

I tried my best to imitate Beyoncé, her evangelical conviction. I got carried away.

When the song ended, Steph boomed: "This is an example of the spirituals of slavery reincarnated through the twentieth-century Afro-American gospel tradition and thus corralled via auto-tune into contemporary rhythm-and-blues pop that straddles both Christianity and secular individualism in its quest for a lover with a halo in lieu of baby Jesus himself!" She sounded deranged. "Beyoncé is a light-skinned African American woman with dyed blonde hair and Caucasian features who wants it and gets it all ways at once: she wants girls to run the world as long as they are sliding around in the dust wearing nothing but bikinis and sucking their forefingers."

"Hey," I said. "Don't say that. I love Beyoncé."

"I know you do," said Steph. "I know you do. The problem with you postfeminist girls is that you love with all your hearts what you know in your heads to be wrong. You love it ironically."

There was silence.

"I don't!" I said. "I love her truly. She's a career woman. She's equal to Jay-Z. They've got one of the best relationships in the industry."

Steph laughed. "You speak as though you're part of

that industry. But you're not part of any industry. Except mine."

The song began again, and again, and again.

"Louder!" screamed Steph.

But it was never good enough.

I tried harder.

She castigated me harder.

Finally, on the twelfth or thirteenth go, she said she liked the sound of my harmony.

I was going hoarse.

Then she told me I'd fallen off.

"Fallen off what?" I rasped.

"Fallen." She shook her head.

By the twentieth go, I was almost mute.

Steph stood up and clapped. "Well done, you."

I sank back in the box, exhausted.

"That signified the exaltation typically associated with the early feelings of love," said Stephanie. "Now the mood changes. We are remembering the first time. We are in the middle. This is your second most-listened-to song . . . a song to die for."

It began: "The First Time Ever I Saw Your Face." The monitor showed Roberta Flack on *Top of the Pops* in 1972. She was wearing a black-and-gold African top and she had an Afro. She was playing the piano.

"Was it you who made them play it at the strip club?" I croaked.

Stephanie shrugged, faux-naïf. "You've listened to this song 5,873 times. You have given yourself brain damage listening to this song."

The rigmarole started again; she made me sing it, again, and again, and again.

"Your husky voice suits this perfectly." She hugged herself. "This takes me back to the days when I fell in love with Leo. He was a brilliant man. An ice hockey player. I'll tell you about him sometime."

Hours had passed. There were no windows and no natural light.

I begged her for a glass of water. She gave me some iced tea.

"Can I have a cigarette?" I said.

"No." She said things had changed now since I hadn't learned my lesson and I was in danger of running away.

"Who said I was going to run away?" I rasped.

"Now we smash through the pain barrier!" She raised her fist in the air. She gestured for me to do the same. "You've listened to this last song 11,785 times."

I began to panic. "Please don't play this song," I said. "Please. It really brings back a lot of memories. I hate this song."

But the chords of "I'll Be Your Mirror" had started, and now she was dancing. "This is *my* era," she was saying.

Nico was promising to reflect her lover, reflect her lover, reflect her lover.

My heart was beating too fast. I tried to grasp the microphone but it slipped out of my hands. I took the headphones off.

There was silence.

She was screaming, but I couldn't hear her. I lip-read: "You're going to sing. Sing, sing until there's nothing left."

I scrabbled at the door of the box. She marched through the glass wall, opened the door, and slapped me, hard.

I could hear the song faintly through the earphones bouncing on their wire.

"How do you feel?" hissed Stephanie. She pressed a finger to my lips. She produced a fountain pen and a pad. "Get down." She pointed to the floor. "Write."

I sank to the floor.

Steph was screaming at me about the semiotic chora that I was riding right now, transporting me to a time outside of time before I loved and lost, when my heart was still whole, not hopelessly splintered by the dictates of gender normativity.

But it wouldn't come.

Nothing would come.

FOURTEEN

THE NEXT MORNING, I did run away.

I returned to Clapham.

The crazy lady with the Cabbage Patch doll was telling me why she preferred minimalism these days. Her cart was covered with flattened white cardboard boxes. Her baby wore a white paper bag as a bonnet. "After an era of great busyness," she was saying. "There must be simplicity. Everything must be stripped down." She paused. "Or maybe it was the snow that inspired me."

Clapham Common was green again. It was Thursday.

"They put me inside for the night," she said. "But I got out. I got out."

We were standing outside the Chinese takeout place on Clapham High Street. Raegan had begged me not to go, but I felt sure that it wouldn't be long before bars were fitted to my bedroom window at Stephanie's. I had taken James's pussy with me.

The sewage had risen still farther from the basement of our apartment. It had become an odor that I could taste. It tasted of tonic water and shit. The shit was real, as though a whole army of schoolchildren had been invited to shit all over the floor for want of any other way to entertain themselves. The remains of a Russian salad had fallen over the counter and dribbled down the cupboard doors. The fridge door had been left open. The TV was on. A copy of Steph's novel *Abreaction* had been tossed onto the chaise longue. The bust of Professor Frank had been hacked at. The electric meat carver that my mother had bought us as a housewarming present lay beside it. The hacking had been aborted because the tires were so thick. It appeared that Freddie had resorted to stubbing his cigarettes out on the Professor's conceptualized fore-head. No one was home.

I went upstairs.

Freddie's room was filled with balloon animals that must have been blown up days before because most had deflated to become wisps, poor unfortunate souls of bal-loon animals. My bedroom door was closed. The smell got stronger.

I heard something move inside.

I opened the door.

Vic was sprawled across the bed, naked. His eyes were glassy.

I screamed.

"I've been waiting," he said. His black hair hung lanker. His penis began to stand up, but I was more concerned about the state of my bedroom. It had been terrorized. The walls were smeared with feces. There were handprints of shit everywhere, but also nods to the history of twentieth-century art: de Kooning-like gestures in shit that coalesced at times into shit figuration. A naked woman had been sketched in shit on the wall over my bed. Her nipples were fingerprints, her eyes were fingerprints, her whole body looked as though it had been poked into being. I covered my nose and mouth.

"It wasn't me," said Vic. He sat up and held out his arms.

I waded through the piles of clothes that had been turned out from the chest of drawers. My feet crunched. I looked down: dozens of broken eggshells were strewed over the carpet. Their yolks had transformed into a variant of milkshake. There were sachets in which the remnants of a black substance swirled. There was a tiny hammer on my dressing table. The mirror inside the wardrobe door bore the black word: "Butchered."

"Fucking Allegra," I said. "God. She's so melodramatic."

"It was like this when I came in," said Vic.

I sat down on the bed. He tried to stroke my hair and I let him for a couple of seconds but then I pushed him off and stood up.

"She hasn't even got any new ideas," I said. "She already did this performance like two years ago. With the squid ink." I laughed at the memory. "She puts a sheet over her head and then tapes eggs to her eyes. She's already got her assistant Sue to inject the eggs with squid ink. Then

– 218 –

she looks like this crazy ghost or nun or something. She gets Sue to tap the eggs with a hammer." I picked up the hammer. "So that the squid ink kind of squirts out of her eyes. It's hilarious."

"You know the person who did this?" The pits in Vic's face had expanded to become holes. "I thought you'd had a break-in—the door was open."

I managed to get Vic dressed and out of the house with threats to call the police and, when that didn't work, I promised to call him.

"I'll call you, I'll call you, I'll call you," said Vic, mimicking my voice. "All I ever hear from you is *I'll call you*."

"How else do you expect to hear from me, Vic? By pigeon? I've just been so busy with work commitments—now that I've got a new job at the bank." He didn't believe that I'd turned into a "square" just at the moment when he'd stopped being a "square" so I had to go into elaborate detail about my daily administrative tasks and how organizing other people's money was a sobering way to fill one's time. I said that now he and I could afford to go on dinner dates to Carluccio's like other couples. I gave him a pair of Freddie's old brogues to wear, but I noticed when I tried to find an outfit that most of Freddie's clothes had gone. His camera equipment had gone too.

I gave the key to the apartment to the homeless lady with the minimalist cart. I told her she could stay there as long as she cleaned it up.

Freddie wasn't answering his phone. I called Jasper. He told me that they were shooting on location. He said that Freddie never wanted to see or speak to me again. I used the forty-eight pounds leftover from the halal chicken to buy a train ticket to Suffolk.

There was a little boy wandering out of the gates of Hammerton Hall. He was wearing a top hat and tails and his face was cut. He looked stunned. I asked him if he knew where he was going, but he ran away from me. He went in the direction of the village.

Maxine the housekeeper was riding a horse around and around the paddock. I knew her well; she had fried us all black pudding the morning after the night of the crème de menthe, which had taken place in a drawing room here. It had been filled with Sarah Lucas sculptures: stockings stuffed with oranges and aggressive tabloid montages. Freddie always said that his father was a follower; he'd caught the Young British Artists wave a couple of years too late. That night, Maxine had assisted our game of truth or dare by fishing the bottle of crème de menthe out of the recycling bin and rinsing it. She had remained in a dark corner, watching. The fire reflected in Jasper's face as he brandished the bottle. Allegra was prostrate. I looked away. Afterward, Freddie saluted Maxine for being unshockable. She had been an artist herself back in the 80s, but it never worked out.

Now Maxine got off the horse and told me they were in the dining room, but that Freddie had said he'd kill me soon as look at me. The bright green English countryside appeared refreshingly blameless and boring, as though nothing could ever happen here. A crow flew above. The pigs were asleep, Maxine said.

Freddie was wearing a black balaclava with a top hat and a black poncho. He was jousting with Jasper who was dressed the same except that his hat had fallen off in the effort to stab Freddie with the point of his sword. The ceiling was high and the walls were paneled, but instead of portraits of successive generations of Freddie's family, there hung Bruce Nauman neons, kicking their legs up in fascist uniformity or lying in chain gangs of oral sex.

"Are these originals?" I called from the far end of the room, and my voice echoed back: "Are these originals, originals, originals?"

Freddie the caped crusader ran at me with his jousting stick and didn't stop, so that I was forced to exit the room and close the door behind me.

"Can we be friends?" I said through the door. "Didn't you get my text? I told you I was sorry."

I heard the sword hit the door and twang.

I moved away. "Sorry," I repeated.

Freddie opened the door. He pointed the sword at my throat.

"Look," I said. "We're even, okay? You got Allegra to fuck up my room so badly and all my stuff is just fucked up and you let that psycho Vic in. He's dangerous, Freddie." I could only see his eyes through the balaclava.

"Do you have any idea how long my uncle has lived?" said Freddie.

I shook my head.

"Ninety-four years. Do you have any idea how many days and hours it will take him to recount his life fucking story? Hhhmm—well." He waved the sword. "The Greenland years alone were fraught with daily risks to life and limb thanks to his rugged determination to hunt like the Inuit man, to fuck like the Inuit man—"

"Freddie can you put your sword down, please? I'm really at the end right now. I'm exhausted. I'm at the end." I sat down on the floor and started to cry. I was wearing one of Stephanie's smocks and one of Stephanie's duffel coats; I had stolen them from the dirty laundry basket before I left.

Freddie sat beside me. He pulled down the balaclava. "To keep the apartment, I have to write up Uncle's whole life in the form of an oral history," he said. "Not a biography. He wants it in the form of *folktale*, a *myth*. To ensure he becomes a *legend*."

I laughed.

Freddie laughed too.

We sat in silence for a while.

Finally he said: "I didn't tell Allegra to fuck your room. She found out that Sebastian met up with you and went really fucking nuts. I think she thinks he's still in love with you or something. She said that when he got back from seeing you, he was just moping around the apartment, saying he didn't want to go to Mexico anymore."

We were sitting on the floor in Freddie's studio. It was in the attic at Hammerton Hall. The windows looked over the forest, turning blue in the afternoon. A harsh light shone down on a high-backed chair. There was a bottle of black shoe polish, and a rag. There was blood on the green carpet.

"There is nothing to dream of," Jasper was saying. "So nothing connects with nothing." He was drinking a bottle of ale. "That's how one always feels after a bout of booting." He lay on his back.

"It'll get picked up," said Freddie. "For sure."

Another young boy dressed in top hat and tails appeared at the door. Maxine stood behind him. She disappeared. He was different from the stunned boy that I had seen by the gate; he wasn't bleeding.

"Please sir, can I have some more?" said Jasper, falsetto.

He and Freddie laughed.

The young boy looked as fresh as an apple. He held out a piece of paper in a plastic sleeve. "Here's my extra-curriculars," he said.

Jasper stood up and stretched. He sat in the chair.

"Wet bob. Good. Dry bob. Kneel there." Freddie pointed to the space at Jasper's feet. "Now I told you this is artistic, hey, so no recompense but you will be in my show *Making A Racket*. Jasp is doing tech."

The boy nodded. "I've always wanted to be in the arts," he said. "I've always been arty."

Freddie turned on his Bolex and beamed the light into the boy's eyes. "Now shine. That's right."

The boy started shining Jasper's shoes, which were already shiny. "Is this right?" said the boy, working the cloth back and forth.

"Say nothing," said Freddie.

The boy shined each shoe for a long time.

And then Jasper kicked the boy swiftly in the face.

The boy staggered back, clutching his nose. Dark blood leaked out of his nostrils and trickled over his lips. His eyes showed terror.

The boy staggered to his feet.

Jasper stared into the distance.

The camera kept rolling.

I followed the boy out of the room and around the fountain in the courtyard. It was guarded by a ring of stone toy soldiers, shooting or being shot. They were replicas of components of a Chapman brothers installation that Freddie's father couldn't afford to buy.

The boy must have thought that I was part of Freddie and Jasper's creative team, because when I tried to catch up with him, shouting that I wanted to help, he ran faster.

I got on the train and returned to London, desperate. I had no money, no job, and nowhere to live.

I walked all the way from Liverpool Street station to Soho. A girl who I didn't know had taken over the reception at William's. She wore a Minnie Mouse bow on her head. She asked if she could help me. She had never heard of me before. I went down to the kitchen and asked the new sous-chef if I could have the staff meal. It was nearly ready: gray mutton and chips. He hadn't heard of me either. I swore on my life that I had been a door bitch here for five solid months until Monday morning. I asked the other chefs to corroborate but they kept their heads down and whittled away at their zucchini flowers.

I found Madeline the head waitress in the cloakroom and she accused me of stealing the lost property box. She told me to pay for it. I said I didn't have any money and besides you couldn't put a price on things that were lost, could you? Surely that was the beauty of lost things?

She threw me out.

I wandered around the block.

I returned to William's and persuaded the new door bitch, who was called Bethany, to let me print out my CV. She told me that she was working on a project about the aesthetics of Americana as part of her Fine Art BA at Saint Martins. She had spent the previous afternoon taking pictures of different branches of Ed's Diner.

I went into every restaurant, bar, and pub in Soho, giving out my CV. They all told me that there was nothing. I went into Ed's Diner and told them that my friend was a famous artist who had just taken pictures of the place for a big exhibition on the aesthetics of Americana at Gagosian Gallery, Beverly Hills, but they said they'd never heard of Gagosian.

"But you've heard of Beverly Hills, right?"

"What's that got to do with us."

I tried every retail outlet in Covent Garden. My vision got hot and demented at the sight of all those clinking gold and silver charms in Accessorize, hanging on their racks. The music jangled, the lyrics self-obsessed and love struck. Everyone said no. I went down a narrow street off the piazza. A back door was open. I went downstairs. Now I was in another American diner, decorated with neon tubes like the Naumans hanging on Freddie's father's paneled walls. But these neons were advertising Coca-Cola and peach melba. "Hit the Road Jack" was playing. It was empty.

I went back upstairs.

There was a woman smoking by the back door. She was wearing a T-shirt that said "Give It Wings" over a picture of a flying, smiling hamburger. I asked her if there were any jobs. She said one of their promo girls had just walked out. She took my CV.

I pointed to her T-shirt and asked what it meant.

"Hurry the fuck up," she said.

Hi Olive!

Hope you're well!
    Was wondering if I could stay in Sebastian's bed for a while? I've just run away from this cult.
    Thanks so much.

Ann-Marie X

Three hours later, I was sitting up in Sebastian's bed, wearing Sebastian's childhood pajamas and navy-blue dressing gown, nestled under Sebastian's familiar old duvet. Olive was sitting on the bed, her back against the wall. Her legs lay over mine. Her husband Hal was serenading us both with a song that he was currently working on. His face screwed up with anguish as he strummed the guitar. "You promised," he sang. His voice sounded a bit like Bruce Springsteen. Hal was from Jersey just like Bruce, said Olive.

"You promised you'd be different this time, that you weren't like all the other guys, but you weren't different, you let me down and blew my mind, just like they did."

"Is he talking about a former . . . boyfriend?" I whispered to Olive.

"No," she said, solemnly. "He's talking about Obama."

"I trusted you, you motherfucking asshole," Hal went on. The song caved into Martha Wainwright's "Bloody Mother Fucking Asshole," which was about her absent father.

"I mean," said Olive. "I had my doubts but you know we all hoped he wouldn't screw us in the ass like the last guy."

Hal stopped, finally.

Olive and I applauded.

Sebastian's parents were at work. Most of the intersex siblings were at their independent day school, except for one, who was pretending to be ill. He/she was scraping the bow back and forth over his/her cello in the next room.

"You know you can stay here as long as you want," Olive was saying to me. She had lent me £500 and her old laptop. "Mum and Dad are going to be psyched."

They went for a walk in the park.

I checked my email.

Ann-Marie,

I pushed you too fast, and for that I'm sorry. Let me try to explain.

I've been propelled toward excess in my actions by a sense of the overwhelming tragedy that has befallen the good name of feminism. Now feminism is a dirty word, a synonym for hairy lesbian. All my life, I've wanted to prove the detractors wrong. I've wanted to maintain myself as an example of otherness, of what the other can be. I've hoped to inspire, but I can see that with you, I've gone too far.

When I was browsing through my teenage notebooks a few years ago, I came across a charming picture of Zelda Fitzgerald that I had taped inside with a quote: "Hysterically, she began to run." It was taken from Zelda's novel, *Save Me the Waltz*. At that age, I fetishized madness to the extent of daydreaming constantly about being locked up in a mental asylum, about watching the yellow wallpaper begin to crawl and writhe of its own accord. To be out of one's mind and beside oneself. I too wanted to run.

However, I soon realized that hysteria— dependence of any sort—is anathema to survival. One must retain one's own inner balance. To do so is a political act.

Only later would I dare—and I did dare—to even conceive of the idea of writing. Of writing about my own experience as a means to write about women in general. Yes, I was accused of universalism—how could I possibly speak for the particular? But what those blue-blooded Ivy League bitches failed to understand was that I was the particular. They had more in common with their class than their sex. I was destined to be a hairdresser.

This is all terribly incoherent. What I mean is—I apologize for becoming that which I have spent my career condemning. Hysterical, inchoate.

Today, the Symbolic constitutes our flesh and blood, our very souls. It is clear to me that you, Ann-Marie, are an embodiment of the Symbolic. Looking into your sarcastic eyes is like looking into the postfeminist whirlpool itself.

I shouldn't be surprised—nor, in fact, disappointed. We are all made by history.

I want to tell you about my ice hockey player. I want to tell you what happened and why the sistahood hates me and why I can never go home to America—except for the occasional publicity tour. I want to shine a light for you, so that you may rise where I have fallen. Yes, I have fallen. One becomes preoccupied with the subjects that most captivate—no, capture—one. I must confess that I remain a hopeless romantic.

Please come back.

Stephanie

P.S. It was Beckett who said: "Fail better." Failure is but a route to creativity. For that reason, and to prove to you that perfectionism only serves to sap one's white milk dry, I have taken the liberty of scanning the tabula rasa that you left on the floor of the recording studio before you ran out and abandoned me just like Leo. The page remains virgin snow—its virginity is perhaps more meaningful than anything you could possibly write. It is a testament to the silence of your generation of young women, who neglect to vote despite the fact that your forebears starved to death to win the vote. There is a beauty to the blankness of your page, imprinted, as it is, with the ever-so-slightly sweaty marks of your growing anxiety as I bore down all the more heavily on you and the night turned to day. It is now available to download on my website.

In order to access Stephanie's website, I had to watch an animated cupid aim his arrow at the heart of an unsuspecting little girl, wearing glasses and reading a book. When the arrow hit her, the little girl immediately dropped the book and stamped on her glasses. Her eyes were stunned and blind; this was illustrated by her bumping into furniture. Cupid was laughing. The girl held her arms straight out in front of her like a zombie and then proceeded to walk over the edge of an animated cliff.

The blog post was titled: "Cat Got Your Tongue?" Steph reminded her readers that in Spanish *lengua* meant both the tongue in your mouth and your language—like mother tongue. My blank white sheet stood like a monument on the screen, a tower of nothingness, to which

I had contributed—nothing. The tags were *trauma*, *disenfranchisement*, and *voicelessness*. Steph had written an emotive caption about how she couldn't possibly reveal the identity of the (un)author, but suffice to say that she (un)spoke for a whole bottled-up generation of young women. The bottled-up part was a play on the fact that people in my generation were all alcoholics who sought escape from the dictates of the meritocracy in the form of drink. Girlwithacurl456 had commented underneath:

> I <3 getting fukd because its fun, it makes me wanna get fukd more.

I also had an email from Vic:

> I don't know how you got down into that submarine, but I saw you, waiting your turn with no shame, wanting it with no shame. Your hair was blond, not brown. You dyed it, slut. Think you can escape me? Letting all five sailors do it all over you, holding you open. I could see all the way inside of you and I didn't like what I saw. Your tits were orange and bigger. You were loving it. They didn't buy you a drink or warn you when they were going to do it and then they bukkaked all over your face. They gave you a pearl necklace and then you licked it all up and snowballed with your friend, who looked just like you too. I never want to see you again.

"Yeah, I joined a cult once," Olive was saying.

It was evening. I was face down on the bed. She was trying to feel out my root chakra. It was somewhere at the base of my spine. Apparently, it was blocked. I had been telling her about Stephanie.

"But I only lasted like one day," she went on. "Before Hal came and got me. I had been trying to get away from Hal in the first place because we had a fight. I wanted something of my own—I was on the verge of training as a physiotherapist. But then this girl came up to me at a café when I was crying. She was very beautiful but she looked zonked out of her mind. When I got to the ranch everyone was drifting around, like, totally placid, but the daily routine was actually really regimented. There was this one guy—Matt—real charismatic. He was the leader. He read books, Wilhelm Reich and stuff, and tried to practice it on the girls."

"What, the Orgasmatron?"

"Is that the box you go in to come?" She laughed. "Yeah. Shit like that. It was deep. There was a lake there, and I remember thinking this whole place is like a placid fucking lake. And just below the surface, there are sharks."

"That feels good," I said. Her hands were hovering above my shoulder blades.

"They tried to stop Hal from taking me because they'd already changed my name to Paula."

I laughed.

"No, it was serious. This guy Matt twisted everything. It was a mindfuck."

"Yeah," I said. "Stephanie was a mindfuck. But I kind of feel sorry for her. She's lost."

Olive leaned forward and whispered very close to my ear: "No, honey. You're lost."

That evening, Sebastian's parents were having a dinner party. They asked me to join them.

Leonard Cohen's "Dance Me to the End of Love" was playing as the amuse-bouches were wheeled out: plates of halloumi and baba ghanoush. A balding man with glasses was sitting on the sofa, trying to engage Hal in a conversation about Syrian politics. Sebastian's miniature father slung an arm around my shoulders and told me how pleased they were that I was staying. He introduced me to the balding man, who was called Phillip. His bald head glowed as he rammed some of that halloumi in his mouth. "Oh, your mother never stops talking about you," Phillip told me.

A few minutes later, my mother turned up, wearing a red dress and red lipstick like mine and red shoes.

Phillip's head glowed more aggressively. It was obvious they knew each other well.

I stood squarely in front of my mother and asked Phillip how he came to be at this party. He said that he was a human rights solicitor. I asked Phillip if there were likely to be any human rights abuses at this party.

He laughed nervously.

"Ann-Marie," said my mother. "Don't be like that. I've wanted you to meet Phillip since . . ." Phillip the bald beau was moving into her house, it transpired. My old room was going to be turned into a study where Phillip could examine in total privacy the shocking wounds of torture victims.

"That's a bit of a sick job, isn't it?" I said to him.

"No," said my mother. "It is a very important job. Phillip helps people from all over the world."

"Seems to me that people who want to help other people are often just suffering from narcissistic personality disorder," I said. "Yeah, I looked it up on the Internet."

Sebastian's mother was basting a goose in the kitchen. It was mammoth, more like a pterodactyl. I helped her with the potatoes and the curly kale.

"We're so glad to have you," she said. "I can't tell you. You know you can stay here for as long as you like."

"Thank you," I said. "It's such a relief. I've been moving around so much."

"How's Freddie?"

"He's beating up young boys in Suffolk."

"Is that a gay thing?" asked Sebastian's father, coming into the kitchen.

"Harold," said Sebastian's mother.

Another couple arrived. They were book critics. They talked at length about the pluses and minuses of historical fiction. "The prose perpetually runs the risk of descending into the purple, or merely kitsch," said the woman. She was swinging her glass of red wine around as she talked.

"God." The male book critic bashed the heel of his

hand against his forehead. "Can we not use that word, darling? What does it even mean?"

They all laughed.

The female book critic was laughing too, but then she slammed her glass down on the counter and said: "Why do you always have to undermine me?"

"Kitsch means the aftermath of experience," I said. "It's like a ghost of experience. A ghost."

They stared at me. I opened the AGA to toss the potatoes again.

The male critic said: "Is that a quote?"

"Yeah," I said. "Stephanie Haight told me. She's a world-renowned intellectual."

"We know who Stephanie Haight is!" said the female critic. She produced *Falling Out of Fate* from her handbag.

"Haight was such an influential figure for my generation," said Sebastian's mother. "She made feminism so cool, so sexy. She was so fierce and dignified."

"And she's still got it," said the female critic. "Her interpretation of the master/slave dialectic is scintillating. Like reading a thriller."

"I'm a feminist," said Sebastian's father. "I've always called myself a feminist." He reached on tiptoe to kiss Sebastian's mother.

"But I still have to remind Harold to help with the child care," said Sebastian's mother.

They all laughed.

Two of Sebastian's intersex siblings wandered into the kitchen. The bigger one helped the smaller one to water a mint plant.

"We don't believe in nannies," said Sebastian's mother.

Soon dinner was served.

I watched my mother canoodle in the candlelight with Phillip. She was flushed, like a girl. He kept on smiling at me. I smiled at the cucumber and pomegranate salad.

"Speaking of Haight," said Sebastian's mother. She looked ravishing tonight; her long black Allegra-esque hair flowed free.

"Hate?" said my mother. "Susan, this sangak bread is divine."

"Thank you, angel," said Sebastian's mother.

"I still find it a bit weird that you lot are friends now," I said.

"Well, I'm glad that they are!" said bald Phillip. "It was Harold and Susan who introduced me to your mother. Harold and I were at Birmingham together back in the Stone Age!"

"No, Stephanie *Haight*," said Sebastian's mother. "Who your daughter knows."

"Does she?" said my mother.

"Yeah, she was my supervisor at Cambridge," I lied.

"You know, that was the thing," said Sebastian's father. He was already drunk. "Sebastian never could forgive you for getting into Cambridge. He simply loathed UCL. Loathed it. Thought they were all beneath him."

"Sebastian was always gifted," said my mother.

"Gifted or got the gift of the gab," said his father. "Who knows?"

Sebastian's mother put down her knife and fork and pressed her fingertips together. "It's a crucial age. Each young person has to recognize at some point the gap between his ego ideal—his ideal self—and who he really is. Now, the question is. Do you strive to close that gap or just accept your shortcomings?" She looked at Sebastian's father. Then she turned to me. "Haight tweeted her blog post today about a young postfeminist woman who tried to write but couldn't come up with a word."

I laughed. Then I stopped laughing. "Oh?"

"That blank page was so resonant to me," said his mother. "I remember when I first tried to give psychoanalytic papers at those big fancy conferences. I was petrified."

"That's so true," said the female book critic. "It is a female thing. Because Carl." She looked at the male book critic. "Can drink as much as he likes and get up in the morning, and write. Hungover or not. I can't do that. I can't afford to be complacent."

"But is that really a gender thing?" said the male book critic. "Because I like to enjoy myself?"

"Women have to work ten times as hard," said Sebastian's mother. "We have to overcome that voice in our heads which says: 'No. You can't do it. You must fail.'"

I helped her clear away the starters.

"You should take a look at that blog," she said. "It got retweeted by Mental, the mental health charity. I do a lot of work with them."

I blushed. "I don't think I'd be interested in that." I excused myself and went outside for a cigarette.

Hal was strumming his guitar while we waited for the goose to rest. Everyone's faces looked happy and dazed. My mother looked happier than I had ever seen her.

We were halfway through the goose when the front door opened and Allegra appeared in the kitchen. She was wearing a tiny black minidress and a pair of ripped black tights. Sebastian appeared behind her.

"This is all very nice," said Allegra. "How nice."

There was a long silence.

Sebastian was looking at the goose. "Is there any left?" he said.

"We thought we'd just drop by because we're all out of mosquito repellent," said Allegra.

"Can't you buy that at the airport?" said Sebastian's father.

"Nonsense," said his mother. "We must have some somewhere. But—oh dear. There isn't any room."

Allegra and Sebastian had to sit with the kids on the collapsible card table. Sebastian gnawed the remains of the goose carcass. I could feel the nihilistic pull of Allegra's presence. This went on for a few moments. There was conversation about the state of the economy.

Then I stood up. "Get out!" I shouted at Allegra. "Get out! This is my house!"

She stood up too. "This is not your house!"

"And what the fuck, you smeared your shit all over my walls."

The party went into shock.

"You'd moved out," said Allegra. "That was an experiment. Haven't you ever heard of Mary fucking Barnes?"

"Yes," said Sebastian's mother. "She was a very interesting woman."

"She was like a schizophrenic who came off medication thanks to R. D. Laing," said Allegra. "She smeared her shit over the walls because she didn't have any paint and then they gave her paint and she became an internationally acclaimed fucking artist."

"So what?" I screamed. "Smear your shit over your own walls if you want to!"

"Now, now," said Sebastian's father.

"This needs to run its course," said Sebastian's mother, sagely. "This is abreaction." She turned to me. "Have you read Haight's novel?"

I shook my head.

"It's wonderful."

I clattered the dishes in the sink. "When are you two actually *going* to Mexico?" I said. "Because you've been leaving for like a week now."

"I don't know," said Sebastian.

"He doesn't know!" said Sebastian's father. He raised his glass. "He doesn't know. He never knows."

"That's enough, Dad," said Olive. "Leave him alone."

"When are you going to make a man of yourself, Sebastian?" said Sebastian's father.

Sebastian stood up. "I would like to make a man of myself. Let's see now. I broke my fucking leg so that I could be a fucking short-ass like you. I maimed myself just to get your approval, *Dad*."

"That was an accident, Sebastian," I said. "Because I made you dance with me on that slippery floor. *And*

I imagined a different space, where no dancing is. Do you remember that poem I wrote for you?"

"What?" the book critics were saying. "What? What?"

"He did it unconsciously on purpose," said Olive.

Hal began to strum his guitar again so that we had to shout louder over the music. His song was rambling and tuneless.

"And playing the Hooray Henry," Sebastian's father went on. "Going gambling in that godforsaken boater. Going to formal halls, when you didn't even belong to a college."

FIFTEEN

ABREACTION: A NOVEL

Chapter 1

Sisyphus was named as such because her parents intimated from her startling hazel eyes that she was doomed to roll a rock up to the top of a hill, only to have it roll down again, so that she would have to roll it up again, and so on, for all eternity.

They would have her believe that her fate was inscribed in her name.

When Sisyphus won a scholarship to St Anne's College, Oxford, she was ecstatic. She surmised that there was no need to hold a pillow down over her well-meaning parents' faces as they slept because now she was free.

She had fallen twice thus far.

The first boy she fell in love with was a local gangster called Simon. He was born of Chinese descent but his parents anglicized his name. He wore a diamond in his ear and he starred in black-

and-white TV ads for oriental-style noodles. It was a time when Chinese cuisine had barely entered the UK.

All the girls loved Simon. Sisyphus knew she would never get him because she was so morbidly obese. He was subject to much racism from the teachers and she longed to position her whalelike body in front of him in the form of a human shield, but he bullied her along with the rest. It was then that she came to understand the veracity of the Auden line: "Those to whom evil is done / Do evil in return."

She prayed to the moon that Simon would love her back. She devised superstitions, wishing for particular patterns of numbers to occur. Soon, she became a slave to those patterns. They ruled her with a logic that she herself had created.

The moon's face remained impassive outside her bedroom window. Simon continued to appear in flickering black and white on the screen, and sometimes in the form of a jingle on the radio. Sometimes she doubted that Simon was real at all.

On the upside, she discovered a mystical inner world. Her desire for him was celestial, not sexual. It belonged to the stars; stars exploded within her. He seemed to be the most powerful person in the universe. He was the sun around which she revolved, just like the songs said it should be. But if he didn't exist then maybe her circular path had no center?

Her second love was called Billy. He fell in love with Sisyphus because she was assertive, like a man. She bulldozed people on the way home from school like a man. And if he closed his eyes, he could just about imagine that she was in fact a man.

Billy had fantasies of being tied to a lamppost and beaten by Sisyphus. While researching her thesis on romantic masochism in the work of Simone de Beauvoir years later, Sisyphus would come to realize that Billy had been using her as a way of punishing himself for his own illicit homosexual desires. He wouldn't come out of the closet until he was married with two children.

Billy made her the aggressor in the relationship. She felt herself to be an aggressor in any case because she was always compelled to defend herself. She was angry as hell. She was defensive as hell. She had to be. It's called survival. She would fight and fight and fight, and Billy would whimper and cry. She would wish that he was a real man, a macho man, but then all the macho men ridiculed her mercilessly. They wanted childlike girls, who had no ambitions of their own.

Sisyphus had nothing *but* her ambition. She allowed Billy to make her orgasm from behind but all the time she was plotting her escape from her family and his terrible silhouette cast on the wall of his father's shed. That's how she knew she didn't love him: she abhorred his silhouette.

Years later, when her head was bent over the tomes in the Robbins Library, Harvard, she would realize that both Simon and Billy had been mere pretexts for her to seethe with a solipsistic passion. It was a private passion, on which they could not trespass.

On an unconscious level, she had ensured in both cases that reciprocity was impossible. She loved Simon; he didn't love her. Billy loved her, but she didn't love him. He only loved her because he was lying to himself and the rest of society.

Someone was always turning away. But did it have to be so?

The rock that Sisyphus rolled up her hill would soon become heavier still. Indeed, soon the hill would turn to ice. The surface would become so slippery that rolling the rock would be nigh on impossible. She would meet Leo, an extraordinary American ice hockey player.

I read Steph's novel on the night bus headed toward Camden Square. I didn't want to stay in Sebastian's bed after that furor. And I couldn't be sure that the crazy woman had cleaned all the shit off my bedroom walls in Clapham yet.

Stephanie promised to reinstate her cleaner, Ilka. She promised that there would be no more sadism, no more chores. She said she loved me, and that without me, she was nothing. She said all this in a stream of consciousness while Marge stirred and stirred that damn chicken soup for the soul, made with my halal.

Raegan was the only one I was happy to see.

There was a hamper of Harrods bespoke offal on my bed. It had been there for some time; it was rotting. The urinal scent of kidneys overwhelmed the Florida Water.

There was a note:

Ma cherie Camille,

Did you receive the garter? Oh, how I drive myself to the point of dementia of a night imagining you slipping that elastic over your lithe thigh. I imagine sinking my sorrowful teeth into that thigh. Sorrowful because you do not write, you do not call. Do you think of me? Can I hope that you do?

Our night together was incendiary. Incinerate me again, my precious one. Let me incinerate you. Jouissance comes in clouds across my vision and I can't think, and I can't see. I yearn to take you up to the Chartreuse Mountains and sample that monkish blue liqueur. Oh, how we would scandalize them! I yearn to make the Fathers disavow their faith and their guilt. They would, after one look at your silken skin.

You have brought out my playful side! I want to see you in the white of Miss H. before she stopped all the clocks and let the rats gnaw at her cake. Will you wear her dress for me?

Salud,
James X

I had taken Stephanie at her word that she would give me anything I wanted so the following morning we went to Selfridges. I wanted to· buy a new outfit for the Samuel Johnson Prize that evening. It was Friday.

The personal shopper was throwing Oscar-style gowns at me: a yellow satin Cavalli, a bustier McQueen printed with dragonflies. Finally, I settled for a Lanvin contrast silk. The front was black and the back was red. It cost £2,320.

"Are you sure you don't mind?" I asked Stephanie, when we were seated at HIX Restaurant Champagne & Caviar Bar on the fourth floor. I had already disposed of the receipt for the dress in the ashtray outside.

"Sure."

"I mean I'm gonna need shoes to go with it," I said, my mouth full of osetra caviar and hot buttered toast. "Can't wear these." I gestured to my old, door bitch ballet pumps.

Her phone rang. "Yes," she said. "Yes. Yes, of course she will. Protected? No problem. Thanks, Francesca."

"Who's Francesca?" I said, when she got off the phone.

"She's a researcher on *Woman's Hour*. They heard about your (un)authored blank page from the MD of Mental. They want to run an item on it." She tried to look excited. "They want you on the show!"

"Excuse me," I said, gesturing to a waiter. "Can I have . . ." I checked the menu. "The white duck egg with the osetra again. Thanks."

"This will be great for your profile," she said.

"I don't want a profile. Do you mind if I go outside for a cigarette?"

"I am trying to help you, Ann-Marie." Steph wasn't eating. "I wouldn't even be going to this phony award ceremony tonight if you didn't want to go."

"But your book might win."

"Me or that awfully boring history of Elizabethan

ceruse. Like a man could understand the historical significance of a cosmetic that causes death by lead poisoning." Steph snorted. She tugged at her straw-blonde hair. "Well, do you want to go on *Woman's Hour* or don't you?"

The duck egg arrived.

"What's my fee?" I said.

"Victims don't get a fee just for being victims. That's not how it works."

"How does it work, Stephanie?" I pulled out *Abreaction* and flipped through it. "I'm looking forward to finding out what Sisyphus did to Raegan and Marge."

She took the book out of my hands and put it on the table. "You'll need a bag too," she said. "I spotted an adorable Mulberry spongy leather medium hobo that you could use day-to-day. Not just for tonight. Not just for tonight." Her eyes returned to the Erzulie state. Then she smiled briskly and said: "I know what! We'll call on Gabriella on the way to the BBC! That'll be wonderful for you, won't it?"

Gabriella's studio was in London Fields.

Hipsters wearing white surgical masks and gowns were bent over what looked like a corpse. Its flesh-colored feet were protruding from one end of the operating table. The studio was huge and white with compartments everywhere. Images of operations were propped on shelves. One face recurred: that of a woman turned yellow by the antiseptic fluid wiped across her skin, turned yellower still by the bruises left by incisions. Here, her eye was cut open, the iris a technicolor blue.

Here, her breast was removed, leaving a textured red mess. Here, her breast had been appliquéd back on, the stitches made of hot-pink wool.

One of the masked hipsters made a big fuss of Stephanie, who strode over to the corpse and demanded: "Gabriella? Gabriella? Is she under?"

The hipster pulled the sheet away from the corpse's face to reveal a hyper-real fiberglass dummy. Its eyes were that same Technicolor blue. I tried to get a look at the gaping wound on which the hipsters were working and saw that there was yet another fiberglass dummy tucked inside the stomach. The second, smaller dummy was likewise being operated on. There was yet another dummy inside of her, inside of her. The dummies got smaller and smaller so that the last was no bigger than a finger.

"It's called *The Russian Within*," said the hipster. "It's a comment on *Anna Karenina*. And like, Russian dolls."

"Where is she?" said Stephanie.

The hipster led us through another studio where something was being blowtorched. It was obscured by a sheet.

"Gabriella was always interdisciplinary," Stephanie said.

We entered an office.

Gabriella was slouched behind a large, white desk. "Tell them I don't care about the cost," she was saying down the phone. "I want ostrich. It's the soft—yes, the soft. And the fire in the grate and the ice in the glass. I want a lot of ice in the glass and I want the glass to be very big. And I want lizards—two, maybe three, crawling up the wall. I want the walls to move. No—I don't want the walls to actually move, I want the lizards to make the walls seem like they're—yes." She had been doodling a lizard on a pad. Now she looked up. "Etienne," she said. "I have to go." She opened her arms wide to Stephanie. "*Mum*."

"I wish you wouldn't call me that," said Steph.

"You love it," said Gabriella, lighting a cigarette.

Steph lit up too.

So did I.

We all three stood in silence, smoking.

I tried not to stare at Gabriella.

She was a specter. Her skin showed no sign that anyone lived inside it. Everything on the outside had been changed. She looked like a 3-D dragon touched by the old-world glamour of Elizabeth Taylor. Her cheekbones were like rocks, her lips like wet, full slugs. She was dressed like a French provincial housewife, but her accent was English.

When we had all finished our cigarettes, Gabriella said: "And is this your new daughter?"

"She's a friend," said Steph.

"Oh, we're all friends," laughed Gabriella.

Her eyes were the same Technicolor blue as the eyes in the photos. Was she wearing contacts?

"And what are you doing here, Mummy?" Gabriella asked Steph.

"I thought you might like to tell Ann-Marie all about your beginnings!" Steph turned to me. "Gabriella has got a midcareer survey coming up at MOMA. She's doing just great."

"Yeah, I'm great," said Gabriella. "My beginnings? Wow. Okay." She hobbled over to a filing cabinet. Her legs seemed to be fitted at awkward angles to her upper body. She selected a white folder. "At first, I was looking for something," she said.

"You see?" Steph turned to me. "We're all looking for something!"

"But I was looking for something real," said Gabriella. "The Lacanian Real, more precisely—which isn't real, of course. But the Unnameable darkness. And all the more powerful for it." She sat down on the edge of the desk and winced. "Something that I could *feel*, in any case. Not some bullshit quasi-spiritual mantra in India. Like Marge Perez. Patronizing the shit out of the Indians." She opened the folder and tossed a handful of stills on the desk. "This was the *King Cake* project. My first art installation, 1993."

The image showed a much younger, plumper, and more natural Gabriella prone and naked and covered in what looked like icing.

"Explain how you did it, Gabriella," said Steph.

"Yes, *Mum*." Gabriella laughed. "The king cake is a cake that is traditionally eaten in countries all over the world, from Spain to Lebanon. They bake a little figurine of a king—more precisely, a baby Jesus—in a cake and then slice it up and eat it on the sixth of January. That happens to be my birthday. Whoever finds the figurine in their slice is lucky but also runs the risk of breaking a tooth. It's also known as the Epiphany cake, and sometimes, the thing in the cake is a bean, not a Jesus."

The second image showed a carving knife looming toward Gabriella from the left.

"Go on," said Steph.

"So I just took that idea and ran with it," said Gabriella. "*I* was the cake. There was a thing—like a little figurine, a king, a father—inside of me and I wanted to find it."

"So you . . . swallowed a figurine?" I said.

"No. The figurine was a metaphor, only. It was the Unrepresentable. Trauma. It was ephemeral, impossible to pin down. That's why I wanted to pin it down. To persecute it. I pinned myself down in the process, since it was a part of me. I didn't know where it was inside of me exactly, but I wanted to cut it out. I was prepared to cut my whole self to pieces trying to get it out."

"That's abreaction," said Steph.

"Possibly," said Gabriella.

She showed me a third image: her, bleeding, in a bathtub. There was a gaping wound in her stomach. Her face was mournful.

"That's not fake," said Steph.

"The thing inside of me, I would later learn, was the Thing called It that Žižek refers to. *Das Ding* in German. Slavoj has become a personal friend of mine." Gabriella smiled. "We met when I was invited to give a lecture on the *King Cake* project at the European Graduate School."

"Slavoj is a charlatan," said Steph.

"He knows what I'm talking about," said Gabriella.

The fourth image showed Gabriella in a hospital bed. "I did some serious internal damage in the course of the project," she said. "I accidentally gave myself a hysterectomy. I couldn't have children after that. I was only twenty-three at the time."

Steph looked at me. "Your age," she said.

"I had killed all my future fetuses for the sake of my art," said Gabriella. "Which seemed appropriate. Art is like giving birth, again and again. And putting your baby in an art gallery. Or a biennale." She held up the last image, which showed her looking pale and wan and much thinner in a wheelchair. "I never did find the Thing I was looking for," she said. "I'm still looking."

"Gabriella's interest in surgery became multifarious from then on," said Steph.

"The point is." Gabriella looked at me. "I don't *want* to find It. If I found It, I would have no reason to make art anymore." She got up and gripped her lower back. She produced another folder from the cabinet. "More recently, this is for the Venice show. It's called *Clamshell* something. It's going to have *clamshell* in the title."

These images showed the various stages of a labiaplasty. First the distended asymmetrical labia minora were marked in purple ink. Then they were injected. Then they were cut off.

"That's when the cauterizing kicks in," said Gabriella. She lit another cigarette. "Well, it's very nice to meet you, Annie-Marie."

I didn't bother to correct her.

"Those labias are just the crash-test dummy if you

will," Gabriella went on. "One of my interns, very eager."

"You know it's remarkable," said Steph. "Gabriella, you don't need me to tell you that Orlan did this in the 70s. She was cutting herself open way before plastic surgery became de rigueur. She was like a tribal woman, creating her own body. Still is, I should say. It was a beautiful moment when Orlan's interventions chimed like music with Haraway's "A Cyborg Manifesto." But you—"

"Are you trying to tell me I'm derivative, Mum?" Gabriella laughed.

There was silence.

Finally Steph said: "I just think you could cite her."

"Was Orlan looking for *Das Ding* though?" said Gabriella. "Did Orlan write as *well*? Was she a *writer*? Was Orlan looking for the Real, the bad part that must be exorcized from the living body in order for that body to go on living *at all*? Did Orlan know that unsaid words contaminate you from the inside *out*?"

"No," said Steph. "All of that you learned from me."

"Maybe I learned it from you." Gabriella stood up. "But you only theorized that shit, Mum. You are a theorist. I *did* that shit. I did it to *myself*. The gravest acts of violence. The most pure—stitching my cunt up to make it look like a Barbie. That's what I'm doing in the spring."

"Do you have to be so childishly provocative?" said Steph.

"You see." Gabriella looked me. "I'm just gonna sew that shit up to make absolutely certain that nothing else can come out or get back in."

"Gabriella is from Brixton," said Steph, as though that explained everything.

An hour later, we were sitting in a hallway at the BBC, drinking coffee.

Francesca the researcher said that, due to the presence of a webcam in the studio, would I mind wearing a black bag over my head to protect my anonymity? No, scratch that. Would I mind wearing a white bag over my head to color coordinate with the blank page that had appeared so strikingly pure on the blog post?

"That's fine," Stephanie answered for me.

When Francesca had gone, Steph said: "You want to be famous, don't you? Don't all you little girls these days want to be famous?"

"But how can I be famous if I've got a bag over my head?"

Stephanie stared at the framed portrait of Bruce Forsyth hanging on the wall. "God, Gabriella can be so recalcitrant," she said. "She might not even come to my ceremony. You know when I met her, she was just a little nude model—"

"I heard you. At William's."

"She was nothing but an ingénue—at Chelsea."

"I thought you said you discovered her at the Slade?"

"It was I who urged her to pursue installation," said Stephanie. "It was I who urged her to go to Goldsmiths, right at the time when Michael Craig-Martin was tearing down every disciplinary membrane known to man—or woman. Gabriella had the drive because she was crazy.

Her father raped her when she was a child, did you know that?"

I shook my head.

"So you didn't read her cuttings?"

"No."

"Have you read my cuttings?"

"What do you mean—cuttings?"

"Have you googled me?"

"No. I'm very busy, Stephanie." I paused. "Why does Gabriella want to stitch up her cunt so that nothing else comes out if she's already had a hysterectomy?"

Stephanie was silent.

Finally she said: "She's paranoid." She turned to me. "You're going to have to think of something good. Something real good. Because 'I was just tired out from singing so I couldn't think of anything' isn't gonna cut it. That's not what's gonna get the hits. And don't tell them about the singing part." She had lipstick on her teeth. "If I were you, I'd dig deep."

Francesca led us into a studio. Once again, I was shut inside a glass box. This one was more spacious. A white felt bag was handed to me; it smelled of shoes. L. K. Bennett was printed on the side. I put the bag over my head.

"We're gonna use your real voice, okay?" said Francesca.

"Okay," came my muffled voice.

I saw a black object come closer; it was the microphone. Soon a woman with mellow tones was telling her listeners to contact their local leisure centers for more information on Zumba classes. Then Stephanie was introduced. She must have been sitting in another box because I couldn't smell Florida Water. She was explaining that while the hypersexualization of society had been commented on at length in the media—

"What do you mean?" said the mellow presenter.

"I mean porn," said Steph. "It's everywhere. What I'm talking about are the parallels between the mass-produced *product* called love and sadomasochistic pornography. Because all mainstream porn is sadomasochistic to a greater or lesser extent. Right."

"Can you give us an example?"

"Like the erotic classic, *Story of O*," said Steph. "The main girl, O, is a successful fashion photographer. She's got her own gig. But she's in love with this guy, René. So René invites her to come to a secluded château at Roissy."

"We're going off topic!" said the presenter.

The lights of the studio burned through the bag.

"If you'll just wait." Stephanie was irritated. "So O goes to the château but it's not like a romantic weekend away. Oh no. It's a sexual slavery camp, Sadeian style."

"Sadeian?"

"The Marquis de Sade. The eclipse of religion by science at the end of the eighteenth century threw the whole world, or at least the whole of Europe into doubt . . . basically. Look, Sade figured that any and all pleasure was up for grabs—bestiality, torture, you name it. It was pleasure without conscience. Unbridled jouissance."

"Yeah, I know about jouissance," I said. But my voice wasn't amplified.

There was silence; maybe Steph and the presenter were looking at me.

"Sade's encyclopedia of perversions is mechanical," said Steph. "Dry as a bone. It is love as hate. Sex without respect for the other."

"I'm sorry, Stephanie." The presenter chortled. "I thought we were talking about *Story of O*. Wasn't that written in the 30s?"

"Nineteen fifty-four," said Steph. "By a woman. No one knew her identity until the 90s. But the point is that René puts O in this hellish situation. There are strict rules governing her every move. She must be 100 percent available to her so-called masters every minute of the day and night, she must open every orifice to them, she must never look them in the eye, she must never speak unless spoken to."

"That's shocking," said the presenter. "I'm sure that still goes on in some parts of the developing world. Maybe even the developed world. It's terrible when women are taken against their will—"

"But that's the point." I heard a thud; Steph must have banged her fist on the table. "O isn't taken against her will. O consents. She consents because she loves René. She is a slave to love."

"She must have self-esteem issues," said the presenter.

"No," said Steph. "My argument in *Falling Out of Fate* by Stephanie Haight, published by Penguin, £18.99 hardback available in all good bookstores and on Amazon and in a Kindle edition, is that O is an archetype. She is an archetype of normal femininity."

"Excuse me," said the presenter. "At no point have I consented to sexual slavery in the name of love."

"What about mental slavery?" said Steph. "Why do you think *Fifty Shades* did so goddamn well? Because women found a mirror."

"That book is pure fantasy. It's wish fulfillment."

"Exactly." I heard Steph sit back, satisfied.

"I want to hear what some of our listeners who've been calling in think about your argument. Here's Jean from Vauxhall."

"Hi Jean," said Steph. "Wait—isn't this show prerecorded?"

"Jean's been waiting on the line," said the presenter.

"Hi," said Jean. "I don't understand what you're talking about. You're talking about things that only make sense to a tiny percent of the population."

"You tell me, Jean," said Steph. "Haven't you ever waited for a man? Haven't you ever paced the room, wondering what he's thinking, what he's doing, where he is, who he's with, whether he loves you enough or at all?"

"Men wait too," said Jean. "When Chris and I started seeing each other—"

"Not in the same way," said Steph.

"I don't want to buy your book," said Jean.

"Thanks so much, Jean," said the presenter, warmly. "We value your input. Now." Paper was moved. "Vanessa is a young woman who has found recent fame thanks to a bad case of writer's block. Am I right, Vanessa?"

The lights got brighter. Someone tapped me on the shoulder.

"Yes," I said.

"But your writer's block is more than a block, isn't it?"

"I don't know," I said. "I'm not a writer."

"Take your time."

Time passed.

"Can you tell us what happened to make you get so pent up inside?" said the presenter.

"Yes," I said. "I can. I was a sexual slave."

The presenter inhaled and then exhaled, slowly.

"Not to a man, but a woman," I said. "Not to my lover, but—"

"Vanessa means slave in the metaphorical sense of the word," said Stephanie.

"I was a slave in the literal sense," I said. "But that wasn't what made me not be able to write. I couldn't write because of guilt."

"The guilt of being a successful woman," said Steph.

"No," I said. "The guilt of what I did."

"What did you do?" breathed the presenter.

"It was my mother," I said. "She started it off. She met the man only casually, in a pub. It was karaoke night. They did a duet together. I think it was Johnny Cash, 'Ring of Fire.' And then before you know it—bang. She's pregnant at the age of fifty."

They waited.

"Well, I wasn't too happy about the whole thing. I was seven at the time. I thought my mother had been highly irresponsible. I didn't like my territory being encroached on."

"Sibling rivalry is a very visceral emotion," said the presenter.

"Yes, it is," I said. "So one day I was sitting at the kitchen table with my little brother on my knee. He was about nine months old. He had a little pink face. He was a very happy baby, always smiling."

"Hm," said the presenter.

"I was jiggling him up and down and he was laughing. In that moment I felt the power in my hands. You know like at school when you study biology and you find out about the different types of energy? I remember this diagram we had to draw of kinetic energy. It was a ball on the edge of a cliff. The ball wasn't moving, but the point was that it *could* move. It had the *potential* to move."

"Yes."

"Or be moved."

More silence.

"So I dropped him," I said. "On his head."

"What happened?" breathed the presenter.

"He got brain damage."

"*Good lord.*"

"And then he died." I paused. "They couldn't press charges because I was a minor."

"And that's why you couldn't write?"

I hesitated. "When I was staring at that blank page, I was thinking: Why should I be able to express myself when he will never be able to express himself? He never even learned to talk."

I was waiting at a table in the BBC cafeteria while Steph bought me a chocolate éclair as a special treat for doing so well on the program.

There was an exceptionally good-looking man at the next table. He looked almost exactly like Sebastian, except that Sebastian didn't have gappy teeth. This man was blond and bestial like Sebastian. He was fondling a large, rectangular box that seemed to contain a flat-screen TV.

"Excuse me," I said. "What is that?"

"It's a SAD lamp," he said. "For people who suffer from seasonal affective disorder. It simulates sunlight."

"Wow," I said.

There was a silence.

"Are you with Mental too?" I said.

"No. What's that?"

"It's this organization for insane people. I'm their representative."

He laughed.

"Do you suffer from SAD?" I asked him.

He laughed again. "No! I sell them. Well—I manage the account. We're pitching the product to *Science and Tech*."

Steph was returning with the éclair so I got the man to write down my number as quickly as possible. His name was Dave.

SIXTEEN

Hi Ann-Marie. How about dinner tonight? Dave X

I persuaded Stephanie to let me wander around Hampstead Heath for a few hours by myself in order to contemplate everything that I had learned from her so far. I told her that I'd return to Camden in time to get ready for the ceremony.

But I went down to Clapham instead. The dress that I wanted to wear for my date with Dave was stowed somewhere at the back of my wardrobe in the apartment.

Blue tarpaulin had replaced the curtains in the front windows.

Jasper was eating a salami sandwich in the kitchen, his feet on the table. The homeless woman had cleaned the place up nicely, but he was dropping his mayonnaise all over the floor. I smacked his legs down. Invitations to *Making A Racket* were stacked up. They were printed with an image of a tennis racket emitting musical notes with bee faces.

"What's that buzzing?" I said.

I went into the living room.

A man wearing a beekeeper's outfit was watching a black-and-white film about bees. Real bees were swarming around a hive that hung from our art nouveau light. The bee man was also eating a salami sandwich, but he had to struggle to get it up and under his white protective helmet.

"Out," he said. He was Scottish. "It's not safe."

Wooden 70s-style tennis rackets were propped against the wall.

I returned to the kitchen.

"Where's Freddie?" I asked Jasper.

"Fred's left me in the shit with the show," he said. "I'm hoping it's not going to be a shit show. He's left me to do everything because he's got something wrong with him so I need to send the press releases out and put all the fucking art in there and, like, move shit around and call people up and turn the fucking lights on. Opening's tomorrow."

Upstairs, my wallpaper had been hosed down. The eggs had been swept away. It was pristine. Stacks of wood and bits of metal grate had been arranged on the landing. There was a wicker chair with the seat missing in the corner. The drapes of Freddie's four-poster had been replaced with tarpaulin. It was a blue cave.

"Come back," he croaked from inside.

"I am back," I said. "I'm here."

"Not you."

I stuck my head in. He pointed a trembling finger up.

A picture of a gaunt, geometric ginger model, torn from a magazine, had been pinned to the ceiling of the bed.

"Who's that?" I said.

"Samuel." He turned away.

"Freddie, that's not Samuel. That's just some random guy."

"I don't feel well. I feel unwell."

He didn't have a fever.

"I've become what I hate," he said. "Get the camera."

I found the Bolex on his dresser and began to film.

"I am but a broken dandy," he said.

"Where's my friend who I said could stay here?"

Freddie sat up and lit a cigarette. "If you're talking about that homeless wench, then I threw her out. I mashed her up. I fucked up her face."

The dress that I was looking for was wrapped around a stack of unopened letters from the Student Loans Company. I unfurled its white taffeta. The shoulders ballooned, the skirt ballooned, the bodice was restrictive, fitted with a real whalebone corset. It was the dress that my mother had worn to marry my father.

I put it on.

In the mirror, I looked like Princess Diana on her wedding day.

"You look like the bride of Frankenstein," said Freddie, in the doorway.

"I hope Dave's not a commitment phobe," I said, twirling in the mirror. "This old guy James wants me to wear it for him but Dave is one of the best-looking people that I've ever met in my life."

Dave was waiting by the clock tower at Clapham Common station. I stood across the road outside O'Neill's Irish-themed pub for about fifteen minutes, watching him. The dress was hidden under Freddie's trench coat. Dave seemed to be pretending that he couldn't see me. He turned away. I turned away too, and stared at the Londis on the corner. When I turned back, he was staring at me, but then he turned away again. He hid behind the station. Then he crossed the road in the opposite direction.

I watched him go.

He stopped outside a bar called Be At One. Rugby players were drinking pints. He continued to watch me. I watched him. We stood like that, watching each other, while cars drove between us, for five, then ten minutes. Finally, I crossed the road toward him. He retreated. Now he was outside the Indian takeout place. He ran across the road that I had just crossed, dodging cars, and disappeared into the station.

"Fuck you," I told a rugby man.

I went into Be At One and sat at the bar; it was awful. Painful pinks and disco purples had been carefully selected. A group of women were talking about someone who had slept with someone else who really shouldn't have slept with that person because she knows Lily likes him and besides he's practically married to Fiona. I ordered a sex on the beach and waited while the bartender carved out a pineapple accoutrement.

I saw Dave walk past, outside. He seemed agitated. Then he walked past in the other direction.

The bartender slid my drink toward me. It was exploding with sparklers. "That'll be £10.99, please," he said.

"I thought you said it was on the house," I said.

"When did I say that?"

Dave walked into the bar. He stood next to me, flustered.

My heart started racing.

He paid for the drink and ordered one for himself. "Why did you do that?" he said.

"Do what?" I sipped the drink and winced; it was vile.

The bartender looked crushed.

"Just standing there," said Dave. "Staring at me across the road when you knew I was waiting for you. We said meet by the station."

"I don't know." My hands were shaking. "I wanted to make you wait."

"Why?"

"To reverse the terms of gendered history."

His hands were shaking too.

"Why did you run off?" I said.

"Because. I didn't know. What you were doing. I thought you would follow me."

"I thought maybe you'd felt my evil aura pulsing all the way across the road and changed your mind," I said. "I'm just warning you now that I'm very difficult to go out with. I'm almost impossible to go out with."

Dave's drink arrived.

A girl with straightened hair came over and slung an arm around each of us. She was drunk. "God, you've really hit the jackpot," she told me. "I would." She pumped her pelvis against Dave's barstool.

He blushed.

She staggered off.

"Dave," I said. "If that is your real name."

"Why wouldn't it be?"

"What brings you here?"

"To go on a date with you."

"With me?" I looked down at my drink.

"Yeah."

There was a long silence.

"I like girls who are mad," he said. "I like difficult women."

"Are you a masochist?"

He laughed. "No—what's that? Someone who likes being tied up?"

"No. Someone who likes pain, more broadly speaking. Like if I go like this." I picked up a fork that had been left along with the remains of a Scotch egg bar snack and stabbed Dave's hand.

He screamed.

The fork didn't go all the way in.

He gripped his hand, sweating.

"You see," I said. "You're not a masochist." I sipped my drink. "It's a shame. I think I only like masochistic men. I mean, someone's got to get fucked. And I'm pretty sick to death of it being me."

He asked the bartender for a glass of water.

"So exactly what is it that you do for a living?" I said.

"Advertising," he gasped. "Brand development."

"So you manipulate the masses into thinking they're depressed when they're not, so they'll buy a SAD lamp."

"Kind of." Dave's face was returning to its usual color. "But I'm an artist, really. Yeah, that's what I do. I'm a light artist. I switched to light as a medium after I got the SAD account. It kind of gave me ideas—about how light is, like, awesome."

I looked at him with disdain.

"It's sculptural, you know?" he said.

"I can't deal with another artist. I can't deal with another artist with a messianic complex."

Dave laughed. "Yeah, I've struggled with that myself." He opened his arms wide as though nailed to a cross and lolled his head forward.

An hour later, we were sitting on a steel island in a pop-up sushi bar called Moat. The island was surrounded by a grimy ditch, filled with fish trying to survive. The odds were against them—diners were dangling their rods into the ditch from their positions at steel tables, laughing as their bait squirmed and the fishes' open mouths sucked at what would inevitably kill them.

"Maybe you're a sadist?" I said.

"No." Dave laughed. "I'm not that either. Do you like it here? Peckham's getting more and more wicked."

"You've got to be one or the other. Either/or."

"Why?"

"Because that's how human nature works," I said. "I had to learn it by heart for my social and political science exams. At Cambridge."

He didn't look too impressed.

"Cambridge," I repeated. "Not the ex-polytechnic, the actual Cambridge."

He laughed again.

I blushed. "Yeah, well anyway we had to do all this Hobbes stuff—life is a war of all against all. We need a benign totalitarian dictator to restrain us from hurting each other. Because otherwise we would hurt each other. Life is nasty, brutish, and short."

"I don't believe that," said Dave. "I'm having a very pleasant evening."

"But it will be short." I took off my coat and revealed the wedding dress. The whalebone was cutting into my ribs.

Now he did look impressed. "Are we going to Vegas?"

"No." I closed the coat. "I'm a commitment-phobe. Like a man. I just fuck and go, that's my thing. No hard feelings." I took a swig of beer.

Dave's line had trailed out of the water. It was lying on the steel decking.

"I'd marry you," he said.

I frowned.

"I felt it as soon as I saw you," he went on. "You're psycho. You're just like me."

"You don't seem that psycho."

"What I mean is," he said. "I'm not psycho myself, but I like to look after psycho girls."

"Oh god. The last thing I need right now is a codependent relationship. I've got enough of those already."

My rod started to tug. I was dragged toward the ditch. The fish had the tenacity of a shark.

Dave was killing himself laughing.

"Help!" I shouted at the waiters, who weren't Japanese at all.

The waiters attempted to wrench the rod from my hands, but then I experienced a surge of Übermensch power. I wheeled the thing frantically until the fish rose out of the water, its iridescent body already entering the death throes. I got it on the deck. It continued to writhe. I grabbed Dave's bottle of beer, still half full, and smashed it over the fish's head.

Blood shot out.

I was pleased.

The restaurant flashed red. There was a blast of giggly Japanese electro-pop. The waiters shook my hands high in the air, a prize fighter.

The hipsters cheered.

The waiter removed Dave's rod from his hands. "She got the fish first," he explained. "So that should be enough for both of you."

"Yeah, so after we broke up, I just had to reconnect with myself again," Dave was saying. "Find the part that I had lost by being with someone—the same person—for so long. Do you know what I mean?" He was shoveling bits of my catch into his mouth with chopsticks.

They had skinned, boned, and decapitated the fish at our table. I could tell that the weak English waiter wanted to be sick at the sight of the heart still pounding, the gills still desperate for life.

"I don't really know what you mean, no," I said. "I've never really been in a long-term relationship due to my commitment-phobia. For me, being in a relationship is like being buried alive in quicksand."

"Do you have to be buried in quicksand though?" said Dave. "Don't you just fall in, and that's that."

"Yeah. Like falling in love. You put one toe in and then bang, before you know it, you're fully submerged and you can't breathe. It's terrifying."

Dave laughed.

"You laugh a lot," I said. "You're always laughing."

He stopped laughing.

"No," I said. "I like it." I must have been getting drunk on the sake.

"So anyway I just always had this mad passion for Japan," he said. "Like the goddamn horn for the place."

"Oh dear."

"What?"

"It's just that expression—it's quite distasteful. Some of the things you come up with are a bit not up my alley."

"What is up your alley then?"

"No," I said. "Go on."

"So I went traveling there—Japan—for like six months."

"Did you discover your Zen?"

"Yeah." He put down his chopsticks. "Yeah. Totally. There was this one festival in a place called Kumamoto.

They get all the horses really drunk on sake and blindfold them and parade them through the streets like totally drunk out of their minds. It's worse than a fucking Saturday night in Leicester Square."

"I was in Leicester Square on Saturday night," I said. "Were you following me?"

"No!"

"Because I've got a stalker called Vic. He's properly psycho."

"Anyway, the horses are like totally humiliated. They've lost control—against their will."

The waiter appeared with the pièce de résistance—a cauldron of fish-head soup, boiling over a gas ring. "The eyes are a delicacy," said the waiter. He looked like he would throw up. "If lovers eat an eye each, they stay conjoined forever. So the ancient Japanese saying goes." He placed the eyes on a little dish.

"In that case," I said. "I'm not eating it." I shook my eye into the ditch; the fish devoured it.

Dave ate his eye with relish.

"You're going to stay conjoined forever with one of those fish then," I said.

"I don't care," he said. "The fish will remind me of you."

"Thanks. Do I look like a fish?"

"No, you look like a gazelle."

"What's that again?"

"Something graceful."

I stared into my bowl.

Soon another lucky diner caught a fish and the electro-pop started again.

"Tell me about your art," I said.

"It's like . . . based on the phenomenological turn? Like Merleau-Ponty's concept of being embodied in the world?"

"Yeah, he got that from Heidegger. I've been reading all about Heidegger. How we're just thrust into the world and it's not our choice so we've got to make the best of it."

"That sounds like self-help. And he didn't get it from Heidegger. He got it from Husserl."

"Whatever."

Our plates were cleared away.

"This date is so cringeworthy," I said. "I hate myself, I hate Heidegger, whatever. I hate fish. I don't like England. I don't like you. Or your teeth."

He covered his mouth. "Hey. I'm really self-conscious about my teeth."

"No." The room was starting to spin. "I do like your teeth. I love them. And I love you. There, I said it. I've fallen madly in love with you so now you can just fuck me up so just get it over and done with, would you?"

Dave pushed me against the betting shop next to the restaurant.

We were kissing, he was stroking my hair, he was telling me that I was beautiful. I didn't kick him in the nuts or even bite very hard.

"One day I'll take you home with me," he was saying. "I'll take you back to Devon with me. You'd love it there. I'll introduce you to my mum and dad. There's just miles and miles of fields and the sky is endless. You'll feel free."

"I don't want to feel free," I said. "I want to feel constrained by something that's not evil, something that I can trust. Dave, how old are you?"

"Twenty-seven." He took my hand and we walked to the bus stop.

"I suffer from anxiety," I told him, as we sat down on the top deck.

"That's okay. I've got loads of downers."

I rested my head on his shoulder.

In front, there was another couple, and a man sitting alone, wearing a red, woolly hat.

"Can I tell you a story?" said Dave.

I kissed him again. "I like kissing you," I said.

The man in the red hat jerked.

"Go on," I said.

"There was this one time that me and my friends went down to this little cove, called Mill Cove, near where I live. We stayed up all night doing shrooms."

I was watching the red hat.

"It was way intense. The world looked so beautiful, I almost couldn't bear it. That's when I decided to be an artist."

"That's a nice story," I said.

"No. That's not it. I started getting all these stones and stuff that were lying around on the beach and organizing them in these circles. They were totally random, but kind of complete in themselves. You know what I mean?"

The man in the hat stood up; he sat down again.

"I felt like I was creating order for the first time in my life," Dave went on. "Not artificial, hostile order, but true, pure, natural order. And I looked at my friends and they were just as they were—complete."

"Yeah, it's like that when you're high."

"No." He pulled his hand away.

I took it back. "Sorry," I said. "Go on."

"We were all sitting around this fire and the night sky looked so beautiful, and then, as dawn was coming, we saw this ship on the horizon. At least, we thought it was a ship." He paused. "The ship's lights seemed to be blinking on and off but it wasn't coming any closer. The sky was insane—just amazing, open, falling color. Then the girls started to cry. They said the light was blinking because the ship was in trouble and it wanted us to help. They said the ship was sinking, but it was too far away and we couldn't swim that far out to help so we better run to the village but the village was too far away so . . ."

"What happened?"

"The sun came up. They said the ship wanted to be seen for just an instant before it disappeared entirely—"

The man in the red hat twisted his head round.

It was Vic.

He seemed to be flinching from an imaginary threat. His lips were horribly elongated.

"Don't listen to a word that comes out of her mouth," Vic told Dave. "She'll tell you she's not an actress, but she is. She'll tell you she's not acting, but she is." He stood up. The parka that I had lent him flopped open to reveal his gnarled nakedness. His penis began to stand up. His nipples looked like blind eyes. Hair crawled over his shoulders from his back like a monster trying to throttle him to death.

"Do you know this man?" said Dave.

The couple had stood up too. They were backed against the front window.

"'A' is for 'all's well that ends well,'" said Vic. "'M' is for 'murder on the bus.' 'Murder on the Dancefloor.'" He laughed. His tongue was scabrous. "I see you in all the scenes of all the films that you said I should never watch. With that woman. That Hispanic woman, eating her out, licking her out."

"Vic," I said. "Porn's not real." I turned to Dave. "I swear I've never been in a porno."

An empty bottle of Lucozade rolled across the floor, knocking into the metal legs of chairs.

"I saw you with your schoolgirl uniform and then you were in the woods with Jeremy and Jeremy told you that you'd been a very bad girl."

The bus had stopped.

The driver was coming up the stairs.

Vic picked up the Lucozade bottle and smashed it over the railing that ran along the backs of the seats. Orange-tinted glass flew everywhere. The driver moved to restrain Vic, but he brandished a shard of glass and started laughing again.

"Do you know that Ann-Marie is a Dutch name?" said Vic. "I looked it up on the Internet. Are you Dutch?"

I said nothing.

"Are you fucking Dutch?"

"No!" I said. "No. Vic, I'm not Dutch."

"Ann-Marie means 'bitter grace' in Dutch," he mumbled. Then he used the sharpest end of the shard to engrave into the skin of his stomach: A.M.

My initials were a pink line then a running red gash.

SEVENTEEN

AS SOON AS the driver opened the doors of the bus, I began to run, hysterically.

Hallelujah! Hallelujah!

God is love, God is light. Light is Dave, the light maker!

Where is he?

I looked back. I had left him attending to Vic, who had collapsed on the floor of the top deck. I had expected Dave to run after me; he hadn't.

I ran into Tesco on Clapham High Street.

I grabbed a basket and skipped down the fluorescent meat aisle. I swung the basket as though it were a holy thurible able to bless the packets and packets of gleaming red-ruby meat, rippled with a fat so white it hurt. There was purity in the world. There was passion in the world. I was alive. Hallelujah!

I stopped, entranced, at the offal section. The hearts, ripe and obscene, seemed to morph into Dave's pendulous testicles—I was sure they would be pendulous—blood bursting and full of the promise of future generations. We would mate! We would mate!

I clawed at the hearts with love streaming through my veins. There would be twenty, thirty children! There would be eternal children! Dave and I would move in with his parents in Devon and I would waddle about the rose-covered cottage, as happy as a fat, pregnant duck. His kindly mother with twinkling eyes and flour on her hands from making so much bread would pat my stomach and possibly perform an age-old family ritual of swinging a locket around my stretch-marked belly in order to tell whether I would be gushing forth a little Dave or a little Ann-Marie. If I had a boy, I would call it Sebastian.

I put the packet in my mouth and tore at it with my teeth. The watery blood that swirled around the edges of the meat ran straight into my throat. I bit down on the heart with urgency. It crunched like a hard peach. Dense, slaughter-heavy scents overwhelmed me. I had an urgent need to masturbate. I put the brown and messy meat between my legs, crouching awkwardly on the floor. The fluorescent lights became gamma ray bursts.

"Ann-Marie!" Dave was running down the aisle toward me. He stopped, sweating. "What are you doing?"

I threw the packet back on the shelf. "It should be perfectly obvious what I'm doing, Dave." I stood up. "You've ruined it now."

"Ruined what?"

"I was having a wonderful time—remembering you."

"Well, here I am!"

"No, Dave. You don't understand. It's better if we skip

this part. If we fast-forward to the beginning and the middle and the end and let the tragic chorus begin and let me feel sad and maybe I'll even write a poem about it. Maybe I was close to writing then—with the meat." I gestured to the hearts, which looked as though they had been mauled by a pack of wolves.

A Tesco worker came striding down the aisle with a mop. She was irate. "Didn't you hear the announcement?" she was saying.

I ran out of the supermarket, grabbing a copy of *Grazia* on the way. I didn't stop until I reached the train. I hid behind the public toilets. There were no police cars. Then I saw Dave, panting. He was looking for me. I watched his discomfort for a while, then, when his back was turned, I ran and jumped him from behind, just as I had jumped Vic on our first date. Dave didn't fall though; he was stronger. He held onto the park railings, saying nothing, until I began to feel foolish. I got down.

"You're playing games," he said. "You're always playing games. What about that poor guy, Vic? You didn't even wait for the ambulance. He was on a stretcher—"

"Was he strapped down?"

"They said he'd lost a lot of blood, that he had hypothermia as well. They said he was homeless."

"He's not homeless. He lives with a whole load of operators—as long as he's not dead, that's the main thing."

Dave stared at me.

"I hope they put Vic in a secure enough straitjacket,"

I said. "Because I can't imagine the lengths he will go to if he's allowed to roam the streets as a free man."

I explained to Dave on the train that I had run to the meat aisle for protection because Vic was terrified of meat. Dave said he wished he'd bought me a packet of pork chops as protection, like garlic is protection against vampires. I was thrilled that he was entering into the spirit of things. People were staring at us in the carriage; probably because we looked like a couple from a romantic comedy, totally made for each other, both appearance-wise and personality-wise.

I got out *Heidegger: An Intro* and said: "I won't be needing this anymore." I offered it to the man sitting opposite; he had a bushy beard and looked vaguely like a philosopher himself.

"Who needs knowledge and even education at all when you have love?" I said. "I was only getting an education anyway because that's what you're supposed to do. And I never really understood any of it. All I ever really wanted was someone to love, who loves me. The rest of—all of it—just seems like a waste of time."

"Really?" said the man opposite. He was holding the book as though it were a bomb.

"Yeah," I said. "See." I snatched it back and flipped to a random page. "Concept of authentic life: my existence is owned by me." I gave it back to the man. "I mean, who needs authenticity when you've got romance?"

Dave laughed uncertainly.

We were nearly two hours late for the Samuel Johnson Prize, but the winner hadn't yet been announced.

Steph went completely apeshit when she saw Dave and told me that under no circumstances was he coming into the ceremony. I told her that under no circumstances was I coming in without him and so she better make sure an extra place was set at our table. She had brought the Lanvin contrast dress in a zip-up sack, carried by Marge, who was wearing a steel-gray fishtail dress. Raegan was wearing an early 90s grunge ensemble of floral dress, DMs, and plastic jewelry bearing the letter R. Steph was stunning in a man's brown suit and fedora.

I changed in the toilet. Raegan did my hair and told me that I was pretty and that she'd fallen in love with my new boyfriend Dave because he was totally hot. She told me all about a documentary that she'd watched on YouTube about Drew Barrymore becoming a coke addict at the age of nine and how she couldn't believe it because *E.T.* was one of her favorite films and if Gertie could be a coke addict then why couldn't she?

I told her I didn't think that was a very good attitude because Drew Barrymore was already an extremely high-grossing star by the age of nine so she could no doubt afford to spend millions of dollars on rehab.

Raegan pulled out a sachet of white powder and a twenty pound note and told me that she'd bought it off Steph's cleaner Ilka, who'd been rehired. She racked up a few, very fat lines on the toilet seat and I told her that I didn't think she should be doing that seeing as she was only twelve but she said it was a rite of passage for all preteens with broken homes.

"I come from a broken home too," I told her. "My father left when I was born. I never knew him. I only ever knew my mother."

"Cool," she said.

She did a line with deftness, pinched the bridge of her delicate, American nose, and threw her head back. She offered the note to me.

"You look at least sixteen in that outfit," I told her. "Maybe you are sixteen. Maybe you're eighteen."

"No," she said. "I'm twelve."

She blocked the cubicle door so that I had no choice but to do a line too.

Nothing happened.

"I think Ilka was getting her revenge on Steph for sacking her," I said. "This is like acetaminophen or something."

But Raegan's pupils had dilated; she was gurning. She kept tucking her hair behind her ears.

"Okay!" I said.

Dave was waiting in the hallway. "You look beautiful," he told me.

"Do I look beautiful?" stuttered Raegan. "You look like Justin Bieber. Or Justin Timberlake. Or a blond Justin Bieber. I mean Justin Bieber after he dyed his hair blond."

Our table was laden with flowers and stacked with copies of *Falling Out of Fate*. Steph and Marge were already seated. Dave was not dressed for the occasion at all; he was wearing a pair of red jeans and high-tops.

"Didn't you get my texts?" Steph hissed at me.

I checked my phone:

> Why have you run away again after everything I've done for you? Steph

> Come back, darling, I'm sorry. Steph

> If you come back, I'll tell you the story, the whole story, whether I like it or not. Steph

> I guess this is karma. Erzulie must be punishing me. Steph

> When will the badness flourish to its fullness and die? Steph

"Steph," I whispered. "I told you I was going for a walk on the Heath. I was gone for like two hours."

"You were gone for five hours." She looked at Dave. "Who is he?"

"I met him on the Heath," I said.

"But wasn't he in the BBC cafeteria this afternoon—" She shook her head. "You missed the dinner." She looked distraught. "There was a dinner before."

Dave leaned across me and told Steph: "My ex-girlfriend was a big fan of your work. She did an MA in gender studies. Never stopped talking about your rereading of Deleuzean destratification. She said it was important as a woman to retain a small amount of the strata, to not let go of the strata entirely."

"Yes," nodded Steph. "Don't burn all your bridges, not all at once." She looked at me.

"Victoria said that was why she was going out with me," said Dave. "I was the strata."

Steph smiled at Dave warmly.

The waiters were pouring champagne.

Raegan reached for a flute.

Marge slapped her arm. "What's wrong with you, honey?" she was saying. "I know it's exciting but it's not that exciting."

Raegan gripped the edge of the white-clothed table. "It's exciting," she was saying, over and over, her eyes whorls of black. She leaped up. "I've got a trick." She attempted to pull the tablecloth out from under the miscellaneous flutes and ice buckets.

"No," said Marge. "No. We'll have to talk to Dr. Garrison when we get home about increasing your Ritalin prescription."

"See?" I said to Dave. "Americans are *obsessed* with prescription drugs."

The chatter of liberals at leisure was silenced by the appearance on the stage of a round woman who looked like an opera singer. She was wearing a blue velvet tent. The blue seemed outrageously vivid to me.

Dave put his hand on mine. He asked if he could have some of whatever I had had; I said there was none left.

"Where's Vic?" I was saying. "I'm so scared that Vic will come, please don't let him come."

"Don't worry," said Dave. "I'll protect you."

"You see?" I said. "I don't need knowledge if I've got

love." I turned to Steph. "There's nothing else you can do to me. More than what you've done. The future is uncertain."

"The future is always uncertain," said Raegan.

The opera singer went on and on about the state of nonfiction and the state of publishing and the threat of the Internet and the exciting possibilities of ebooks and the danger that ebooks were deregulating the world. "In the words of David Lynch," she quipped, "we take our screens to bed."

Everyone laughed.

Raegan bashed her fork too hard against her empty flute; it cracked. Marge tried to escort her outside for a telling off. Raegan held onto the edge of the table again, but Marge pried her fingers away. They disappeared.

A tall man in a bow tie appeared on the podium and read out the nominees. He described *Falling Out of Fate* as the culmination of a life spent in women's letters.

Steph snorted. "Or just *letters*."

Along with the cultural history of ceruse, the other nominated books included a history of the London sewer system in the Victorian times, a biography of the butler of Lord Douglas-Home, an account of the demise of ash trees, and a recently discovered account of the Boer War from the perspective of a man who had been shot for desertion.

"Then how the hell did he give an account?" I said.

"He wrote it *before*," said Steph.

"And finally, a heart-wrenching memoir of one man's struggle to be reunited with his daughter after his wife discovered that he was having an affair with one of her best friends," said the host.

A picture of a Hispanic-looking man with red-framed glasses appeared on the screen. His name was Greg Perez. It was Raegan's father, Marge's ex-husband. Raegan had shown me a photo of him when we were drawing at the kitchen table a few days ago. His book was called *Distance*.

Marge returned with Raegan, whose eyes were looking all over the place. Water had been splashed on her face. The Drew Barrymore makeup had run. She got more excited when she saw her father on the screen.

"And the winner is . . ."

There was silence.

"Stephanie Haight for *Falling Out of Fate*."

Steph stood up, too fast. The table tipped; Marge caught it.

Steph walked to the podium and assumed the calm authority of a professor. She thanked her publisher, her agent, Marge, Raegan, me. "And most of all," she said. "I'd like to thank Greg, for making our affair public."

Gradually, people began to clap.

Steph didn't return to the table.

"It starts with lesions," the short, fat, serious man was saying. "Lesions the shape of lenses that appear on the branches." He shuddered. "And then there are the fungi that sprout. They look appetizing—one is almost tempted to make a fungi risotto. But oh no they're not." He slurped his gin and tonic.

Dave and I looked at each other.

"Here." The man pulled his iPhone out of his pocket. "Have you heard of the Ashtag? It's an app that spots dieback."

"I'm sorry you didn't win," I told him.

Raegan had attached herself to her father's leg as he accepted consolations. She had a hunted look in her eye, like Freddie at the peanut factory. The liberal intelligentsia had turned into a mob; they bumped and grinded to one of Adele's more upbeat numbers, letting their hair down, letting it all hang out, letting the joy of being liberal lift the sense that the wrong horse won. Greg had been the favorite. Greg had managed to mix erudition with emotional pain, contextualizing the latter within the ongoing debate about the rights of fathers and the dubious rights of mothers to wreak revenge via the children. "It was Stephanie who got revenge," I overheard a renowned panelist remark to an even more renowned commentator and critic. "They should have given it to that fabulous work on ceruse. I read it. It was fabulous. His insights on red and how it is not what we think it is and Elizabethan purity more generally were really startling."

"Startling how?"

"They were just really startling to me."

Dave and I were dancing with the expert on Victorian sewers, who was only twenty. It transpired that he was a child prodigy who'd gone up to Oxford at the age of fourteen, chaperoned by his father, who was eager to buy a tandem so that they could ride around Oxford together in the style of another child prodigy from the 70s whose name the sewer man couldn't remember. He didn't mind that his sewer book hadn't won because he said he'd had a jolly good time splashing around in the sewers with a flashlight strapped to his head. He said he had the rest of his life to win. He screamed with joy every time a new song came on; "Twist and Shout" got a particular rise out of him.

I checked my phone:

Come to the pool. Please. Stephanie. Leave your man behind.

There was another:

The hotel pool. Not the pool at home.

Steph was sitting in a deck chair with her back to the black shape of London. The pool was on the roof, lit from within. It deserved to be filmed for an R&B video. A few people were laughing by the bar in the corner but they didn't seem to belong to the award ceremony. I sat in the deck chair next to Steph, then got up and turned it around so that I could see the view.

"I can't believe he beat me," she said, lighting a cigarette. She lit one for me too.

The waitress came over and she ordered two bourbon highballs.

"Who?" I said.

"Greg. I can't believe I let him win." She shook her head. "He won. If only I'd written harder, if only I'd tried harder, I could have done it. But there was something inside of me saying don't do it, you can't do it. That thing inside of me will never go away."

Our faces were slanting in different directions.

"I tried to kill it in a multitude of ways," she said. "I did everything. But the voice telling you you're shit is a self-fulfilling prophecy."

"Stephanie," I said. "What are you talking about? You won. Where's the award?"

"Don't laugh at me. I can take it."

"Take what? You *won*."

"No."

"Do you mean that he won metaphorically or what?" I said.

Steph laughed. "Ann-Marie, you're delusional. Were you *there*? Or were you too absorbed in your new zip-less fuck? That's what we used to call it—back in the old days." She unbuckled her ankle boots and kicked them off. "Greg won *in real life*. It was my punishment for doing what I did to Marge. It's karma. I fucked the balance. But Marge is worse. Marge internalized the negative voice on a scale that even I can't fail to marvel at." Steph laughed again. "She stays with me because I'm the one who killed her spirit."

"Marge seems quite spirited," I said.

"No." Stephanie shook her head. "She's dead inside. So am I." She tossed her cigarette on the floor. "My hope is that things will change generationally. But you've fallen at the first hurdle. You're falling."

Our highballs arrived.

"I—" I started.

She cut me off.

"I met him on the ski lift," she said.

Her eyes glazed over.

I had no idea what she was talking about.

I waited.

Her eyes went back to normal again. "Yes." She downed her drink and waved for more. "It was snowing, obviously. It was chance. We went up, up. That night in the cabin was a bliss that I can't tell you. I can't tell you what it is to stare into the eyes of a man with whom you are in love and come simultaneously."

"With Greg?!"

"No."

More drinks arrived.

"With Leo. My American ice hockey player. He held my hand in a way that—He held my hand."

There was a long silence.

"I became an American for him. I followed him there. He told me that this was it. It *was* it. I changed my name, got a green card. I changed my heart. I made it pliable. Open." She grimaced. "Every night, night after night."

I waited.

"I enrolled in grad school at Harvard. He had gone to Yale. He was very well-bred. We didn't have much to talk about, looking back. In fact we had nothing to talk about at all. I was so bored, sitting in restaurants. I kept the smile on my face but I just found him tedious as hell."

I laughed. "Dave's quite boring."

"Yes." She lit another cigarette. "But my *god* is he cute!"

We both laughed.

"Leo never made me wait," she said. "That's why I loved him. He was always there. Sure—I could be tricky at times. Some nights I wanted to work on my thesis but I would go to a movie with him or watch him play or hang out with his friends. I didn't mind because I was with *him*. I let my studies slide. I didn't mind. I let my mind slide. I didn't mind. I let myself slide into him like . . . something inevitable."

A woman staggered over and asked for a light. Steph handed it to her.

"But he got poached," said Steph.

"By a woman?"

"No! By the Toronto Maple Leafs. He went pro. He was that good."

"Is that an actual team?"

"One of the best. We carried on long-distance. I was twenty-five. I wrote him every week, great, massive out-pourings of love. And he wrote me, the best he could. Not so poetic. But I didn't care. I used to get so excited by his letters." She looked at me. "They were mostly about Maple Leaf strategy, league tables, chances. The letters got shorter. And then no letter arrived. I kept writing. I wrote for six weeks. I can't tell you the anxiety I went through. I became superstitious, again. Eventually, I went up there because I was worried that he had had an injury and the coach hadn't told me. But he hadn't had an injury. No. He wasn't hurt at all."

There was another long silence.

"I'm sorry," I said.

"He'd got engaged to a Maple Leaf cheerleader. Do you know they can skate and cheer at the same time?"

I laughed.

Steph stood up. "I want you to go," she said. "Go free."

She wrote me a check for £5,000.

I stared at it for a moment, and then I put it in my handbag.

I returned to the party without Stephanie.

Dave was on the dance floor. He and I danced until four in the morning, and then we took a taxi back to Clapham.

The window-shattering power of Nina Hagen's 1978 *Rockpalast* performance of "Naturträne" greeted us in the hall, drowning out the hum of bees.

It was coming from the basement.

The stench in our screening room was compounded by the alarming vision of Nina, stretched from floor to ceiling on the screen, baby dummies hanging from her ears, opening her mouth too wide to be human.

More urgently, Freddie was standing in dandyish regalia on a chair in the center. One end of the cord of my red silk kimono was tied around his neck; the other end was attached to a makeshift scaffolding, fashioned out of the bits of wood that the homeless woman had collected and left upstairs, nailed together with all the ineptitude of one who has never done a day of manual labor in his life.

Jasper was steadying the chair on which Freddie stood. He looked delighted. The bee man in his white, astronaut-like outfit was slouched against the wall, watching the video of Nina, batting a tennis racket back and forth, saying: "She was extraordinary."

"Change it to No Bra," commanded Jasper. He was wearing some kind of purple college gown.

"Freddie, get down from there," I said.

"Oh good, you're here," he said. "I wanted you to see me. Perhaps you most of all."

Bee Man changed the video; a picture of a grim-looking topless woman appeared on the screen. Her long brown hair was positioned over one breast. *Hi, my name's Munchausen, how are you?* came a man's voice, accompanied by jittery electro.

"Right." Jasper moved behind the tripod. The Bolex was ready.

Freddie turned his plagued face toward Dave. "Sebastian?" he said. "Sebastian? Ha, she got you back."

"This is not Sebastian, Freddie," I said. "This is Dave. Dave, these are my friends."

"My god," said Jasper, looking at Dave. "You've found his doppelgänger, Ann-Maric. The likeness is uncanny. Congratulations."

"What are they talking about?" said Dave.

"I did an installation about doppelgängers back in 02," said the bee man from beneath his helmet. "I got loads of twins to, like, bump into each other on a busy street."

"Who's Sebastian?" said Dave.

"He's just this guy I went to school with," I said.

"The love of her life who she was with for seven years

until she destroyed him by sleeping with *him*." Freddie pointed to Jasper.

"You said you'd never had a long-term relationship," said Dave.

"I was joking," I said.

"Enough," said Freddie. "Go."

The bee man casually kicked away Freddie's chair.

Freddie's body fell, then lurched. His eyes bulged; he began to choke.

"Relax," said Jasper.

Freddie continued to writhe. I tried to grab the chair off the bee man but he wouldn't give it to me.

"In Switzerland, we believe in the right to die," he said. "No one should deny that right."

"You sound Scottish, not Swiss," I said.

Dave went crazy; he tried to get Freddie to sit on his shoulders, but Freddie kept kicking him away. Freddie was about three feet off the ground. Jasper was laughing.

Then Freddie's body went limp.

"Fuck." I was going into hysteria. "Fuck."

Dave managed to half throttle the bee man, ripping off his bee helmet in the process. He looked like an ordinary man in his mid-thirties beneath. Dave grabbed the chair. I grabbed the chair off Dave. Jasper attempted to block both of us. I climbed on the chair and tore at the knot around Freddie's neck. That magazine ad of a ginger boy who wasn't Samuel was stuck to the sweat on Freddie's palm. When I finally managed to haul him down, it came unstuck and floated into the mouse shit on the floor.

EIGHTEEN

"WHAT'S THE PASSWORD?" said the mouth.

"I don't know," I said.

"Use your imagination."

The mailbox was very low down.

"I don't have an imagination. I don't have time." I kicked the door.

It opened.

The green girl from the peanut factory was standing in the entrance hall of what was once a boys' prep school. "The password is 'squat,'" she said, and disappeared through a door to the right.

A meeting was going on. "He seemed like a nice guy," a girl with a bolt through her nose was saying. "But I knew from the way he was dancing that he was a spy."

Boys' names were engraved on the wall in silver. Headmasters' names were engraved in gold. The place was clean, but I could hear the menace of minimal techno warbling from below. They were having a rave in the basement. I went upstairs. Classrooms with blackboards

- 296 -

had been turned into ill-defined lounge areas. Beds were piled on top of beds. A dog was chasing a dog. I wandered through corridors without knowing where I was going. There were stickers on a window: "Ambition: The Desire To Tread On Others." And: "Stop Mad Cowboy Disease."

I found Samuel sitting on a cot in the last room on the third floor. One of his heinous Disney remixes was spinning, botched and repetitive. He was staring at his laptop, earphones in, back to me. This had been the sickroom. Ointments were still lined up on shelves. I lifted the needle off the record and yanked out Samuel's earphones. He jumped; the laptop crashed to the floor. He was watching *Splash*. Daryl Hannah with her crimped blonde hair was wandering around Bloomingdale's in a man's suit.

He reached out to me. I let him cry into my hair for a long time.

"I'm trying," he said. "I'm trying to get past the cartoons and move onto to some real live pictures."

"They're not real or live," I said. "It's a film from the 80s."

"I was thinking about you." Samuel wiped his nose. "Because in this one, the mermaid's got the upper hand. She doesn't sacrifice anything. She returns to the sea and Tom Hanks follows her. He sacrifices his life in New York for her and becomes a merman. He sacrifices his life in *New York*." He shook his head, baffled. "Freddie told me what that woman Stephanie told you about Ariel, but I don't believe it. Or maybe I believe it."

"So you have seen Freddie?"

"No. Not since that night." He started to cry again.

"Samuel," I said. "This is serious. You know I don't like you. I've never liked you and I don't like your sister either."

"I thought you did like me!"

"No," I said. "I don't."

More crying.

"But Freddie tried to take his own life last night."

Samuel stared at me.

"Yes," I said. "That's right. Commit suicide. He would have died if it wasn't for me." I sat on the cot. "It pains me to say it but he's madly in love with you."

Green Girl appeared in the doorway, brandishing an old Nando's chicken box. She didn't recognize me at all. "Dude," she addressed Samuel. "Is this girl bothering you?"

"No." He looked happy.

Daryl Hannah was shoplifting. Tom Hanks was trying to stop her.

"Okay, well do you have any, like, detergent?" said Green Girl. "Or bleach. I need really strong bleach to really fuck the stains."

"What stains?" said Samuel.

"Here." Green Girl produced a pair of pink gingham underpants from the chicken box. She twirled them around her finger. Ants swarmed out of the crotch and over her hand and arm. She didn't react. "Or I might just go to the community garden and just, like, *leave them there*."

I escorted Samuel and all his belongings back to Clapham in a taxi.

It turned out that the balloon animals in Freddie's bedroom were the brainchild of Samuel, who had been promised a balloon animal installation in Freddie's show.

"Don't you know that Koons did that back in the 80s?" said Dave. He was sprawled on the chaise longue in the living room. I was sprawled on top of him.

Jasper had made a Lancashire hotpot, which he was forking into his mouth straight out of the pan. He passed the pan to Dave, who lifted it up and drank the gravy.

"Mate," said Dave. "This is fucking sick."

"Cheers," said Jasper.

Samuel was playing with his balloons in front of the Victoriana screen. "Who's Koons?" he said.

"Samuel's a genius," said Freddie. There was a deep bruise around his neck. "He's my pet. He's superlative."

"Superfluous, don't you mean," said Jasper.

"Koons is like the proper Damien Hirst," said Dave. "His puppy is, like, legendary. It's as big as a building and it's wicked. It's made out of flowers."

I went upstairs to check my emails.

Dear Ann-Marie,

Why do they insist on reporting in the press that I won?

The people who I love the most always die. It's patently obvious that Greg was just a zip-less fuck, albeit prolonged, because he's still alive. Did I tell you already? "Zipless fuck" was

a phrase coined by second wave feminist Erica
Jong in her seminal 1973 novel, *Fear of Flying*.
Why don't they paste his face on top of mine in
all the publicity shots of that ghastly ceremony?
Did you read the master/slave chapter of *Falling
Out of Fate* yet?

Until I see you.
Steph

Sebastian called me on Skype.

"Hey." He was in his bedroom at his parents' house. "You were brilliant on the radio."

"Did you hear it?"

"Listen," he said. "I want to tell you something. I think if I tell you, things will be different between us. Maybe we can start again. Maybe we can."

"Sebastian, I'm really busy at the moment."

"Wait. I never told you this before."

"What is it?"

"I didn't get kicked out of boarding school for fighting. That was a lie."

"What?"

"I just wanted you to think that I was strong. You were always getting into fights."

"What did you get kicked out for then?"

"I was sleepwalking. I used to get up in the middle of the night and just wander around the countryside around the school and just kind of end up in weird places, like in the woods and stuff."

"Were you actually asleep though?" I said.

"Yeah. Except they never believed me. They thought I was just being a juvenile delinquent. But I was scared when I woke up in the woods and I had no idea how I got there."

"You never sleepwalked with me."

"No . . ."

"Do you sleepwalk with Allegra?"

"Yes. I started sleepwalking again after you and I broke up. I don't walk very far now. Usually I just walk to the kitchen or the living room and start watching TV. But she loves it. She says Artaud sleepwalked."

"Did you wet the bed as well when you were at boarding school?"

He sat back; the lens pointed at the corner of his ceiling. His face looked very tall.

"Look, Sebastian," I said. "I have to confess something to you, too. I've met someone else." I paused. "I never thought it would happen, but it has happened. He's unbelievably charismatic."

He said nothing.

"Dave works hard, plus he's just a gifted conversationalist, which is the ideal combination. The problem with you is that you're quite talented but you're also lazy so you need Allegra to pussy-whip you into doing anything the whole time."

"Fuck you." He disappeared. The screen showed a series of moving abstractions. His laptop must have landed at a bad angle on the bed; I saw dark blue. Then there was nothing.

I had tried to persuade Freddie to wear a turtleneck for the opening of *Making A Racket*—to hide the bruise around his neck. But he wanted people to see that he had suffered for the art. Jasper had enlisted a team of his father's employees to do everything. He had flown someone in from Cologne to do the lighting. *VICE* was filming. Scene & Herd from *Artforum* was here. Everyone was here, it seemed, except the bee man, who had apparently gone into anaphylactic shock. "Which is strange," said Jasper, watching the backside of a waitress as she shouldered a tray of devils on horseback.

Dave was whipping out business cards, saying: "There's a person who matters. There—that person. He really matters."

"It's off-putting," I told Jasper.

We were standing at the bar. The crowd was contained in the first gallery, which was separated from all the others by a black curtain. The walls were exposed brick. There was no art on display.

"We get them fucked first," Jasper explained. "They're more inclined to review well and buy this shit."

"Is it shit?" I said.

Jasper laughed. "Freddie knows it's shit, I know it's shit. More to the point, Freddie's father knows it's shit and he's paying for the space."

The space had recently housed the remains of defunct trains. Living trains still thundered overhead.

Dave came over.

"Sebastian, I was just saying to Ann-Marie," said Jasper.

"Dave," said Dave.

"How fucking hot it was when Ann-Marie and I were in the back of my Alfa Romeo," Jasper went on. "When we were parked outside Allegra's parents' house in Buckinghamshire that night after the crème de menthe. We had all driven straight from Hammerton Hall because Allegra wanted to leave the scene of her spoliation. She said the smell of mint had penetrated the whole county of Suffolk. She said she would never chew chewing gum again, or brush her teeth with mint-flavored toothpaste. 'What other kind of toothpaste is there?' I asked her." Jasper laughed. "'Babe, you're cornered.' Allegra was always moaning. But she and I." He gestured to me. "We literally tore it down. The leather interior was cannibalized, but I didn't care. It was worth it to see her sullen face crease in an orgasm that seemed to have no end."

Dave put his arm around my shoulders. "Hey," he said. "That's my girlfriend."

"She's incapable of love," said Jasper.

"I'll ask you to kindly leave your drinks at this point," Freddie announced. "The work can't take it."

Everyone laughed.

We went through the black curtain.

Allegra was sitting cross-legged on a raised platform in the second gallery. Her glorious black hair was hidden under a frizzy blond wig and she wore a loose white dress. An opera began to play.

"*Madame Butterfly*," said Jasper.

To the right of Allegra, there was a transparent acrylic

bath, filled with water.

The crowd gathered.

A light fell on her. Everyone else was in darkness. The light turned into an image, projected onto her face, so that her blank white skin became another face, a man's brown hair, a business suit. The image rippled away from her; it settled on the bath, and became clear. It was Michael Douglas.

Sue came out of the crowd. Her bob was concealed under a brown wig. She was carrying a box that thudded from within.

The water in the transparent bath began to boil.

Allegra relieved Sue of the box. She opened it, and, with an expert grip, produced a live white bunny. She held it aloft by the ears. Its eyes were pink.

"Why do you have to make things so difficult?" Allegra asked the bunny.

The image of Michael Douglas had drifted to the rear of the platform. Sue stood beside it, an arm around its phantom shoulders. A second image appeared: that of a little boy. No, it was a little girl who looked like a boy. I remembered the child actress being particularly cute and undeserving of the violence inflicted on her pet bunny by Glenn Close.

Allegra dangled the rabbit over the boiling water. *Madame Butterfly* got louder. The crowd went "ooohhh." Maybe they didn't think she would drop it in because she was so pretty but yes she did—there it went—body writhing, visible through the side of the bath so that everyone could watch it die.

Blood came out of its ears.

Eventually, the bunny floated to the surface.

Sue maneuvered her squat body into a position of attack. She pulled out a butcher knife; a departure from the movie, in which Michael Douglas's wife is a model of harmlessness. But Allegra had no intention of remaining faithful to the movie or to anything else for that matter because now she grabbed the knife out of Sue's hands, scooped her up, and dropped her too in the boiling bath. Sue flailed next to the bunny corpse. I could tell by the expression of pure panic on her face that this had not been part of rehearsals.

Sue begged Allegra to get her out.

"I guess this is what they call the sublime," said Allegra.

There was only one artwork in the second gallery. It was very small and low down on the floor. Our view was blocked by the crowd.

Samuel was garbling about being so proud of his sister because she was going to get, like, loads of kale. Dave seemed to know what Samuel was talking about; he agreed that Allegra was tubular but was she doing a carpet?

Samuel shook his head vehemently.

"My debut is dedicated to you," Samuel told me. "For bringing me back to Freddie." He led us through the crowd.

The artwork was a mangled balloon polyp, freshly inflated.

"It's a lark!" said Samuel. "Like having a lark!"

"Man, I wish I'd met you sooner," Dave told me. "Your contacts are beyond. You could have totally put me in this show."

I let go of his hand.

Allegra was talking to a man with a thin face and a flamboyant tie.

"That's Der Santo," said Dave. "He's a significant collector. I can't believe he's interested in her."

"I can't believe it either," I said. "That performance was terrible."

"What are you talking about?!" said Dave. "It was arresting."

The third gallery had nothing in it but a beehive in a glass box.

The fourth gallery contained a series of black-and-white films called *Shine Me*. Each showed a different boy, first bending to polish Jasper's shoes, then being kicked in the face. The boys' fear was visceral, as Dave put it. Jasper's face had been censored.

One wall of the fifth gallery was covered in a screen that showed me, ludicrous in canary yellow, going under. The magnolia bubbles in the vast martini glass drenched my feathers, got in my eyes. Flack's "The First Time Ever I Saw Your Face" was playing. That rancid ballad. In the center of the gallery, a normal-sized martini glass stood on a plinth. There was a single yellow feather inside.

"I'm going to kill Freddie," I said. "He must have—how the fuck did he get that footage?"

"The found object really enhances the Bergsonian sense of duration," said a redhead.

"Yes," said her friend. "The glass functions almost like a visual madeleine."

People were sitting on the circular leather sofas of a private members' club in London Bridge, holding jars containing limited edition dead bees, thrilled that they had had the opportunity to fork out £500. The bees had been killed and jarred by the bee man's assistants. He still hadn't turned up. The after party was supposed to be sponsored by Grey Goose, but Jasper had forgotten to get in touch with them or any other drinks manufacturer. Jasper had paid for all the vodka himself. "Still, it looks better if people think brands are willing to invest," he told Dave and me. "Investment being a kind of belief."

"This is an investment," said Dave, brandishing his own dead bee. "This could be worth like five million in five years."

"Or nothing," I said.

"Fred told the bee man not to show up," said Jasper. "It just looks better if he doesn't show up. Someone already offered to buy the hive and the glass box and the rackets. It's like absence as presence."

"Yeah." Dave nodded, earnestly.

Jasper addressed Dave: "You know what, Sebastian?"

Dave didn't correct him.

"I remember this one time that I was sucking your girlfriend's cunt. And I suddenly had the unmistakable impression that I was eating a sea urchin."

"Shut up, Jasper!" I said.

"Don't get me wrong," Jasper went on. "She is a delicacy. But she won't let you do it unless you make her feel that you really like her personality." He shuddered. "See, Allegra knew that she had no personality to like, so everything was much easier."

"How can you let him talk about me like that?" I said to Dave.

"Relax," said Jasper. "I'll let you sit on my face any time you want. Urchins are among my favorite crustaceans."

The art people had been overwhelmed in numbers by Freddie's two thousand Facebook friends: old Etonians and people from Cambridge who I had hoped to avoid for the rest of my life. One girl with a double-barreled surname had broken into the Bank of England and managed to stage a protest for thirty seconds. She had posted the video online, which went viral before she was put in solitary confinement and her laptop was confiscated. Another girl had already starred in a BBC period drama; she was set for Hollywood. Yet another had already inherited the family property business and lost it.

Samuel came over, clutching his lark. He sat down between Dave and me.

"Aren't you supposed to leave that in the gallery?" said Dave.

"Oopsy daisy!" Samuel covered his mouth. "Freddie's going to be mad at me." He asked Dave to look after the lark and pulled me onto the dance floor.

"I feel like Ariel waving to her father from the shore

right now," Samuel shouted. "Like right at the end when King Neptune gets surrounded by golden light and accepts her for what she is. I always wished my parents would accept me like that. But I guess I don't need them to accept me anymore because I've got you and Freddie as my family."

"I still see you as you were when Freddie and I first met you," I shouted. "When you were into chess."

"That wasn't the first time we met," shouted Samuel.

Public school boys around us were pogoing up and down, straining against gravity to soar as high as possible. A girl to the right was attempting to bogle.

"When did we meet?" I shouted.

"Freddie and I met at school when I was thirteen. We saw each other once when I first started, then I only ever saw him from afar." Samuel looked ecstatic. "That's where he got the idea for the shoe polish films. I was a lower boy and he was in pop—a prefect. I was a chug. I deserved it."

I pushed Samuel away.

The bogling girl was doing the butterfly now.

"So he kicked you in the face?" I shouted.

"Yeah!" Samuel held me close. "I was never the same after that." He whispered in my ear: "I think that's when I fell in love with him."

It was five in the morning. I was backed against the fire escape. Dave was trying to hold the attention of Der Santo, who was coked out of his mind and talking non-stop about how he'd bought Allegra's bunny boiler piece and how he wanted to buy every other goddamn piece that she would ever make. He said he was particularly fascinated by her plans to extract hearts at the top of pyramids in Mexico but that he had forbade her from going. He wanted to fly her out to LA instead, where he said they could construct a goddamn pyramid from scratch.

I smiled.

Dave went on about his light fixtures until Der Santo growled: "Tell me how your concept of barren rooms is any different from Dan Flavin's concept—nay, celebration—of barren rooms back in the goddamn 1960s?"

I slid out from under them.

Public school girls and boys had melted into and mated with the art people. The scene looked like a Hieronymus Bosch: body parts had been unscrewed and screwed afresh into uncanny orifices. The circular sofas seemed to swirl and rise. Sebastian was sitting on the far end of one, staring into his glass of water.

I staggered over, and fell across him. "I've got a confession to make too, to you," I slurred. "I need to tell you what I couldn't tell you on Skype."

He was sober.

"It never really ended between you and me because of Jasper. Or her." I pointed to Allegra. She was doing an avant-garde waltz with Sue, whose face and arms had blistered.

"Why did we break up then?" said Sebastian.

I tried to sit up, but I couldn't. "Because of that time we were watching TV."

"Oh, yeah. *That* time."

"I know we watched TV a lot of times but there was this one time we were watching it and *Flashdance* came on. Do you remember?"

He shook his head.

"The girl was dancing and dancing in front of the judges," I said. "They were judging her. There was so much at stake. And she fell over—she couldn't do it."

"Yeah."

"And I looked at you, watching it. You looked so handsome. You always looked so handsome." I tried to stroke his face but my hand missed. "You look handsome now."

"You're drunk."

"I'm high."

He stood up.

"Wait," I slurred. "Wait." I dragged him back down by his shirt. I tried to hold his hand, but he wouldn't let me. "But then the girl got up. She started dancing again. The song started: 'Once, there was nothing . . .' but I can't remember what. A dream, I think it was. There was nothing but a dream."

"You always were sentimental."

"What else is there to be? Let me ask you that question. Freddie believes things just decay, but I don't believe that. I believe that things become—but you've got to make them become." I sat up. "Stephanie taught me that."

"Weird," said Sebastian.

"Wait!" I shouted. "I'm trying to confess to you. I need you to understand." I tried to hold his hand again.

He let me this time. "I need you, Sebastian." I paused. "I love you."

He waited.

"The second time, the woman could do it! She could really do it! And I looked at you, watching her do it, and I thought to myself: 'If I stay with Sebastian, then I'll never do anything.'"

NINETEEN

THE FOLLOWING MORNING, I got a call from Emma, the manager of the diner in Covent Garden. She wanted me to do a trial shift as a promo girl. It was Sunday.

After three hours of traipsing around in the snow in a miniskirt and a tank top bearing the slogan All the Way above an image of a hot wiener topped with mustard, celery salt, meat sauce, and onions, Emma conceded that yes, I was allowed to run into Boots and buy a pair of flesh-colored tights. They didn't have any flesh-colored tights, so I bought black, twenty denier. My skin still showed through. I continued to hand out flyers to angry, snow-covered shoppers, promising two for one on all bun pups and black cows.

"You're selling a black cow?" said one backpacker from New Zealand who couldn't find his hostel. I knew he was from New Zealand and not Australia because of the flag stitched onto his fanny pack.

"Yeah, it's a chocolate soda with a scoop of chocolate ice cream in it!" I said, excitedly.

"You wouldn't be allowed to call it that in Auckland," he said.

"It's from Minneapolis!"

"Where are you from?" he asked me.

I looked around at this desecrated, white death sentence of a city and said: "I'm from here."

Two hours later, Emma the manager stomped toward me in her All the Way bomber jacket, which was white. She looked like the abominable snowwoman.

"How come you get to wear that and I don't?" I said.

We were outside Paperchase.

She told me that my trial was not going well. She said that unless I pulled my finger out, I would not be joining the team. She said the black tights were the last straw—how the hell was anybody going to be enticed to eat a stack of blowout patches if they couldn't see at least part of the way up my skirt?

"What's a blowout patch?" I asked her.

She grabbed me by the shoulders and escorted me back down the dirty old stairs into the diner. It was warm. The blue of my skin blossomed into a broken-vein red.

"This," she said, positioning me in front of a smiling picture of a pancake. "Is a blowout patch."

A girl who looked like a gorilla sidled up to Emma and said: "Can I go on my ciggie break now?"

Emma nodded. She whipped the waitress pouch off the gorilla and strapped it around my waist. "You can work the floor," she said. "See if you can survive."

Five minutes later, I was balancing four plates of surf

and turf on my forearms, trying not to look at the way the microwaved prawns were defrosting into the liquid collected around the microwaved bun pup. I remembered to smile as I slid the plates onto the table but some of the steak liquid splashed onto the Juicy Couture tracksuit of a Chinese woman with very thin penciled eyebrows. Emma didn't see, but the Chinese woman complained. I went and hid in the changing room. The gorilla was reapplying her raspberry lip gloss in the mirror and regaling a dishwasher with describing how she couldn't wait to get back to Dubai and dance in that cage, just as soon as the season started.

I checked my phone:

> **Do you want to come with me to an alumni dinner at your alma mater tonight? I can pick you up from wherever you are in an hour. Steph**

Steph had parked her car between the rows of people pretending to be statues. They were waiting for money, despite the snow. She seemed oblivious to the fact that Covent Garden was a pedestrianized zone. Shoppers flowed around the car. I got in. She demanded to know why I was dressed like a roller-skating Hooters girl. I said that I wasn't wearing roller skates and didn't Hooters girls go topless?

"You know what I mean." She lit a cigarette and reversed at speed. "What about that money I gave you?"

I told her that I'd put it in a savings account.

"You're crazy," she laughed, crazily. She looked out of

the window to her right as she drove, ignoring the front view entirely. "It's such a picturesque thing when something comes back that you thought had gone away."

"Who, me? Stephanie, please, can you watch the road."

"No," she said. "Not you. The snow. It makes me think of my childhood in Alhambra, Illinois. Oh, how we used to kick it about, my brother and I! Mother would throw her hands up at us so!"

"Weren't you born in Bermondsey?"

She looked at me with alarm. "Bermondsey, yes. But father was a traveling salesman. We traveled."

"I thought you owned a candy store?"

"Yes." She fiddled with the radio and turned the air conditioning on. "Fuck." A jet of freezing air blew in our faces. She banged the vent until the air turned hot. "He sold sweets." She placed both hands on the steering wheel, calmly.

We were leaving the city's outer suburbs, when she said: "Do you know your alma mater is giving me a lifetime achievement award? Which just goes to show that spring must follow winter. Because I've been so downhearted since that terribly disappointing loss—to a man that I know for sure is a monster." Her tone became wistful. "Greg seduced me, you see. It was terribly humiliating for Marge. She was at a postnatal yoga class one day and I went over to see if she wanted to come with me to a book reading. At a bookstore. I can't remember what it was. Raegan had just been born." Steph rolled down the window; snow blew in. She rolled it up again. "He used coercive tactics to get me where I didn't want to be—that is, horribly in love with him. It's a terrible curse to be in love. Did I ever tell you that?"

"Words to that effect." I pulled my leather jacket tighter around myself and sunk lower in the seat.

"I wanted to stop it, but he persisted. He wouldn't let me go. We were together—off and on—for years. For most of Raegan's life so far. You see, I *had* to leave New York." She paused. "And then of course Greg moved over here and got a job at the London School of Economics not long after." She laughed. "What a surprise."

"I think I must have failed my trial for the diner. Emma won't have me back after I ran out."

Steph was silent for a moment, then she said: "Oh, but you can do so much better." Her face tightened. "Haven't you absorbed one goddamn thing that I've tried and clearly failed to drum into you?"

I looked out the window.

"Did you ever get around to reading the fiftieth anniversary edition of *The Second Sex* that I bought for you especially?"

"No."

The green fields of England raced away from us.

"But I'm thinking of doing an MA," I said. "In poetry. Yeah, that's what I might do."

Stephanie slammed her foot down on the brake. We were on the highway. The car behind us braked too, and the car behind that. I heard nothing crash. Horns blared. Steph revved the engine and swung into a Little Chef.

She turned off the engine and stared straight ahead.

A little girl was screaming in the snow. She was holding a purple furry alien. "I didn't want this one!" she repeated again and again, until her father strode over, and smacked the girl so hard in the face that she staggered sideways. Stunned, she stopped crying. I tried to open the car door to help the little girl, but it was locked.

Steph seemed not have seen what happened.

The girl continued to lean to one side, paralyzed. Her father bent down and kissed her. She followed him to the car.

Steph turned to me. She had the Erzulie look. "What do you think a creative writing *class* will teach you, may I ask?"

"Uh—to write."

She exhaled. "And do you think that the vocation of the creative writer can be learned in a *class*? Do you not think that that vocation has a sacrosanct, a sacredly transgressive quality that is anathema by its very nature to the structure of an institution?"

"I just want some direction, Stephanie."

"Some direction." Steph honked the horn. "Have I or have I not been trying tooth and nail to implant some direction in you? Did you read the master/slave dialectic part of my book yet?"

I shook my head.

She fumbled with the glove compartment. I thought she might pull out a gun, but she pulled out her book instead. "Here. Read it now. Page 267."

My eyes moved across the page.

"Aloud."

She thinks she is alone in the world and that all the others have died. Then she sees another she. She is of the same sex. But this other she is different: she is quiet, docile, obedient. This other she is prepared to bat her lashes and pucker her lips to find a way through the darkness. Because there is darkness all around.

Steph lit a cigarette; the car filled slowly and totally with smoke. "Go on," she said.

You and she fight to the death because only one of you can survive. It will be the one who is prepared to risk death to gain life. To gain meaning in life. It cannot be both of you.

"I don't really agree with this," I said. "Why does it always have to be one or the other? Why can't both survive? I mean, Stephanie—are you master or are you slave?"

"I'm both," said Steph, sucking ravenously on her cigarette. "We're all both. Go on."

You want it more. You triumph. But instead of killing her when you can, you enslave her. You put her in bondage and make her work for you.

Steph opened the window; the freezing air sucked the smoke out.

Now the slave-girl toils night and day while you,

master-woman—shall we call you mistress?—sit back and relax. You delegate. She does it all.

More children were streaming out of the Little Chef, clutching purple aliens.

But as she works, a change occurs. It is her work, even if it belongs to you. After all, she is the one doing. You are just being. She is the one breaking her back, making her eyes water with the effort of getting where you want her to go—that is, nowhere.

You are doing nothing, living off the spoils of her labor. She is learning.

As she learns, she plans. She gets better.

By now, you are fat and slow. She is strong and quick.

"Stop there," said Steph. "I fucked this bit up. I couldn't figure out if there was another fight to the death or the princess slave simply overthrows her mistress through a process of evolution."

"So is it like a fairy tale?" I said.

"No," said Steph. "Skip ahead to the unhappy consciousness."

Now the former slave is herself a master-woman. She is a mistress. Only, she has no subjects. Her only subject is herself. She wants to be rid of hierarchy once and for all, rid of all the forces of domination and submission. Her former mistress is dead. She is alone.

"Now," said Steph. "Listen to yourself."

The former slave now feels a presence within her. She misses her mistress. She has internalized her mistress. The slave was ruled over for so long that she has no idea how to be free in the world. She has no idea how to live without a ruler.

Steph revved the engine and rejoined the flow of traffic.

After a long silence, I said: "I meant that I wanted to study poetry, as in analyze poems and write essays about them, not do creative writing classes. Just so you know."

There was no one to meet us in the front entrance of my college, and the guards didn't have Steph's name down on the list for the dinner. They were all ex-policemen, refined in their peaked caps, pleased to polish the souvenirs on sale in the special glass cabinet, next to the Parties and Events bulletin board. Their ties were branded with a ewe: the college insignia. Everything was branded with that bloody ewe.

I was beginning to feel both dread and angst. There was my old pigeonhole, in which I had received numerous notifications that I was late, behind, wrong, bad, or just inadequate. In that hole, hand-scrawled letters from the Christian Society had begged to save my soul. I had been invited to audition for numerous Patrick Marber plays via that hole. It was in that hole that I finally received notification that I was no longer permitted to live in college accommodation.

The guards pretended not to recognize me.

Steph was making a fuss.

I sat on the long sofa that faced the pigeonholes and hyperventilated. Girls who looked stricken, traumatized, raped, weird, mad, old before their time, drifted past. Girls who had given up on men by the age of eighteen. Girls with death in their eyes. Girls with pigtails at the age of eighteen. They were not ironic pigtails; they were just pigtails. The place reeked of arrested development and chronic perfectionism. The women-only college had begun to entropy sometime after its second wave zenith, when the admission of women to the university was still radical. But soon all the colleges admitted women. It was an atmosphere of despair.

"Steph," I said, pulling at her sleeve. "Come on. Let's go."

Then Gabriella turned up. Once again, I was horrified by her appearance. Her Technicolor blue eyes stared out.

The alumni coordinator—Simone, according to her name tag—had chaperoned Gabriella from the train station. Simone recognized Stephanie. She told her how much she loved her book, how much of a lifelong fan of her work she was. Simone castigated the guards for not rolling out the red carpet and said that of course she could find a place for Ms. Haight and guest at the dinner that evening when Gabriella would be winning the Alumni Society's Lifetime Achievement Award.

"Gabriella's winning it?" I turned to Gabriella.

She nodded.

"Did you go here?" I asked her. "I thought Steph said you went to Goldsmiths—when Michael what's-his-name was breaking every disciplinary boundary or something?"

Stephanie laughed riotously.

"No, I never went to Goldsmiths," said Gabriella. "I was here at Cambridge—1989 to 92. I studied history of art. I always believed that the idea should come before the work of art so I went down the academic route!"

Simone the Coordinator nodded.

"I made the *King Cake* project straight after I graduated," said Gabriella.

Stephanie laughed more.

"It's embarrassing, really—to be honored with a lifetime achievement," Gabriella went on. "I've not done much and I'm still only twenty-one!"

Now they all laughed.

Then Stephanie stopped laughing and said: "You were twenty-one the year the Berlin Wall came down, Gabriella."

"What's that got to do with anything?" Gabriella kept laughing.

Simone ushered us into a sterile room that I remembered well from the drinks reception that followed my nongraduation dinner. They must have sent the invitations out before the exam results were processed. I wasn't going to go, but then I got stoned. I thought it would be funny. Allegra had been sitting over there, by the window. She was engaged in conversation with a quantum physicist. I hadn't seen her since she fucked up my whole life. She pretended not to notice me. The coat of arms with the gold-plated ewe still hung on the wall. I stole a bottle of port from the drinks table, and she saw me do it. I went outside for a cigarette. She followed me. I told her to go away, but she didn't go. I didn't want to look at her so I looked to the left, at a hedge. Behind the hedge, there was a giant tin drum sculpture with a ball inside it that was supposed to represent the vulva. The ball was supposed to be the clitoris. We had laughed at it together, long before. She asked for a drag on my cigarette and I reminded her that she didn't smoke. She asked for some of the port; I handed her the bottle. Soon we were passing it back and forth. She said something funny and I laughed. I can't remember what she said. I remember how beautiful she looked and I remember thinking that she would always be more beautiful than me, and probably a lot nicer than me, and certainly a lot more charming. She was the better human being overall and Sebastian had been right to go with her. Then she went back inside.

"I'm thrilled," Gabriella was saying, her face unmoving. "I just can't tell you how fabulous it is for me to walk down memory lane."

"Ann-Marie came here too," said Steph.

"We remember," said Simone the Coordinator.

"And I came here back in the dark ages too!" said Steph. "So we're all old gals together!"

"I thought you went to St Anne's in Oxford?" I said. "That's what it said in the blurb."

"Oh," said Steph. "The press always lie."

"But it wasn't press," I said. "It was the blurb on your book."

"Steph forgets where she goes," said Gabriella.

I wanted to ask Gabriella if she'd ever been a nude model, as Steph had said, but the gong was banged. It was dinner time.

There was the painting of the woman wearing the hijab, crouching in the desert with the Kalashnikov. It hung above the long table. The woman in the painting seemed to be pointing the Kalashnikov directly at the head of my former director of studies, Professor Kyle. He had sloping shoulders and watery eyes. His teeth were yellow, but all the girls liked him because he was only about thirty-five. He had made a brilliant breakthrough on Karl Popper a few years ago, apparently. He too pretended not to recognize me.

Another gong was banged. Latin words were read out.

History of art undergrads had been selected for their virtue and seated near Gabriella. They had long hair and long legs. History of art alumni had been trooped in from all four corners of the earth, said the president, who was a quiet and judicious bluestocking. She had written me a decent enough reference when I applied for the job as door bitch at William's. I watched the woman in the painting very closely, hoping she would fire.

The ravioli arrived—singular. When I pricked it, a yolk burst inside.

Steph put her hand up as though she were at school and called to the president: "Excuse me, is this free-range?"

The president said that she was sure the produce was of the highest quality.

"But is it free-range?" Steph demanded.

The president requested the presence of the chef. He too was an ex-policeman. He had started out at the college as a guard. "No," he told Steph. "It's not free-range, but it is local."

"So it's from a local battery chicken farm?"

"Stephanie," I said. "Leave it."

The chef looked at me. "You've got nerve," he said.

The main course was rose veal.

Steph began a tirade about how she wanted it tough. The chef was called again; he explained that he could only do justice to the veal if it was tender.

"Then what is your job exactly?" said Steph. "Because the yolk was raw and the meat is raw. What do you actually do back there?"

"The chef makes everything wonderful," explained Simone the Coordinator.

Between the veal and the lemon syllabub, the speeches began. A series of old girls stood up and described how they had successfully commandeered hedge funds and households and dogs and cats. They were living proof that women could really have it all, said the president. "And now please put your hands together for Gabriella—" She listed Gabriella's achievements.

Steph was holding a toothpick; I watched her dig it farther into her thumb.

Gabriella thanked the authorities then held her hands up in self-defense at the Kalashnikov-wielding woman in the painting.

Everyone laughed.

"I always did feel under surveillance and under threat," she said. "Here."

Everyone stopped laughing.

"I would love to say that it was all down to the fine feminist principles instilled in me by these white corridors," said Gabriella. "So redolent of *Girl, Interrupted*. Has anyone seen that film?"

A few of the history of art undergrads nodded enthusiastically.

"I bet you have." She laughed. "I wish I could say I transcended my immanence because of this place."

Everyone waited.

"But I can't. We make art out of our pathologies as much as our strengths. This place ruined me—maybe I was already ruined. But the ruins gave me something to rise out of." Again, she laughed.

Stephanie laughed—too late.

Gabriella went on: "I might have been content instead of wanting to unstitch the very parts that held my soul together, to spread them out calmly, to see what was there. To see what was worth saving. And to see what urgently needed discarding."

The president put her knife and fork together.

"This place was the part that urgently needed discarding. One of many parts. It's a shocking place, full of sexless pain. Full of the impotence of eunuchs. So it's an irony to me that you wanted me back, possibly to claim my success as your own. Because I did it in spite of." She didn't seem to be drunk. "This whole place is just like my father."

"And I eat men like air," added Steph.

I looked at Dr. Kyle across the table and he looked right back at me.

Drinks were served in the college bar, which was not a bar but a youth club where no youths resided. Everything was purple and green and white—the colors of the suffragettes, as Steph pointed out. Simone said this was not intentional. The bar was sponsored by a budget airline because the Seven Sisters funding drip had dried up in recent years.

"Yes." Steph nodded, earnestly. "Wellesley. Bryn Mawr. Vassar. Radcliffe—"

"That's right," said Simone. "They've all gone, mostly. They can't support us anymore. We're the last all-women college."

"He's not a woman," said Steph, pointing at Dr. Kyle, who was informing the bud-like breasts of a pretty undergrad about Kant's *Critique of Pure Reason*.

Simone went to get more drinks. There was no bartender so she had to reach across the bar herself. Steph continued to stare at Dr. Kyle.

"He's dangerous," she said. "He's hot."

"Don't." I made her look away. "I had a terrible experience with him in the spring. It was just before my exams. I wanted to seduce him so badly so I turned up to a supervision session in a really short go-go skirt. I don't know why I wanted to—because I hated him, probably."

Steph nodded, furtively.

"Maybe I wanted to seduce him because I wanted to seduce this whole institution." I gestured to the bar. "This whole *place*." I was tipsy. "Because if *it* was inside of me then *it* would approve of me. Maybe if I could make *it* come, if *it* had me on my knees then *it* would redeem the whole experience—somehow."

"*Yes*."

"It had ruffles—really nice ones. The skirt. It swished when I walked, and when I bent over, it rode all the way up. I thought about bending over his desk on the way to the faculty building. I did arrive on time, but then I bought a Mister Whippy at the last minute, and sat on the wall outside, and ate it, slowly. It took me a good ten minutes to eat it. The sun was shining—it was so hot. I thought I would be more mysterious, more sexy—making him wait. I didn't have time to wash my hands, so my hands were sticky. I felt him recoil when I turned up at his door and offered my hand so that he was forced to shake it, but then he dropped it and told me I was late and so he was canceling the supervision session. He didn't stand up. He said that I was in danger of never fulfilling my potential, and I said, still trying to be the coquette: 'But what potential can you mean, Professor?' He told me that I should leave his office. 'Really?' I said. 'Yes,' he said.

I told him that I wanted to overcome myself in order to become myself—or become anything at all. But he just turned back to his computer." I took Steph's hand. "I was nothing at the time." Her hand was limp and damp. "You have to understand that I was nothing." I too was sweating. I could see Gabriella sweating across the room. "I was nothing."

"Yes," said Stephanie.

"When I went next door to get some bureaucratic form or other, the secretary told me that I had white stuff around my mouth. I went to the toilet. I looked in the mirror. It was the ice cream."

There was no way the guards would trust me with keys to any room, so Gabriella told them that it was she and not I who wished to see the seminar suite. She said she wanted to reminisce in there.

"Yeah," I said, closing the door behind us. "This was where they made me come and sit for the rest of my exams after I walked out of the first one. They wouldn't let me back in the main exam hall after all that screaming."

"Why did you walk out?" said Steph.

Tubes of light ran around the ceiling; the room was bare. We were all very drunk.

"I ran out of time," I said. "There was no more time. I was supposed to be writing, but I was thinking about Dr. Kyle. I thought about Dr. Kyle. I thought about how Dr. Kyle would never fail—or fuck me. It was the pressure. I'd had it up to the eyeballs." I laughed. "But they stopped the clock. They put me in here." I moved to the back of the room. "I was alone. Except for the proctor and this one other girl. Bizarrely, she was called Mary-Anne. Which is almost my name, backward. She sat at the back. Here." I stared at the whiteboard from where Mary-Anne had sat. "She was doing engineering. She had a twitching jaw and, every time I came in, she did this demented thumbs-up. After the second or third exam, I came to welcome her thumbs-up."

Stephanie picked up a marker pen. She was about to write something on the whiteboard, but then she changed her mind. She put the pen down. Very slowly, she said: "*It's a disgrace.*"

"So they segregated you," said Gabriella. "They quarantined you because you wouldn't conform."

"Well, they said I was a threat to the ability of my fellow exam candidates to concentrate. They said I would be better off in here."

"So you passed?" said Gabriella. "You passed?"

"No," I said. "I failed."

It was hours later. The sun hadn't yet come up over the red star of the Texaco gas station across the road, but soon it would illuminate us, illuminate Castle Mound just beyond, where Allegra had staged her communion with the elements and failed to feel anything at all. Soon the signs to keep off the grass would be illuminated too, and soon the rowers would start rowing, and the earth would keep turning. But for now it was dark, except for that weak red light across the road, making the face of my director of studies, Professor Henry Kyle, BA (Oxon),

MPhil (Cantab), PhD (Cantab) look sorry.

"Please forgive me for being so powerful," I was saying, as Gabriella and Stephanie danced around the room to the ringtone on Gabriella's phone: "What Difference Does It Make?" by the Smiths.

Dr. Kyle couldn't respond because he was gagged. He was bound with the standard-issue bedsheets that the cleaner had diligently left folded in the wardrobe.

We had bumped into Dr. Kyle on the way back to the bar from the seminar suite. He had been photocopying handouts in the admin hall, drunk.

This had been my room. I hated it.

Dr. Kyle twisted from side to side.

"It's the overhead light or darkness," I told him. "Because there's no bulb in the sidelight. Someone forgot to change the bulb."

He twisted more.

"Do you want to see what is happening to you?" I said.

He nodded. Then he shook his head.

Gabriella and Stephanie held hands and formed a ring. There wasn't much space between the bed and the desk. Steph kept banging into the desk chair. We had got his trousers and his boxer shorts around his ankles but his shoes wouldn't come off. I pulled and pulled, attending to each foot. Finally, the first one gave. I fell against the wall. The second one gave more easily. I unbuttoned his shirt.

Gabriella was explaining that she was an amateur surgeon in the eighteenth-century tradition. At that time, women were only entitled to be amateurs, but they took their work extremely seriously. She talked about the difference between the scatological and sentimental in contemporary art. Then she got out her surgical travel kit.

"Are you listening?" she asked Dr. Kyle.

He nodded. He was trying to recoil but the sheets were bound too tightly.

Gabriella sat down on the edge of the bed. She lit a cigarette.

I fixed one of Dr. Kyle's socks over the smoke alarm.

"Do you include a module on doomed romantic love in your social and political science syllabus?" said Steph. She lit her cigarette off Gabriella's.

The professor was trying to breathe.

"Well, do you?" said Stephanie.

"No," I said. "They don't."

"Do you plan to include one?" said Steph.

He nodded, frantically.

"Because let me tell you." Steph wafted her smoke around the room so that it curled in the shadows. "It's really a key aspect of human culture that has been neglected by the humanities of a quasi-scientific bent. Those who have pretensions to *empiricism*." She stood over him. Then she sat down next to him.

His sweat had soaked the bed.

"The rise of the individual has coincided with the invention of romantic love as we know it. It's all about free choice." Steph laughed.

Gabriella laughed too.

His eyes looked stricken.

Steph moved around the glass partition separating the

bed from the sink. I saw her double-glazed form bend over the rushing tap. She returned. "Like if we think of the myths. Tristan and Isolde, Romeo and Juliet, Heloise and Abelard. They all experienced a preternatural feeling of truth in relation to the other, a purity so deep that they would prefer to be together in death than apart in life. Isn't that right, Ann-Marie?"

"Yeah." I told Dr. Kyle: "It was really humiliating that time with the ice cream."

"The latter is a particularly fascinating case study," Steph went on. "Abelard was a brilliant man. A scholar. Heloise was brilliant too. He taught her. But then her father got mad, as fathers tend to do."

Gabriella laughed. "Oh, Steph, you can't generalize about *all* fathers."

"True," said Steph. "The problem was that Heloise and Abelard weren't careful enough. They took risks. Because they were both literate, they wrote to each other. The letters survive." She stared down at Dr. Kyle. "Have you read them?"

He shook his head.

"Oh, you must." Steph became wistful. "They are too beautiful. The sentiment is so—*there*. They described in detail how they made love in a church, I think it might have been Notre Dame. This being the eleventh century I'm talking about. Maybe it was an act in praise of God— but it was punished as an act against him."

There was a long silence.

"Heloise's father was a powerful man of the cloth and he simply had to send his wayward daughter to a nunnery," said Steph. "Abelard, on the other hand, was castrated."

Dr. Kyle twisted harder.

"Oh, you like that, do you?" said Steph. "Gabriella."

Gabriella flipped open her pouch of instruments and produced a small scalpel. She handed it to Steph.

"Like this," Steph said. "Like this."

She cut off Dr. Kyle's balls with dexterity and threw them in the wastepaper basket, which was standing clean and empty under the desk, ready for the next girl.

TWENTY

I TRIED TO enter the church near our apartment in Clapham, but a man of the cloth said: "Sorry, we're closing," and shut the door in my face. I wanted to ask for forgiveness. I went around the side through the bushes. I could hear the murmur of a prayer meeting through the window. Bespectacled women had their heads down, Bibles open in their laps. I wanted to tell them all what had happened, but Steph had instructed me with unnerving calm as we drove back to London from Cambridge in the dawn light that if I ever uttered a word, she would ensure that my tenure on the insane celebrity spokeswoman circuit had ended before it began. "But I don't want to be on it," I said. She seemed not to hear. By way of a bribe, she said she'd organized a spot for me on *Sunday Brunch*, a live Channel 4 morning talk show—very blokey and jokey, but you want to reach outside your target audience, don't you?

"Who is my target audience?" I asked her.

"Oh," she said, flitting a strand of peroxide hair off her face. "The mad, the bad, the sad—women, basically."

I managed to get in the back door of the church and joined the prayer group. The man of the cloth handed me a Bible, but he didn't tell me the page so I had to read over the shoulder of the woman sitting next to me. She looked Scandinavian, around forty, with albino-blond chair. She smiled and pointed to the passage.

The man sitting next to her raised his hand: "But why did God make him sit in ashes while he scraped broken pots over his skin?"

"Darling," said the Scandinavian woman. "It's broken pottery, not pots. It was *Satan's* suggestion."

"But God told Satan that he could suggest whatever he wanted." The man looked like a laid off banker; he was rumpled and boyish.

"God was testing Job," said the man of the cloth. "That's where the boils come in."

I raised my hand. "Excuse me, what religion is this?"

The circle swiveled to look at me.

Then the Scandinavian woman laughed. "This isn't a religion," she said. "This is a faith. We include all religions—we're omnists."

"Only on weekends," said her husband.

Nick was pouring Campari into glasses, crosshatched and solid. I wanted to get my hands around that glass. I wanted to hold something tightly for a very long time and never let it go. I checked my phone; there was a message from Steph. I didn't read it. I heard a siren in the distance and pinched my twenty-denier tights until a hole and then a ladder ran down my thigh. "Oh, forgive me," I said, rubbing the ladder.

Toril the Scandinavian looked at my hand, rubbing. Nick, who was in fact a laid off banker, looked too. Their living room was decorated entirely in cream so that the Campari appeared like a vicious, red threat.

The siren reached its peak and then died.

"Thank you so much for having me here," I told them, gulping the drink. It tasted like blood too thin to be used for a blood transfusion. I needed a blood transfusion. Someone, somewhere, needed a blood transfusion. I tried hard to make the cream walls transform into a carte blanche, a means to start again, but the sun passed behind a cloud at some great distance and it all became dirtied with shadow.

"It's our pleasure," said Toril. "Please. Tell us a little about yourself. Tell us about your journey."

"My journey? Oh, I don't have one of those." I tried to laugh.

"Everyone's on a journey," said Toril. "Even Nick."

He flopped into an armchair and grinned like a fool.

"Life is a journey," Toril continued. "Only, it doesn't end." She shook her head vehemently. "No. Life goes on and on. It goes on and on and on."

"Really?" I said. "I'm looking forward to the end. I think it will be a blessed relief."

"Never say that." Toril moved over to the mantelpiece, picked out a book, and handed it to me. "Have you read it?"

It was *The Prophet* by Kahlil Gibran. I shook my head.

"You must. I can give you a reading list if you like. There's so much to read! Once you realize that you're on a journey."

"Life is a constant process of self-improvement," said Nick. "At least in this house." He'd already downed his Campari.

The drinks cabinet looked antique; wooden owls with electrified eyes were entwined with stems that metamorphosed into snakes.

"Nick has much time on his hands these days," said Toril. "So he is free to explore."

I checked my phone; there was a message from Dave:

Woke up this morning feeling buzzin, A. I'm like a baby with a rattle now that I've got you.

I wrote:

Dave, I don't know if I can be your rattle.

I still didn't open the message from Steph.

"Do you have any spare rooms here?" I asked Toril.

"Of course," she said. "Nick and I are childless, sadly. It was one of our greatest misfortunes, but we've had to clamber over adversity to become stronger. Um." She held out her empty glass to Nick.

There was another cabinet, bigger, its façade teeming with a greater diversity of wildlife, in the right hand corner of the room.

"It's our *Wunderkammer*—our cabinet of wonders," Toril explained. "Toys. Have you ever heard of the tragedy of success?"

"Is that a band?" I felt my phone vibrate. It was Sebastian:

I have to see you.

"No," said Nick. "It's a philosophy that Toril had time to concoct despite being the sole breadwinner."

"I made it up on the train," said Toril. "On the way to work. And compounded the finer points at a retreat that Nick and I go to in Idaho called Skearth. The name is a fusion of sky and earth." She smiled at some fond memory. "The tragedy of success is what afflicts the very successful, those who are predisposed to win. They suffer a superabundance and so run the risk of exploding."

"Yeah, I know what you mean." I nodded. "That's like how I felt after finals. It's what Nietzsche talks about in *Thus Spoke Zarathustra*. The prophet comes out of the wilderness after so many years of being alone because he's got so much honey that he can't contain it. He's got to give his honey to . . . someone." My eyes met Nick's.

I excused myself and went into the garden to smoke.

I paced in a circle seven times.

Then I opened Steph's text.

I told him that if he presses charges, the president of the college will receive an anonymous email about his affair. He claimed that he wasn't having an affair but I said no doubt you were thinking about having an affair. We all saw the way he was looking at that history of art piece of ass. I said I'd tell about the others too. He's married with children. It will finish his career. Plus does he really want everyone to know that he's got no balls. Steph

The message from Dave was full of unhappy emoticons. He said that he wanted to hold me right now. I replied that it was the middle of the afternoon and people only hold each other at night. He replied straight away that he would hold me day or night, which I was sure was a song lyric. Finally I wrote:

You can have my emotion or my sexuality, Dave. Which one? I'm afraid you can't have both.

As Toril showed me out, she made me promise that I would return to the church the following week, when we would be studying the book of Leviticus.

I arranged to meet Dave for lunch at Lorelei on Bateman Street in Soho. I texted Sebastian and told him to come along too.

When I arrived, Dave was sitting in front of the

wall mural of the Rhineland mermaid, waving to her doomed sailors. Her naked breasts and long blonde hair were out of focus.

"This place is sick," said Dave.

"Freddie and I used to come here all the time when I worked at William's," I said. "Everyone comes here. Media people, film directors, everyone." I opened the menu. "I think I'll have the penne ragù. I always have that."

The waitress came over; he ordered the same as me. I changed my order to the amatriciana.

"I thought you said you always have the ragù?" said Dave.

The waitress went away.

The restaurant's front window was fogged artificially so that the view of the street was obscured. Still, I saw the blond beast himself come striding up Bateman Street.

The bell rang.

Sebastian stepped inside and shook off the snow.

"Hey," said Dave. "Isn't that the guy from last night?"

Sebastian was flushed and intensely good-looking from the cold. I stood up and he kissed me hello. When Dave stood up too, I saw that Sebastian was taller than him.

"Hey," said Dave.

"Hey," said Sebastian. "What's he doing here?"

They stared at each other.

The waitress returned with our food.

Sebastian ordered the ragù and then changed his mind when he saw that Dave had ordered it.

"I'm surprised you've got the nerve to actually order food," said Dave.

"Why?" said Sebastian. "I'm hungry." He ordered the T-bone steak, the only thing on the menu that cost more than five pounds.

"I want a steak too actually," said Dave. "Yeah. I really feel like a steak."

"But your food's already arrived," I said.

"Well, I want a steak *and* pasta. The pasta is only the starter."

Sebastian had brought along his fishing tackle. He propped it against the table. He started talking about how Allegra was on the verge of totally smashing it and how he was so in love with her, more in love than ever.

Dave relaxed.

When Sebastian's steak arrived, I said: "You know, it's a real shame. I thought I could kill two birds with one stone but I haven't killed either bird." I pushed my plate away.

"What are you talking about?" said Dave.

"Doppelgängers are supposed to die when they see their twin," I said. "But you're both still alive."

I walked out.

When I got back to the apartment, Samuel was bursting balloon animals with the back of his diamond stud earring. Freddie was screaming in his underwear about how not every single person in the world wants to curl up in a little ball and watch Disney cartoons all weekend.

"Has anyone seen my wedding dress?" I said. "I'm

going to see this old guy, James, and he wants me to wear it. I wore it to the awards thing but I can't find it anywhere. Maybe I left it there." I moved to make a cup of coffee, but Samuel barged into me and pointed the back of his stud in my face.

"You brought me back to him," he shouted. "You only did it to get revenge on me for being related to Allegra, didn't you?"

I said nothing, holding the kettle.

"Didn't you?"

The crazy woman was standing outside the Clapham Common station. She was wearing my wedding dress. She had a black eye. Her cheek was bruised. There was no sign of the doll.

"Hey," I said. "That's mine. That was my mother's."

"I don't know what you're talking about." She looked the other way, toward the common. The wedding dress didn't fit her; I could see that it wasn't zipped up at the back and her arms made the sleeves bulge. She had slipped her grimy fingers through the lace gloves. The hem was already blackened. There was a rich brown stain on the front of the skirt.

"Give it back," I said. "I'm going to have to get that dry-cleaned now. I had to wear this." I gestured down to my white halter-neck summer dress from Primark; it was the only white thing I could find. I had teamed it with leggings and a short, black blazer.

"You look chic," she said, dully. "You look young.

You look like you could do anything. So why are you complaining?"

"Give it back," I whined. "I've got to go."

"No." She opened her arms wide; I heard a rip.

"Where's your baby?"

"Dead."

"Dead?"

"Yes," she said. "Have you heard of death? It's what happens to us."

I got on the train without the dress, and read *Falling Out of Fate*:

> The turning figure of modernity is the figure turned against itself, turned on itself. She is the figure who has grown from a child into an adult and learned on the way that in order to live at all in this fallen world, she must contain and control what she feels to be most natural. She learns that nature means violence; she does violence to nature. She does violence to herself. But what is lost along the way is a tragedy of the highest order. What is lost can never be regained, but it is remembered. Remembered as the hope of love.

I had never been to North Greenwich before.

I expected a baroque villa, too large to fit in the city, but James lived in a red brick retirement village. The river was near. I rang the bell, and waited.

And waited.

Eventually a woman came to the door. She was about

his age. She wore a red dress and bifocals. I could tell that she had been pretty.

"Hello?" she said.

"I'm here for . . . the pussies?" I said.

She smiled. "Pussies?"

"The pussies with the blue fur and the blue light. In the blue mountains." I paused. "With the monks."

"Monks? My dear, I think you've got the wrong address." She tried to close the door.

I blocked it. "The pussies from the refuge?" I said, desperately.

Someone was coming from farther inside the building.

The woman turned back.

James appeared, his comb-over not so slick, a red napkin in his hand. He stopped at the end of the hall when he saw me. "Margaret," he said. "You go and finish your dinner."

James came outside and closed the door behind him.

"What about the pussies from the refuge?" I said. "What about the refuge?"

"Wasn't it *you* who adopted the pussies from the refuge, Ann-Marie?"

I said nothing.

He looked very seriously at me. "What we had was wonderful. But it wasn't meant to last."

"Meant to last?" I echoed.

"Meant to go anywhere," he said. "Meant to be."

When he opened the door to return inside, a cat slipped out. It was brown.

I stared into the black river at Greenwich as though I could divine my future there.

At Clapham Common, I got the crazy woman by the arm and told her to take me to her baby.

She looked at me suspiciously. Her black eye was really terrible.

We walked across the darkening common together, slowly. There seemed to be something wrong with her legs. The cars formed a ring of light around us. We walked all the way around the fenced-off area until we reached the filthy hut on the edge of the park. There was a gap in the fence. We hid her cart and got through. I watched my mother's dress get more and more soiled as her old knees raked through the dirt. There was a mountain of trash, hidden by trees. Baby carriages and TVs and Hoovers. I heard things moving in the bushes. I could smell fire. She took my hand; it was black but I didn't pull away. We walked very slowly to the far corner, where branches from a big tree on the other side sheltered the earth.

"Here," she said.

I got down on my hands and knees and started digging. She stood over me.

Finally I hit a smiling plastic face. I lifted the baby out. One of its legs had been ripped off.

"They did it to us," said the woman.

The birds started singing. They seemed to be shouting their song and it was hateful.

— ACKNOWLEDGMENTS —

THIS BOOK WOULD not have been written without Hannah Westland, publisher at Serpent's Tail, who has mentored me since 2008. Her faith in my writing, encouragement, support, and incredible editing have been more valuable than I can say here.

I feel so lucky to be part of Serpent's Tail, which seems to be one of the few publishers that gives its authors creative freedom. It has been a great pleasure to work with a load of feminists! Particular thanks to Anna-Marie Fitzgerald, Flora Willis, and Ruthie Petrie.

Thank you to my agent Jenny Hewson at Rogers, Coleridge & White for her excellent advice and encouragement.

Thank you to all the wonderful team, past and present, at the Feminist Press, especially Amy Scholder, Jennifer Baumgardner, Jeanann Pannasch, Jisu Kim, Drew Stevens, Julia Berner-Tobin, Elizabeth Koke, and Lucia Brown.

A special thank you to David Lister, my editor at the *Independent*, for giving me a chance and starting me off as an art critic. Thanks too to the *Independent*, and particularly the arts desk.

Plenty of people have let me live in their houses while this book was written. Thank you so much to Mary and Rado Klose for all their kindness. Thank you too to Nigel Horne and Cassie Robinson.

Thank you to Tom Warner, Natasha Booty, and Roxy Smith.

Most of all, thank you to my parents. To my dad, for unfaltering love and support. And to my mum, for encouraging me to write and showing me the true importance of feminism.

The Feminist Press is a nonprofit educational organization founded to amplify feminist voices. FP publishes classic and new writing from around the world, creates cutting-edge programs, and elevates silenced and marginalized voices in order to support personal transformation and social justice for all people.

See our complete list of books at
feministpress.org

THE FEMINIST PRESS
AT THE CITY UNIVERSITY OF NEW YORK
FEMINISTPRESS.ORG